Cult of the Eclipse

ISBN: 978-1-64945-277-1

Author's Note
The following is a work of fiction. Any resemblances to real-life persons or settings are coincidental.

Deadly Sins

Book One

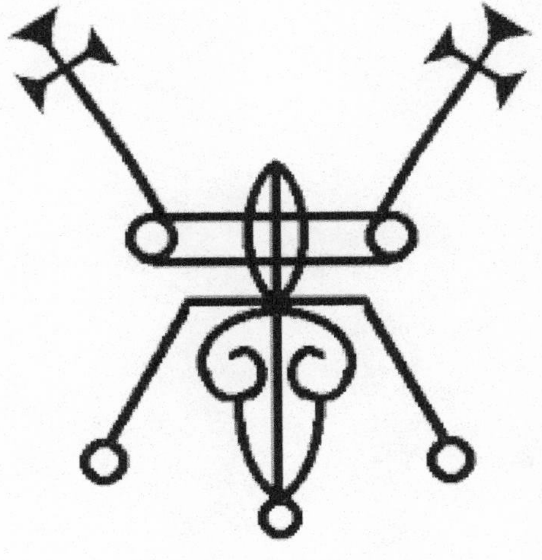

For Helen

Cult of the Eclipse

By

Winfield Winfield

1.

Jaclyn Ellsworth was driving down a lonely stretch of road, thinking any second, her runaway child would turn up. She'd been driving for the past two hours. She finished her nighttime breakfast at the roadside diner, and an old woman at a nearby table claimed to have seen the boy.

Jaclyn was on the highway, but it was just another obscure road among western Pennsylvania suburbs. She knew the route itself went on for miles in both directions, but that didn't matter. There was always money for another tank of gas in her checking account.

The past few roads she'd been on never had streetlights, and this was no exception. Straining her eyes to focus on the misty road, she noticed that the potholes were fixed. The summer rain was light but steady.

"It'd be nice if it let up," she said. "Been like this for days."

Jaclyn switched her wipers to the faster of the two settings. Keeping her eyes on the road and slowing down to five miles below the speed limit, she reached for the console between her and the passenger's seat.

She felt for the small, half-empty paper box there and lifted the flap open. Pulling out a Marlboro ultra-light, Jaclyn held it between her burgundy-painted lips. She reached for the lighter and lit the cigarette. Taking the first drag, she cracked the window open, just enough to fit the cigarette through. A little rain would get inside but not enough to leave its smell in the car.

"Did that old bat at the diner know what she was talking about?" She used careful precision to fit the end of her cigarette out the window, eyes always on her lane. "That lady said she *saw* him."

None of the houses that she passed by had their lights on. Their features were indistinguishable in the dark. The grassy space between them grew larger with every passing, two-storied home. The surrounding, grassy hills were as empty as they were spacious.

Jaclyn glanced at her rearview mirror to check for any cars. To anyone who'd been in the area before, she was a nuisance because of her slow driving. There weren't any headlights approaching. The only things behind her were the faint glow of her taillights and a never-ending, pitch-black darkness.

She bit her bottom lip while glancing between the road and the burning orange glare of the check engine light. Jaclyn imagined her Chevy Cobalt stalling again.

"Fantastic," she said. "That's what I needed."

The road up ahead didn't have anymore houses alongside it. It was nothing but trees and empty grassland. Once she was driving through the abandoned hills, Jaclyn held her steering wheel in a death grip.

If this pile of junk breaks down again, she thought. I'm screwed. God knows I don't have the insurance.

She had already stopped paying the bill months ago. When her eleven-year-old son brought it to her in the living room from the kitchen counter, asking what it was, she told him to just put it back.

"I'm not sure if I can pay it," she had told him. "We can probably do without it anyway. It's not like I've ever been in an accident."

As the unfathomable darkness approached, so did a wave of silent regret. She realized she could probably have borrowed the money at that time. She would've been able to pay it back with her inheritance.

But then again, she was a ways away from home. Why bother?

It was far from the only time Jaclyn got lost, but one of the things she learned from the countryside was: where you had lights, you also had businesses. And from her experience, just going straight was the fastest way to reach the next sign of town.

She had a small coughing fit upon noticing that her tank was only a third the way full. Sliding her cigarette out the window, she could feel her throat starting to get chilly and raw. As Jaclyn closed her window, the car slowed down.

The Chevy decelerated by five miles an hour, whistled as it *kicked*, and the speed increased again. She turned on the radio, drowning out the light whistle with WDVE. The sound of *Black Hole Sun* took her mind off the engine.

A spot of hot pink twinkled on the horizon. It was piercing the darkness like red-hot metal through butter. It caught Jaclyn's eyes, and the needle on the speedometer crept up to sixty-five.

As if uttering a prayer, she said, "Please let me make it. *Please* just let me make it."

The spot of pink grew and turned into a mass of warm fuchsia and yellow light. It scattered through the mist, taking a clearer shape. The yellow expanded, narrowing the hot pink down to a mere outline.

A rectangle with a white outline and yellow illegible letters expanded to its right. As Jaclyn slowed down, she could see a building with dimmed light emanating from the windows.

She groaned, and said, "Thank God."

Jaclyn pulled into a small parking lot underneath the bright neon sign. She looked up at it and the building. Hit by a wave of guilt, she let out a sigh and rolled her eyes.

"Am I really stopping *here?*"

After opening her glove compartment, Jaclyn pulled out a napkin. She fixed her gaze on the neon, cursive lettering along the windows. She brushed the napkin across her lips, enough not to leave too much lipstick.

It was something she did out of habit, when the temptation to get a taste returned from the shadows. At this point, the idea of her glove compartment not having any napkins was unthinkable. She saw them as a crucifix to ward off the desire. And in most cases, it worked.

There wasn't any Juicy Fruit in the car, so it *had* to work.

"It's okay," she told herself, looking in the rearview mirror. "I can control myself now. And maybe someone else knows where he is."

Turning the radio off, she adjusted her straight brown bangs away from her face. Jaclyn looked around in the car and realized it was the one time she forgot an umbrella.

Not a big deal, she thought. *It's just a little rain.*

"I don't need to buy anything," she said. "I'm just stopping by. And if the Chevy breaks down, I can go somewhere for shelter."

Gazing up at the sign above her, it felt like the devil himself was beckoning her. She needed no more than a single word burning from that neon display. That was enough to invite her to a place with the world's greatest pleasure.

2.

Jaclyn looked at the time on her car's digital clock. Eleven-thirty. It was late, but the place had to have been open.

"I won't be long," she said, as if speaking to another person. "I mean it. I really mean it now."

The sign above displayed a smiling, yellow cartoon duck with a white sailor hat, holding a tall glass mug of foaming beer, all within the hot pink outline. To its right was a sign that read, *Happy Duck Tavern.* The windows of the aged brick building had neon lettering that spelled out *Coors Light and Yuengling.*

But if that sign only had a single word, she still would've been sold on the deal: tavern.

"It never fails," Jaclyn said, getting out of the car. "If there's one thing you can count on, every bar in Pennsylvania has Yuengling."

Finding another one of these bars in the region didn't surprise her. But at the same time, an establishment like this being a chain throughout the country was a novelty of its own.

She locked the Chevy and stuffed the keys in her pocket. Then, sprinted to the door and walked inside. As she opened the door, it rang a small bell just above. The sound of the touchscreen-operated jukebox in the opposite corner followed that of the bell.

The piano intro to Miles Davis' *Blue in Green* emanated from the machine and filled the room. It gave the bar a welcoming quality. The tavern was bathed in crimson light coming from the ceiling. It made Jaclyn and the rest of the bar-goers look like they had blood-red skin. The bartender, a petite blonde woman in her early twenties with green eyes, slim-fit jeans, and a black t-shirt with an *Invader Zim* design across the chest turned to her.

Jaclyn thought the bartender was too pretty, mostly because of her freckled face and slim features. Even though she was wearing jeans herself, it made her want to cover her thighs with another layer of clothing.

The cellulite there and on her upper arms felt like an alien parasite that was draining her whenever she looked in a bathroom mirror. She was already wearing a jacket with fake fur along the edges. Nonetheless, she instinctively pulled it closer and tighter across her body. She felt it was the curse of being a woman her age.

Whenever she looked in the mirrors at home, it felt as if decades passed her by in a matter of days. Not long ago, she was a woman of twenty, the world looking like a playground of freedom and no consequences. But soon, youth had left her like a fickle partner would and she'd turned forty.

The customers, along with the bartender, looked at Jaclyn with a curious but unfeeling expression. A second of staring, and the bartender went back to pouring two shots. The first with butterscotch Schnapps. The other with orange juice. As the girl poured, her customers went back to their drinks and conversations.

The sight of an Irish breakfast made Jaclyn salivate. If canned beer didn't do the trick, she thought a shot was a great way to take the edge off when she couldn't make rent on time, when her ex-husband threatened to get the police involved again—

When her son locked himself in his room.

She sat on one of the bar stools next to a man in a black leather coat and Pirates' baseball cap that covered his dark, shaggy hair. As he rubbed his rugged cheeks and chin, Jaclyn noticed this man could've been the only other person without a drink.

Even the bartender had made herself a raspberry kiss. The girl would take a sip between looking at the customers for body language indicating that they wanted another drink. Come to think of it, Jaclyn couldn't tell if she was of drinking age. The rest of her body conveyed that she was ripe for college, but the face said otherwise.

She's got the face of a high school kid, Jaclyn thought. *But all the younger people are like that, I guess. They haven't spent their whole lives yet.*

"Hi," the bartender said to her with a perky voice, but a neutral expression. "Did you need help with something?"

A lot of things, Jaclyn wanted to say. "Could I just get a glass of water?" she asked with a smile.

The bartender cocked her eyebrow, but got a fresh glass, scooped ice cubes into it, and filled it with water. She put a coaster in front of Jaclyn and stuck the glass on top. After another quick look around, she took another sip of her raspberry kiss.

Keep it up, girl, and you might end up like me. "What's the charge?"

Another quick look with her eyebrow cocked and the bartender replied, "Nothing. Don't worry about it."

Jaclyn looked at the jukebox again as the song ended. On her second glance, she *recognized* the machine's specific model. It had the unforgettable *Eclipse* logo with the C styled to look like a crescent in the top-right corner. That was the brand she'd seen in every retailer that carried electronics.

Eclipse was most smartphones, home computers, business hardware *and* software, and from what Jaclyn had seen, it even had a hand in the video game industry. It didn't have a total stranglehold over gaming from what she had noticed, but it had a way of creeping across the shelves.

"Good God," she once remarked in an electronics store in her shopping district. "One day, Charles might even outdo Nintendo."

The machine in the corner opposite the entrance was something she had read about on the news on her phone. It appeared to be an innocent jukebox—playing music was just an installment available to the buyer.

The *Eclipse* Tracker was a machine to keep records of inventory and profits and make accurate predictions of supply to invest in without manual input. Jaclyn stared at it as if it'd try to take her wallet the moment she turned away.

Somehow, Jaclyn thought. *That hunk of metal knows what people are paying, even when they pay without the bartender telling them aloud.*

The model was the first of its kind—prehistoric by today's standards. She imagined it was something not many people cared to read about. This Tracker was something business outlets raved about as being more efficient and cheaper than its competitors. Not only that, it also allowed them to install additional *hardware* components over the *Eclipse* online store.

Somehow, the machine physically adjusted with each purchase. She'd only seen demonstrations over videos on the internet and could have sworn that it gave her a heart attack.

Jaclyn felt her heart leap to her throat on seeing one of these things build itself a new USB drive, or even obsolete parts like disc drives after the transaction went through. But she supposed that's why the company's owner, Anthony Charles, must've been filthy rich.

"Innovative and nostalgic at the same time," one reviewer had said. "The backwards compatibility is phenomenal. Perfect for any entrepreneur who wants to use both old and new tech. Almost its own home computer. All that's missing is office and gaming capabilities."

As the song changed to Chet Baker's cover of *Sultry Eve,* Jaclyn winced at the idea of the cash in her purse being monitored. At least surveillance cameras had an eye that she could *see*. She knew what was watching her. Now, that wasn't the case. The mechanical eyes could watch people through a one-way window.

She looked just past the bar that held the bottles of Smirnoff. The slow, melodic rhythm of the piano and Chet Baker's moaning trumpet made her fixate on the labels. Jaclyn not only realized how late it was, but the feeling of not having slept for days also crept onto her body.

She drank half her water and her eyes began to droop. Her shoulders sank as she slouched against the bar.

Jaclyn jumped as a raspy voice spoke into her ear, "Just water?"

She turned, held her breath, and stared. But after seeing who it was, she let her breath go. It was the man with the Pirates' cap, giving her a friendly smile and lighting a cigarette. He took a drag and stuck out his hand.

"Just joking. Name's Randy," the man said.

"Jaclyn," she replied, shaking his hand with a soft, nervous grip.

"You feeling alright? Maybe you could use a little more water."

"I'm fine. Why?"

"It's just that you were dozing off and saying something about *Corey*." Randy took another drag, blew the smoke away from them and asked, "Who's Corey?"

3.

"Corey," Jaclyn repeated. "He's—" Her speech faltered with the passing thought, *He's my biggest failure.* But she said, "Corey's my kid."

"Oh," Randy said, pleased. "How old is he?"

"Eleven." His age wasn't the kind of thing Jaclyn could forget. She and Corey hadn't shared a birthday since he was gone. The number was etched into her brain.

"What're you gonna do when he's a teenager and starts chasing girls?"

She gave him a fake chuckle and said, "I have no idea. I might need to start praying more when that happens. It's one of those things you don't think about until it does."

"Is he home, asleep?"

"Oh sure," Jaclyn lied, with a reassuring grin and nod. But it was a mere reflex. She hadn't *thought* about what she just told him.

"You should probably be getting back home to him. Kids need their parents, don't they?"

You don't need to remind me, buddy. "Yeah, I know. I don't plan on being here long. And I'm not drinking anyway."

Jaclyn realized the position her lie put her in. It meant one lesser possibility of getting a lead. If she had honest said that Corey was missing, Randy wouldn't have assumed it was her fault. Sympathy and a small eagerness to help would've been the first and only reaction.

That's how it was with anyone else she asked. Why Jaclyn decided to lie *this* time, she couldn't say.

And the internet hadn't given much of a lead either. With the local police already having searched for weeks, she checked social media for other police departments in the county. If the cops found a strange boy wandering around, they would've told the story over Facebook by now.

Just before her phone died and she stuffed it in the Chevy's glove compartment with her napkins and cheap prayer book, she was going through the Facebook accounts for other police departments in the state. They occasionally shared stories about missing people, but nothing hinting at Corey.

For all she knew, he could've been in a different state altogether. Earlier that evening, Jaclyn read a news article online about a boy the same age who took his brother's car and used his dad's GPS to drive two-hundred miles on his own. This kid went all the way from Simpsonville to Charleston to meet some girl from the internet.

Her blood pressure rose at the thought of Corey operating a car. There was no way she'd let him work a small, under-the-table position, let alone learn to drive. At least not at this age. Jaclyn decided he wasn't even close to old enough for any of those things. And he wouldn't be for years to come. Not until he was an adult.

Unless, she figured, her ex decided to interfere. She remembered that he let Corey go down the street on a bicycle without training wheels at the age of seven, and told her, "He's bound to get a few bumps and scrapes. That's just how little boys are. Little boys like to play rough."

A couple years later, after the divorce, he even mentioned the idea of teaching the boy how to hunt deer when he was a bit older. More than likely during his junior high years. At that point, Jaclyn decided she had enough and threw her cell phone against the wall, hard enough to crack the screen.

Even when Corey was eighteen, things like a car and a job would be questionable. The *real* world, she decided, would chew the kid up and spit him right back out. The real world was a cold, indifferent place. After all, there were more independent people than him who didn't make it. She never told a soul, but often thought of herself as one of them.

"Not that it's any of my business," Randy said. "But if ya don't mind me asking, why come to a bar just for some water? There are gas stations a little up the road from here. Just seems a little odd is all."

He was right, and the bartender glanced at Jaclyn with that same puzzled look on her face. A bar was a peculiar spot, but it gave Jaclyn an equally strange relief. It was as if she were soothing herself with her preferred elixir of alcohol without letting the stuff touch her lips. She felt the water was an adequate substitute—not for the beer and liquor—but for the physical act of drinking itself.

"I just needed something on the way," she said. "I guess I'm not totally familiar with the area."

Randy was taken aback, his eyes wide open. "You mean you're *lost?*"

"No, not *lost.* Just taking a different route than usual. I should be heading home soon. It's nothing to worry about."

"I was about to say, you got a *kid* waiting."

"Yeah," Jaclyn replied. "It's nothing like that."

The bar's phone rang. It sat next to the cash register, perhaps one of the few landlines she would ever see again. She started to wonder who still sold those things. Even with the internet, it was impossible to find a seller these days.

It could've been from an obscure little junk shop where they also repaired old machines for a small charge. They didn't pop out much, but they let people send in their appliances in through the post to get them fixed no matter the distance.

Downing the last mouthful of her raspberry kiss, the bartender answered it. Her expression hadn't changed at all, even with the vodka and juice having gone down her throat. It stayed indifferent as ever.

That girl's still pretty damn young, Jaclyn thought. *But maybe she can hold it down.*

"I'm sorry, who?" The bartender asked, plugging her free ear with the knuckle of her forefinger.

Despite how loud Chet Baker's trumpet was, Jaclyn heard a voice from the other side. It was a small and anxious voice, but clear nonetheless. Even though the voice was full of worry, there was no stutter, no hesitation. There were only two sentences over the phone:

"Jaclyn Ellsworth—she's been out there since six-thirty. Is she coming home soon?"

Somehow, Corey had found out where she was. This hit Jaclyn like a sandbag hurled at her face. Strange, she reflected, how he seemed to locate her with ease, yet she couldn't do the same.

Memories began flooding in her mind. It was the latest incidents where that exact question had been asked. The time wasn't always the same though. Sometimes she'd been away at a bar since five in the afternoon, staying later than she had now.

But tonight would be different. This would be the end of a long streak. It'd be the opportunity to find him and start anew after months of having this habit. Tonight would be the night when she could promise Corey, to his face, that she didn't drink.

He wouldn't smell beer, rum, vodka or even mouthwash on her breath. Nothing but an odd mix of Juicy Fruit and Marlboro. Corey would know that she was telling the truth.

"Hey," she said to the bartender. Waving to the younger woman, she said, "Excuse me!"

Her voice was just louder than the music, catching the bartender's attention.

The blonde girl turned to her with a puzzled look and said into the phone, "Hold on for just a moment." She asked Jaclyn, "Yes, can I help you?"

"Give me the phone," Jaclyn answered, as if asking a question. "It's for me. I know who's on the other line."

4.

"I'm sorry?" The bartender replied.

"I said that's for me."

Jaclyn couldn't understand how Corey would've found her here, at this specific tavern. But she always figured that her son was a smart kid. There was no way he wasn't. By the time he turned eleven, the boy decided he wanted to learn about computers, and managed to write basic HTML.

Using Wordpad, coding software and a couple books from the school library, he wrote his first webpage with a solid-colored background, contrasting text and hyperlinks. It was just a compilation of personal information about himself. He wrote his name, what school he attended, made some of the words hyperlinks going to the school's website. None of it was ever published to the public, just something for himself. God knew what else Corey could figure out.

When she saw that little stunt of his, Jaclyn pictured him working for *Eclipse* one day. He'd even be the right-hand man of Anthony Charles, given enough effort and encouragement.

"Uh, I'm sorry. The person on the other end's asking for—"

"I *heard* what he said," Jaclyn interrupted. "He's asking for me."

"Okay," the bartender said, her voice full of doubt. "Here you go, I guess."

Once Jaclyn put the phone to her ear, she heard a different voice on the other end. It was not gentle or childlike at all. It was rough and deep, as if this man had been a heavy smoker for decades on end. Initially, Jaclyn thought that whoever this person was, he must've taken the phone in Corey's place. A kidnapper. It started to make sense.

"Hello?" she asked.

"I *asked* if I was talking to a Jonathan Dell. Where is he? He said he's in the *Happy Duck*, and you sure as shit ain't him. Get him on the phone."

Covering the mouthpiece with her free hand, Jaclyn asked the bartender, "*Hey*, he was asking for Jaclyn Ellsworth, wasn't he?"

"Hmm? No, he wanted a Jonathan Dell, I think."

"Bu-But there was a *young boy* speaking over the phone! I heard him myself!"

"I don't know how you would've heard the other end of the line, lady. Maybe you have supersonic hearing or something, but that wasn't a kid. It was a man asking for Jonathan Dell. Who did you think was calling?"

There was a loud *screech* against the wooden floor.

A man's voice from the other end of the bar called, "Wait a sec, you said 'Jonathan Dell'?"

Jaclyn turned around to see a balding man in his late forties with a forest green dress shirt, jeans, and little streaks of black along his hands leaning against the bar by his elbows. His sleeves were rolled up past his elbows, showing what appeared to be oil going up his forearms.

"Oh," she said in a hushed voice, handing the phone back to the bartender. "Sorry."

The blonde girl took the phone and handed it to Jonathan, keeping her eye on Jaclyn the whole time.

"Hello?" he asked, turning away from everyone. He muttered, "Crazy bitch tryin' to steal my phone call."

The bartender made herself another raspberry kiss and asked her, "I take it you're Jaclyn then?"

"Yeah. Sorry about that. I just thought I heard someone else on the line."

"No, I get it. Everyone makes mistakes. You sure you're feeling okay?"

"I'm fine, for the most part."

"Well," the bartender replied, taking a sip. "I won't force anything, but that usually means something's wrong." She took another sip as she listened.

Jaclyn wanted to tell anyone, even strangers like her. She wanted to explain how Corey was *somewhere* out there. Maybe picked up at this point. Kidnapped. Possibly dead. Perhaps being taken care of. Or even wandering the big open highways of the country by himself. Hell, if that other kid his age could drive two-hundred miles from one end of South Carolina to the other—

She considered telling a perfect stranger what she'd done—how everything was her fault. How she *drove* her only child into oblivion.

But she already lied. Not even for any good reason. The lie had no advantage. But if their first real impression of her was as a liar, they wouldn't want to help. They'd only think of a way to call the authorities on her.

A vision of long vertical metal bars and the rest of the world laughing at her flashed in front of her eyes. Besides, she wouldn't see him again anyway. The tens of voicemails from her ex with reworded threats about dragging her ass to court for the umpteenth time echoed in her mind.

She bit her tongue.

"I'm—" her speech faltered as she swallowed. "I'm trying to get things back together. And I don't know what I'm doing. Maybe I just needed to relax." *But what I need is another chance,* she thought. *Forgiveness.*

"Yeah, I getcha. But what's the problem? What happened?"

Jaclyn hesitated, then replied, "I'm not sure how to explain it. It's just like the rug's been pulled out from under me."

"Oh. Well, did you lose your job?"

"No, I quit my job a little while ago."

"You quit?" the bartender asked. "Then where's your money coming from?"

"I got an inheritance."

"Oh wow, alright then." The bartender gave her a sly grin and asked, "Aren't *you* the lucky one?"

"At first, I thought so too. But lately it feels like there isn't much left. I can get by without trouble, but money can only do so much. I need to make a better life for my kid."

"I think I understand," the bartender said. "Where'd the inheritance come from? If you don't mind me asking, that is."

The ice sliding against her lips, Jaclyn finished her water, set the glass down and answered, "Parents."

"Well, I'm uh, I'm sorry to hear about them."

"Thanks."

"So what's the plan?"

"Plan?"

"Sure," the bartender replied. "Your plan to get things together for your kid."

A few seconds of silence. "You know, to be honest, I'm not sure. I guess it sounds pretty bad, but I don't have a plan."

"Maybe you'll figure it out soon. But you can't do much if you don't have a plan. If it means anything… Hey, you've probably heard of Anthony Charles, right?"

"Yeah, the guy who owns *Eclipse?* What about him?"

"He came from a broken home. He didn't have two nickels to rub together as a kid but look at him now. Must be one of the richest men in the country. He's even about to release a new smartphone. You hear about this?"

"Not sure I have," Jaclyn answered.

"Apparently it starts as a totally blank phone with no applications or anything. Starts off at maybe fifteen dollars or something. But the cost only goes up with every application on it. It's supposed to be totally customized for the user. So if you want, you could have a phone that does Facebook chats and text messages but no calls."

"You're kidding."

"Nope. And if he can be that successful, there's no reason you couldn't make things better for yourself. You just gotta put your mind to it."

“Maybe, but I don’t know if it’s that simple,” Jaclyn said. “Having Corey and the inheritance are really the only blessings I’ve had. A lot of people are really just out to screw you over.”

The bartender took a drink and replied, “If you say so. I might still be young, but sulking didn’t get me a job and a place to live. And it didn’t get Anthony Charles where he is either. You know, I hear that man’s a lot more than just an industrialist.”

“What else could he possibly be doing? It’s not enough that the whole tech world’s in the palm of his hand?”

“To tell you the truth, I don’t know how to explain it without sounding crazy. You’d have to see it to know what I mean. I guess it’s a kind of healing.”

“Would I find it if I looked up his name?” Jaclyn asked.

“I doubt it. For some reason, he doesn’t seem to like *all* his work being on the internet. Apparently when he makes appearances, people aren’t even allowed to keep their phones on. There’s heavy security and if they catch you, you’ll get thrown out. I’ve heard they usually break people’s phones and cameras on sight.”

Jaclyn gave her a puzzled look and replied, “Sounds pretty crazy to me. Destroying property over a little footage is a little extreme, doncha think?”

"Yeah, but I don't make the rules for stuff like that. They're not *my* events, you know."

"How do they get away with it?"

The bartender pondered and replied, "They probably have people sign a waiver saying that other people's belongings aren't their responsibility." She shrugged and leaned forward. "But I've gone and seen him at one of these exclusive presentations of his. He didn't show off any new gadgets or anything."

"Then what was it about?"

"He healed a man."

"Healed? What do you mean?"

The bartender answered, "He brought a man up on stage—this guy, probably in his fifties. Been stuck in a wheelchair for most of his life because of a car accident. Anthony knelt next to him and put his hands on the guy's back. Then, he told him to *stand.* Next thing I knew, I was pretty much about to piss myself because this handicapped guy had *gotten up out of his chair.* And he even started *walking.* He had a little trouble, but still, he was *walking.*"

5.

"Trixie, what are you going on about?" Randy asked the bartender, taking another drag and blowing smoke out in a thin stream.

"Anthony Charles—one of his gatherings. And he's about to come back."

"You're saying he magically *healed* someone who couldn't walk?" There was a natural persuasion in his voice when he asked a question like that. It had this quality that could make someone doubt the existence of gravity.

"I didn't say anything about magic," Trixie replied. "But yes, I said he *healed* a man. When *you* say it, it always sounds like it was staged." She cocked her brow and gave him that sly grin as she said, "Like a parlor trick or something."

"Well…" Randy tilted his head as if to say he didn't mean to be rude. "How do you know it wasn't?"

"You don't just trick someone's spine into working again."

"Was this something you just *heard* about? Or did you see it for yourself?"

"I saw it with my own eyes, Randall. It was in a room full of regular, working people, just like you and me."

"Even then—" he took a drag. "He coulda been an actor—" and exhaled.

"An actor…" Trixie smiled, rolled her eyes and shook her head. "You wouldn't think that if you were sitting next to me."

"I would. Hell, I seen magicians in Vegas before. I didn't go around calling them healers though."

"Maybe that's your problem. Ye of little faith, you only want to disprove everything."

"Trix, you show me a so-called 'faith healer'," he said, making air quotes with his fingers "who *really* cured some old lady's arthritis, and I'll show you a goddamned con artist. If he quit putting on that big, ugly grin of his like he was Joel Osteen, *that'd* be a real miracle."

"But he's already wealthy. Why would he need to con people?"

Randy smiled at her and answered, "Never stopped other charlatans before. Gotta keep the money rollin' in, don't they? But like you pointed out, the guy's a billionaire, yet he keeps pumping out gadgets anyway. He could retire and just live off his money, but he doesn't."

As she was being handed the phone from Jonathan, Trixie replied, "Would *you?* You might've said that if you won the lottery, you'd split the money with your coworkers to walk out of the job at the same time. But would you really stop working altogether?"

"Well, not altogether."

"Right. I don't think being rich would stop you from producing. You're already used to it. And so is Anthony Charles. That's why he won't stop. Besides, he knows how many people depend on him."

Exhaling another breath of smoke, Randy rolled his eyes and smiled back, as if to return the favor. "Spoken like a true believer."

"Damn straight. And why not? I saw him do it with my own eyes, didn't I?"

"I s'pose a businessman can do good for the people, but I just can't trust a big businessman. Let alone some con man. Hell, as far as I'm concerned, sometimes they're the same. Anthony Charles is just more obvious if he's trying to pull some faith healer stunt."

"I'm telling you," Trixie said. "It's not the same thing."

"If you say so. But you said they can't film or take any pictures?"

"Yeah, what about it?"

"But doesn't that sound kinda weird?"

Trixie leaned forward, her elbow on the bar and drink in her other hand. "I guess. Maybe he just likes his privacy."

"Anything you say, Trixie. Just wondering, that your fourth cocktail tonight?" Randy chuckled, as he reached the end of his cigarette.

A voice from the other end of the bar interjected. "We talking about the owner of *Eclipse* over there?"

"That we are," the bartender answered, sipping her drink.

"I mean, maybe she's onto something there, Randy. I wouldn't be so quick to conclusions. What if this Anthony Charles is the real deal?" Jonathan asked.

"A real load o' bullshit. Bad enough to work for one of those big industrialist types. Now you're acting like the fella's a holy man or somethin'. I'm tellin' you, he's probably a con man. They always turn out that way, and they always just want your money."

Trixie turned toward Jonathan and replied, "He didn't."

"He didn't? What do you mean?"

"When I saw him heal that man, he didn't ask for any money at all, Randall. Didn't try to sell us anything. None of that."

"Still pretty weird if you ask me."

"Yeah, well, when did I ever ask you?"

"You're still young," Randy said, putting his cigarette out against the ashtray in front of him.

"So? What do you know, old man?"

"I know you've been helping yourself to free drinks when the owner's not around. I also know he might not be happy if he catches you."

"*I* hope you're right, Trix," Jonathan said, stopping her from raising her voice, placing his roughened hand over hers and smiling. "And maybe you are. I can't speak for him, but I'm still willing to believe."

"Er, thanks," she replied, giving him a fake smile and pulling her hand away. "I appreciate it."

The jukebox was silent. Jaclyn hadn't noticed at first but she realized that *Sultry Eve* had already faded out. There was a faint *hiss*, almost imitating a record player, followed by the sound of Jamie Berry's *Peeping Tom.*

As the piano followed the beat of the drums to perfection, she said, "It still sounds incredible to see." Turning to the bartender, Jaclyn asked, "You said you saw the guy in person. How'd you manage?"

"Oh, I traveled a lot and had a few connections while I was still in college."

"College? So you quit?"

"Yeah," Trixie replied. "I dropped out. I hate to say it, but university was just an excuse to see the world. Studying abroad, all that jazz. I guess I could go back if I wanted. My parents said they'd pay for the tuition and everything, but it really wasn't for me. Seeing Anthony Charles was probably just a once in a lifetime thing. A one in a million chance."

"Sounds about right."

"I don't know if I'd do it again if I had the chance though."

"Huh? How come?"

"I'm not sure how to explain it. He looked sort of—" she motioned her free hand in little circles "—*different* in person, you know? It was amazing, but at the same time, something about him made me feel kind of intimidated. I guess I just felt like I really didn't belong."

"Oh," Jaclyn replied with her brow up. "Yeah, I guess that makes sense."

"But I was fine by the end of it," Trixie said with a reassuring tone.

"I mean, he's pretty famous. Maybe you were just a little starstruck."

"Yeah, *exactly*."

Jaclyn decided to hold her tongue but had a hunch that the young bartender had improvised that last remark. Like she would've said anything to purge any discomfort from the conversation.

"But it'd probably be even more amazing to see it a second time. I wouldn't be so taken aback."

"Right," Jaclyn replied as she got up, her foot inching toward the door.

"You don't want more water or anything?"

"Uh, no thanks. I need to head out."

Jaclyn pushed her chair in and turned to head for the exit when she was interrupted. "*Oh*, before you go—" She turned back to see Trixie presenting a folded-up sheet of paper to her. She said, "Just in case you ever get bored. I do it with everyone here. Good meeting you."

Taking the piece of paper, Jaclyn smiled and stuffed it in her pocket. She gave Trixie a cheap smile and thanked her, already planning to toss the thing in the garbage later that night.

A little too friendly for the first time meeting, she thought. *Maybe she means well, but that girl weirds me out a little.*

"Come back some time," Trixie said.

"Maybe, who knows?" Jaclyn replied, walking out the door and back into the rain.

She got in the Chevy, turned her key in the ignition, and put it into reverse. As she turned and crept onto the shoulder of the road, she felt her breaths growing shorter. It was as if she'd been powerwalking instead of sitting in a tavern.

A wave of anxiety hit her. The shortness of breath that came out of nowhere was a brand-new sensation. It could be nothing serious. Just a sign of getting older.

There wasn't any incoming traffic. She turned onto the road and went further down the rainy highway. The whole stop had just been wasted time and opportunity. No progress on tracking Corey down.

But then again, at least she knew that there was a gas station up along the highway. If not, a place to sleep for the night would be.

6.

"And Jonathan, or whatever his name is, thinks *I'm* crazy," Jaclyn said and shut the radio off.

She could feel an oncoming headache. She couldn't tell if it was the lighting, the music in the bar, or just dehydration. Her throat wasn't feeling raw since she went into the tavern. She checked the digital clock and saw that it was two minutes to midnight.

The Chevy continued its tricks from earlier that night. It slowed down, whistled, *kicked*, and caught back up to speed again. But the whistle wasn't as loud as she remembered it from earlier.

Jaclyn couldn't believe she had forgotten. It was the reason for the radio being on in the first place. An anxious pulse of putrid acid shot through her brain. At any point, the engine would burst and send her swerving off the road. Every yard she drove, the idea became more certain in her mind.

"Jesus *God*," she growled, gritting her teeth. "This son of a bitch better not break down on me. Of all times to have problems…"

Thinking about what she just said, Jaclyn asked for forgiveness in her head, assuring she didn't mean it. She took another ultra-light, held it in her mouth and lit the end. She cracked the window again and took her first drag. It was always a nearly automatic action.

Jaclyn began to reconsider her actions. She was driving down a small, lonesome highway, and thinking Corey could be there had been pure idiocy. She thought she was wasting her time.

What I should be doing is speeding up and stopping before this engine blows out on me.

Her speed went up to sixty-five but slowed down again. The whistle was louder, the *kick* after harder than before.

She felt her heart stop in for a second and slowed down to ten miles below the speed limit. The cigarette wasn't enough of a distraction from her engine. The whistling noise alone sounded like a group of streaming missiles. Jaclyn was just waiting for the inevitable explosion.

Turning the radio back on, she only heard a string of advertisements playing over WDVE.

There're enough ads on the internet. The radio doesn't need to give people a reason to not listen. People want music, not this.

She started switching the stations without looking at the radio. She only needed to pay attention to the road. Jaclyn had heard somewhere that deer liked to spring out of nowhere on these roads. The highways more so than anywhere else. She hadn't been in an accident involving deer but saw enough pictures to not question it.

She took her fingers off the car's buttons when music started playing instead of advertisements and late night, in-studio talk shows. It was something she'd never heard before—Electric Swing Circus' *Golden Hour.*

As the smooth female vocals played, she took a deep breath and flicked her cigarette through the crack in her window. She turned the volume up a little, trying to think of where to go to fix the Chevy.

It was useless. She didn't know the area, and it was the weekend. Most garages were bound to be closed until Monday. And her phone had already died before she reached the tavern, so she didn't have a GPS to tell her which ones were nearby.

"Shit," Jaclyn muttered. "I should've brought my phone charger. Then I could've had a full battery by now."

She slowed down and stopped at the next red light. There still wasn't a single car behind her. It wasn't something Jaclyn had done before, but she figured there was a moment before the light would turn green again.

The fatigue's thick, viscous weight that made her slouch and her eyelids droop in the tavern crept along her entire body again. It made her feel as if a gelatinous ooze were coaxing her body to lie down.

Just for a second, she thought. *It won't hurt. I'll just shut my eyes for a—*

As her eyes shut, Jaclyn heard the faint *click-clack* of footsteps in the distance. Everything was dark beyond the stoplight. Even her headlights couldn't penetrate the sea of shadows that lay before her.

As the *click-click-clack* grew louder, the engine slowed down. The car's natural *purr* relaxed, yawning into the night, and finally stopped. The Chevy was still on, but as Jaclyn anticipated, the engine had given up. All she probably needed was a jump start—something to get her to the nearest motel. But there wasn't another car in sight for the entire night.

She heard the *click-clack* approaching the edge of the darkness. It stopped before going underneath the stoplight. It was watching her. Jaclyn knew it. Cold sweat formed at the roots of her hair.

A deep, monstrous breathing stirred the air. She couldn't identify who was making the noise, but it sounded like a stalking, wild beast. The breathing changed to a deeper, intermittent growl.

Jaclyn found herself gazing into the dark. She hadn't realized that her body paralyzed. The only thing in the world was what lay beyond her eyes' reach.

"*Jaclyn*," a raspy voice whispered to her.

A withered, gray hand reached out from the darkness, underneath the stoplight. It was the left hand of a creature with long, yellowed and gnarled fingernails. They were ridged, as if from age and disease.

The skin hung loose and had tiny bits of protruding hair. The back of the hand had a chalk-white mark. It looked like a birthmark, resembling a symbol of some kind. But she couldn't see well enough to make it out.

All the fingers, except the forefinger, were curled together into a fist. The lone forefinger hung somewhat limp but pointed at Jaclyn in accusation.

"*I* know *you, Jaclyn Ellsworth*," it said to her. "*I* know *you*."

She sprung awake to the loud *honk* behind her. In her rearview mirror, she saw the blinding white light of someone else's headlights. Looking at the stoplight, she saw it had already turned green.

She realized that her car wasn't off at all. It was still in drive, but her foot was on the brake the whole time.

An angrier *honk* from behind. She took her foot off the brake and floored the gas. The engine simply *revved* at first but got her moving at forty-five miles an hour, gradually creeping up to the speed limit. The car behind her didn't turn. It stayed behind her at the same pace.

"What's that guy's problem?" Jaclyn asked herself.

She had to suppress the urge to speed up to put some distance between them. Car maintenance wasn't her forte—she had admitted it to people countless times by now. But she had a strong gut feeling that if she drove any faster, the car would only break down sooner.

Another *honk* from behind. It was longer than the others. The markers on the road didn't indicate that it was okay to pass. But it was just the two of them.

She gestured him to go around. His lights were shining into her face. She figured there was no way he didn't see her waving. But the stranger refused.

Jaclyn couldn't see the person driving behind her. She couldn't even discern the car itself. It was as if two disembodied, glowing eyes were on tailing her.

7.

The area Jaclyn was approaching had dense patches of trees on either side of the road. They were impossible to see through, more so in the dark, even with the stranger's headlights reflecting from her mirrors.

A yellow diamond-shaped sign up ahead warned them of approaching sharp curves. She tried to slow down for safety's sake, but it didn't stop the driver behind her. He didn't decelerate at all.

His raging headlights only gained on her, inches away from scraping her bumper. Another vicious *honk*.

"How do I get that bastard off my ass?" Jaclyn asked, gritting her teeth.

Her body swayed with the Chevy as she made the first sharp turn to the left. The stranger behind her executed the turn much smoother, as if he rehearsed it.

A second sharper turn followed to the right. Jaclyn saw that she was going onto the wrong side of the road but corrected herself. The honking continued in a constant, furious stream.

A final swerve to the left and Jaclyn couldn't believe her eyes. She saw the driver behind her drifting to the left through her rearview mirror. He sped up and the grill of his car was alongside her trunk now.

She wondered, "Is that psycho finally going around?"

She watched him creep up beside her on the road, ignoring the kickback from her engine. It wasn't long until his passenger window met with hers.

The other driver didn't speed up after that. He maintained his speed and stayed next to her. Jaclyn's eyes went from the road to the other car and back again.

That crazy bastard better hope no one else is out. It'll be a head-on collision if he doesn't just pass already.

She glanced at the other car again, seeing that the driver rolled his passenger window down. Jaclyn didn't see the person inside. The other driver was concealed by shadows.

The honking continued. It was grating against her ear drums like a record being played backwards by hand.

The glint of metal flashed in the corner of her left eye. As the projectile coin made an echoing *crack* against the window, Jaclyn saw the face of George Washington on it.

"*Jesus,*" she yelled.

Her window had a blotched white patch surrounded by a little web of cracks. Her only question was whether the web would expand through the rest of her window once the strange car sped up.

He sped up to seventy, drove around Jaclyn and honked one final time. He left a trail of sound behind him until he was out of her sight.

She realized her heart was beating at a hundred miles an hour. Taking a longer drag than usual, she slowed the Chevy back down again. It was moving at ten miles below the speed limit again, and the road was a straight shot.

Flicking the ash off her cigarette, she said, "Fucking psycho. I'm willing to bet there's a body out here somewhere, and he *put* it there. God forbid Corey go anywhere *near* this place."

Driving through this part of the highway made her glad she hadn't found him in the area. If he were at the edge of those woods, there'd be one kind of predator or another following behind him.

But what if he was already in there?

The thought was a real possibility. Jaclyn had to force it out of her mind. She wasn't about to pull over and search through the woods, especially out of paranoia. Having gone down this highway didn't mean he would've wandered through the woods. There wasn't any motivation. He was far too smart for something like that, she decided.

Once the expansion of woodlands ended, so did the road. Jaclyn stopped at a three-way intersection. Both turns led to an area she hadn't heard of.

The left was a road leading toward Quakerston, and the right went to Dourmsburg. From the intersection, she could tell that the left turn went into more empty, grassy hills and eventually the woods. Peering to her right, Jaclyn saw flickering white light in the distance. Even if she didn't find a place to sleep right away, lights were a sign of people.

Worst-case scenario, she always had the option of sleeping in the car. It wouldn't have been her first time.

Turning right, she remembered the innocent little questions she would hear from the back seat during a trip that lasted late enough into the night.

Corey would ask, "Are we going to a motel, Mom?"

Now, there would be no uncertainty about that question, as long as the car didn't break down. She would never consider sleeping in the car. She had money now. Gone were the days of surviving off a maid's wages.

Gone, also, were the days of reminding Corey not to tell her ex that they couldn't find a place to sleep. Once she found Corey, Jaclyn could even buy a modest house. Her parents would've wanted that anyway, wouldn't they?

Further down the road, the cluster of light divided and coalesced into tiny streetlights. Once she reached those, a wave of relief washed over her. Not only were there lights, but single-storied houses also appeared.

"I can finally pull over soon," she said.

She thought back to the diner. What were the chances of the old woman at the table behind her being wrong? The fact that she wore glasses meant that her eyesight wasn't perfect. And this was a stranger. How did Jaclyn know she hadn't been lying?

What if she was wasting her time, gas and peace of mind?

Unless more people claimed to have seen him, the chances of her being wrong were overwhelmingly high. The deeper she drove into Dourmsburg, the more real that idea became.

"If that old bat was wrong, I'm gonna kill her."

The old woman Jaclyn talked to said he'd just left the restaurant and took the following exit west. According to her story, he was being driven off in a black Cadillac.

She couldn't think of anyone she knew who drove a car like that, and the description was vague. But even that was better than nothing. Arriving at a sloping four-way intersection, she stopped and looked to the left.

Jaclyn saw a cluster of gas stations, local restaurants and a small two-star hotel.

8.

Everything was closed for the night, except for the pizza joint, gas stations and the Cozy Moon. Jaclyn's stomach was starting to rumble, but food wasn't important right now. The only two things that mattered were getting another lead and a few hours of shuteye.

Parking at the Cozy Moon, she stepped out of the car, dropped her cigarette to the pavement, and crushed it out with her shoe. The cherry was near the filter anyway, so she figured it didn't matter. Just noticing the tall, plastic bin a couple feet from the glass front doors, Jaclyn thought it wasn't worth bothering. A single butt wasn't a big deal.

"I hate to say it," she told herself. "But one of those raspberry kisses doesn't sound like a bad idea right about now."

But on the other hand, Jaclyn remembered that she still managed not to drink. And at a *tavern.* She went into a snake pit and coming out without a single bite.

Smirking and covering her head from the light rain, she sprinted inside. She looked around the front lobby. It had chrome-colored floors with reflective surfaces, white chairs and couches with arms backs at right angles.

A coffee table with a copper frame and glass surface stood between two of the chairs. An empty martini glass was placed on it with a napkin for a coaster.

A television was suspended from the ceiling at the end of the lobby to her right. It was playing the news, probably as a default for the guests passing by with nothing better to do.

The TV didn't have audio, just continuous subtitles. However, the lobby had a speaker in every corner along the ceiling. The volume wasn't loud, but the twinkling piano of LVDS' *Café Noir* was playing throughout the room. She took her eyes off the tv and looked back at the coffee table.

Temptation rose like a fire given a splash of gasoline. If she took the glass, who would've noticed? She looked over to the front desk and saw a burley attendant standing at over six feet tall. Aside from the black collared shirt and slacks of his uniform, he wore a pair of reading glasses and a crew cut. He was working something into the computer system at his station.

He could've been the type who got so distracted by his own work that the rest of the world ceased to exist. Then again, this gentleman could also have been the type to be aware of everything around him, like a motion sensor that encompassed an entire room. There was no way to tell which.

Jaclyn decided against stealing the drink. It wasn't because of the front desk employee, but the thought of breaking her sobriety. She hadn't touched the sauce for months. It wasn't worth breaking now. If she did, that'd be months of effort trashed for nothing.

Was I really about to do that? she thought. *Someone already drank part of it. God, who knows what was on their mouth beforehand? They could've had a disease.*

She brushed her lips with her forefinger and approached the front desk. Nothing about the man working there conveyed he'd hurt a fly. Yet his size alone made her wish it were someone else instead.

"Hi," she said. "Could I just get a single bed for tonight?"

The employee looked away from the computer and replied, "Sure, I just need you to sign in first." As he spoke, the front desk man handed her a clipboard with a half-filled page.

"Oh, right," Jaclyn said, looking at his nametag, which read *Thomas*.

"How's your night going?" Thomas asked with a warm smile.

"It's going, I guess. How about yours?" She signed in, gave him her American Express card, and returned the clipboard.

Taking it back, he replied, "Not bad, just a little slow." He swiped the Amex, handed it back to her after the transaction went through, and gave Jaclyn the card key for her room.

"Thanks." Putting the key in her pocket, she thought, *Maybe he's seen Corey.* "I'm sorry to ask, but you wouldn't have a phone charger I could use, would you?"

"Oh yeah, we do." Thomas pointed toward the chairs in the lobby. "We have a few chargers plugged over there. I'm sorry to say, but we just have Eclipse, Apple and Android chargers. I hope that's okay."

"Oh yeah, that's perfect. Thank you."

Running back outside to the parking lot, she whipped the keys from her pocket. She hit the unlock button on her ignition key and flung the passenger door open. Digging in her glove compartment, Jaclyn grabbed her Eclipse Gamma phone and one of the wrinkled napkins. She slammed the door shut on her way out and rushed back in.

Jaclyn took another look in the main lobby. She found a multi-outlet cord attached to the wall opposite the front doors. They had a charger for the three kinds of smartphone Thomas mentioned.

They were attached to the multi-outlet itself, and no matter which muscle one used, none of them could be pulled out with brute force. It was a kind of mechanism that only unlocked through the owner's laser key, a laser pointer with an extra feature. Jaclyn and countless others had to admit it was a smart move for anyone with valuables to have at least one of these keys.

She plugged her phone to the charger, letting her body sink into one of the cushioned, white chairs. It wouldn't take long to have enough battery power now. It would only take thirty seconds to revive the battery to one percent again. From there, each percentage needed only another twenty seconds.

When her phone was at two percent, Jaclyn checked her calls. There were none from the police yet. Even if they hadn't called her back, they must've been searching. She noticed there also weren't any new calls from her ex-husband either.

What a surprise, she thought.

But there were still the voicemails. There weren't any new messages from her ex's number, but she still had the cluster that'd been ignored. They were still marked unread, even though she had seen them in her Calls app without listening to them.

"Damn phone's glitching," Jaclyn said. "Didn't expect this from *Eclipse* of all brands."

She exited the Calls app and opened her photo gallery. It took a moment of scrolling but Jaclyn found the picture she was looking for.

Jaclyn stood up from her chair and unplugged the phone after selecting that picture. An ember of curiosity had started burning in her thoughts. Listening to the voicemails wouldn't bring her any closer to finding Corey. She knew that right off the bat.

But another part of her wanted to find out what he had said anyway. It was like the rumor she heard as a schoolgirl—apparently an African child would slap a sleeping lion in the face to try and outrun it as a game of courage.

She approached Thomas again and saw that he was busy, pounding away at the keyboard. Peering at the screen, she discovered what he was doing wasn't work-related. He was texting with an unusually pretty, long-haired woman over Facebook. Jaclyn read something this woman had written about just getting out of the shower and decided to keep her eyes away.

"Excuse me?" she asked.

Rushing to close his Facebook, Thomas replied, "Yes?"

"I was just wondering if you've seen someone."

9.

"*Seen* someone?" Thomas asked, cocking his brow.

"Yeah," Jaclyn replied. "Someone named Corey come by here? Corey Archer?" Although *Archer* was her son's last name, she was reminded that it had also been her ex's.

"Who's Corey Archer?"

"My son. He's only eleven and I've been trying to find him."

"He's *missing?* I can call the police."

As he reached for the desk phone, Jaclyn interrupted, "No, no, it's fine. They already know about it. They've been searching too, but I haven't heard anything in a while."

"Oh wow, I'm—really sorry to hear about that."

"It's not your fault." Returning to the picture in her phone, she held the device up in front of him. "You haven't *seen* him, have you?"

The picture showed a boy with dirty blond hair, with bangs reaching his eyebrows. He was sitting on the stoop of the house Jaclyn used to rent before she was evicted, packed up and travelled elsewhere. The boy had a toothy grin and his elbows were resting on his knees. His cheeks rested on his palms, pushing them up. He was dressed in a t-shirt and pair of athletic shorts—Corey was a part of an image that reminded Jaclyn not only of him but also the house where they had lived a year ago.

"Well," Thomas responded. "I haven't seen him around the hotel. I'm sorry." He pondered for another moment and said, "But now that I think about it, he does kinda look familiar. Can't really put my finger on it though."

"So you think he could still be around here?" She gazed into the picture again.

Memories of the old house resurfaced. It was one of the few times when Corey had his own room, although it was small and drab. It had nothing but a closet, a bed, his small collection of toys and a set of curtains. Even the expense of a dresser drawer had been too much at the time. Corey's clean underwear and socks would be folded up and neatly placed in his closet, but it was still something.

Corey never questioned their conditions—Jaclyn supposed he was too young to really question these things, or he just appreciated what little they already had. How would she have explained to him that she was in-between jobs because she showd up to her cleaning job with her breath smelling of vodka? And how could she just get another job after being fired like that?

"I don't know," Thomas said reluctantly. "But he could be."

"Yeah, I really hope so too." Jaclyn's eyes started looking even more sunken and melancholic as she continued. "I don't know what else I can do. All I can really do is hope the police get back to me and keep looking for myself. I'm not exactly a professional detective, but it's better than just sitting on my ass, right?"

"A *lot* better. To be honest though, I'm kind of filling in for someone tonight. I haven't been here the whole night shift."

"Someone call off?"

"No, the girl who'd usually work the front desk tonight left early."

"Oh, how come?" Jaclyn asked.

"Don't know. She didn't say. Apparently, it was an emergency though. She's had perfect attendance, so it's probably important. I hope she's okay. I mean, whenever she's back, I can ask if she knows anything."

"Thanks. I really appreciate it."

Taking a closer look at Thomas, she noticed a silver pendant on a thin chain around his neck. The pendant's left side was a solid crescent, glimmering in the fluorescent light from the ceiling. The rest of its design, a thin hollow circle, overlaid the crescent.

She couldn't say how, but it looked familiar. Jaclyn could identify the symbolism of every religious pendant she'd seen before. Religions around the world and even the occult were a strong interest of hers, despite her Catholic upbringing telling her that some of these practices were blasphemous.

It was the most common topic across her bookshelf. Besides the Bible and a few Stephen King novels, dream dictionaries, and a couple anthologies from H.P. Lovecraft, this was all of her reading material.

The pendant reminded her of the Wiccan jewelry of the lunar phases. But this was something different altogether.

"I hope you don't mind me asking," she said, pointing at his pendant. "But what's that on your necklace?"

"This?" He pinched the front end of his chain and examining the pendant for a moment, as if he'd just found it. He let it go and replied, "It's just a symbol of my faith."

Jaclyn smiled and said, "Oh, okay."

She thought that it could be harmless as the little gold crucifix dangling around her neck. But she remembered the numerous strange cults that had existed in recent times. Jaclyn was reminded of Aum Shinrikyo, the Japanese cult that attacked the local metro system with poison gas during the mid-nineties.

She realized that although she was just an outsider looking in on Aum Shinrikyo, the people operating it behind closed doors deserved the most suspicion. Recalling how it looked harmless to the public at first, she had a feeling that it wouldn't end well—even as the story first came out when she was a little girl.

"They were secretly making sarin gas and anthrax," she'd heard her dad telling her mother after school.

Stopping the train of thought right there, she realized how silly it all was. Even if this person had some strange ideas, it didn't make him a threat.

Curious as she was, Jaclyn decided not to ask about it. It was far too easy to get in an argument over personal faith. She knew all too well about the long and painful history with the Protestants, despite Catholics and Protestants being Christians.

Jaclyn never liked admitting it, but she knew plenty of stories about her own sect. She wouldn't deny that the jokes about Catholic priests were well-justified.

"Well, it was good meeting you," she said.

"You too. I hope your evening gets better."

"Thanks."

Jaclyn turned around and walked out of the main lobby. She went down the main hall, past the bathrooms and toward the elevators.

There were two sets of elevator doors and a stairwell to the left. She pressed the button to go up and waited until one of the elevators opened. Stepping inside, Jaclyn hit the button for the second floor and stared out into the hallway, as if waiting for other guests to join her. As the doors closed, an icy mist slithered inside and settled against the skin of her neck, whispering:

I know you.

10.

It didn't take Jaclyn long to find her room as she walked through the second floor. She slid the key card and unlocked the front door. The second she opened it, the faint scent of linen and fake lemons wafted around her.

Her eyes instantly fixed on the bed. It was a double-wide bed, meaning plenty of room to stretch out. The mere sight of it was a relief. It was the first small dose of aspirin for a splitting headache.

Jaclyn wanted to run to the bed like an eager lover and cuddle it tight, but her body would only let her drag her feet. She realized that this was her reward for being in the car all day. There was an unspoken joy to being on the road, but the car always sucked the lifeblood out of her.

Jaclyn approached the bed and collapsed, lying on her stomach. There were a few days' worth of clothes sitting in the trunk, but she'd put them in the closet later. But what that really meant was *tomorrow*, and Jaclyn knew herself too well to deny it.

As her body relaxed, she let out all her breath and looked up. Across the small room from her bed was a television mounted into the wall. The remote was placed on the nightstand beside the mattress and there was no doubt that this Roku TV had internet access.

She squirmed across the mattress, reached for the remote and snatched it. Jaclyn turned the TV on and went straight for the YouTube feature. She noticed the TV had an option for regular cable, which surprised her. Who demanded cable TV these days? Even the elderly, who grew up with cable, were doing just fine with it as far as she could tell.

It could've been the nostalgia. That had the potential to sell just about anything.

"All I need is a little music," she murmured.

She checked the volume, saw it was low, and went to YouTube's home page. Going down to the music section, she selected whatever was on display, and put her head down without looking at the song's title.

The television played John L. Nelson's *Lonely*, the slow piano rocking her to sleep. It didn't matter that she was still in her street clothes. Even her shoes were still on. All that mattered was being able to sleep on a proper bed.

The lower end hotel room took her back down Memory Lane. Memories of staying up this late into the night with Corey, microwaving hot cocoa and watching *The Nutty Professor* with Eddie Murphy resurfaced. She also remembered being too embarrassed to tell anyone that she had to get a cheap room, until the money ran out.

As Jaclyn let her body sink with the mattress, a small but potent *squeak* shot through the room. It made her jump. Her eyes were wide open. She found herself propped up on her hands and knees. It was as if she were a cat about to flee.

She panicked and looked around her room. The folding closet doors at the foot of the bed were shut. The bathroom door was ajar. Jaclyn couldn't find anything amiss. Everything looked exactly as it was when she first came in.

She looked around again and relaxed. She smirked at the way she jumped because of a little noise.

So there are *other people here*, she thought. *About time someone else peeped around here.*

She lay back down and listened again, trying to tell which room the sound came from. Footsteps, a cough, the toilet flushing, the tv. It didn't matter. Any other sign of life would be an explanation.

A faint whistle resembling the wind could be heard throughout the room. Jaclyn raised her head, eyes darting around. She walked over to the dresser drawer and opened the window just above it.

But there wasn't any wind outside. The only noise was an occasional passing car. The cool summer breeze fluttered inside her room, and Jaclyn shut the window. She figured the sound must've been her imagination. It was a long day after all. Her ears playing tricks was just a sign of being tired.

Moving away from the window, she sat back down on the mattress and pulled off her shoes. However, the sound inside the room continued. She started to think it was the ventilation, but it morphed into a whispering voice.

It was unintelligible at first, striking her ears as pure nonsense. She thought it had to have been the television from another room. But there was no denying it. The sound was coming from inside the room.

She felt crazy for even considering it, but asked in a hushed voice, "Hello?" Her eyes wandered as she asked, "Is somebody there?"

The jumbled whispers concentrated to the inside the closet, evolved into discernable words, and said, *"I know you."*

Jaclyn's heart was lodged in her throat. It was galloping like a racehorse, filling her windpipe.

She inhaled, stared at the crack between the closet doors, and repeated, "Hello?"

Silence. Not even the phony sound of the wind. Jaclyn breathed out, thinking she was hallucinating because of the fatigue and anxiety.

But a small frightened said came from within the closet, "Mom?"

Jaclyn's throat constricted. A cold ripple traveled down her skin. Just the idea of hearing Corey's voice stiffened her entire body.

"No," she mumbled. "That can't be."

She strained her eyes while looking at the closet, trying to see anything past the darkness inside of it. There was no way Corey could've been here. Yet there had to be someone waiting in the closet. Somebody who already knew them.

She'd see a hint of movement. An arm shifting. Facial features changing. A pair of unknown eyes staring back at her from the abyss. But whatever the body in the closet was, it was completely still.

"Mom?"

And it sounded just like him too. The mimicry was on par with its hiding.

That can't be him, she thought. *That isn't him. There's no way. No way in Hell.*

On her nightstand, there was a small lamp. She yanked the plug out, gripped the base and held it up.

Jaclyn swallowed, carefully got off the mattress, and stood on her feet. She took a deep breath, never taking her eyes off the crack between the closet doors. "Who's there?"

She slowly stepped forward on the balls of her feet. Squeezing the lamp in her right hand, she prepared for whoever was hiding in the dark.

"Mom?"

Jaclyn demanded, "I said, who's there?"

11.

Jaclyn inched to the closet doors. Her fingertips turned white as they squeezed the lamp. The lump in her throat grew.

"Mom?" The voice in the closet never changed. It was like listening to a tape recorder. Or a parrot that perfected its craft.

She pictured an entity with a protruding, elongated mouth, leech-like teeth and a gelatinous body waiting for her. She imagined a pair of semi-human hands with claws that could tear through flesh like scissors through paper, reaching around the closet doors. They were covered with mangy fur and the smell of rot. She thought of a pair of red corneas and elliptical pupils watching her, and a beastly snarl rumbling in the dark.

"Mom?"

Despite the image, she gripped one of the folding doors, raised the other arm holding the lamp, and pulled the folding door open.

The closet was empty, except for a few unused hangers. The red-hot panic in her head settled like boiling water being taken off a burner. Her breath was shorter and faster than ever. She was gasping for air.

She turned away from the closet, taking deeper breaths. Her hands were trembling uncontrollably. Although Jaclyn was struggling, she swallowed, releasing the dry lump in her throat.

Jaclyn knelt on the beige carpeted floor and set the lamp down in front of her. She held her temples, as if trying to hold her skull together in one piece. It was all a hallucination. She had to tell herself that. She needed to believe none of it was real. Nonetheless, there was a moment when it all felt too familiar.

But where did it come from? She started remembering the dream at the stoplight. But even then, her dream had a familiarity that she couldn't identify.

"It wasn't real," she said. "None of it was real."

Wiping the sweat from her face, she stepped out of the room and back into the second-floor hallway. God, she needed a cigarette.

Yeah, that'd bring the panic bubbling within her down to a warm simmer.

Jaclyn entered the elevator and returned to the first floor. She stopped after getting out of the elevator, feeling short of breath again. Bending down, she felt as if something was weighting her lungs down.

As she tried to breath deep, she heard a faint noise in the hallway. It took her a moment, but she caught her breath. She didn't care to listen or find out what the sound was. It was someone in one of the rooms. All that mattered was feeling normal again.

Another customer or, God forbid, the staff, she thought.

Why she even heard it was beyond her. She figured it was just coming from whatever she heard in her room. Her ears were just playing tricks on her, that was all. She told herself that again as she passed a couple of the rooms.

It sounded like a whisper, but she couldn't make out precise words. She glanced at the room number where it had to have come from. Room One Fourteen.

None of my business anyway.

Walking through the main lobby, she noticed Thomas still typing away. Jaclyn had suspicions as to what he was doing but couldn't be sure. The rising redness in his cheeks was all she needed to see.

It proved to be a distraction from what she'd seen in her room. The voice may not have been real, but everything else was, including a young man's testosterone.

It was just a hallucination, she thought, as if to convince herself. *I'm just stressed and tired.*

Looking up from his computer, Thomas asked meekly, "Is everything alright, ma'am?"

The question snapped her out of her thoughts. She felt as if she were yanked back into reality, without specters and ghouls that hid in the bedroom at night.

"Yeah," she lied. "I just need to go out for a smoke."

"If there's anything you need, just let us know," Thomas replied, smiling.

"Sure." As she went to the chargers and plugged in her phone, Jaclyn asked, "Where is everybody? This place just looks awfully empty, even for a small hotel."

"Well, like I said, it's been kinda slow. Plus, most guests just like staying in their rooms around this time. Not a whole lot goes on around here."

"I guess housekeeping's doing the night work?"

"Nah, housekeeping doesn't usually do their thing until morning. Like, around six or so."

She nodded and headed out the front doors, going out to the Chevy. Jaclyn returned with her box of ultra-lights, stood under one of the hotel balconies, and lit a cigarette.

Taking the first drag, she held it in longer than usual. She wouldn't admit it but was under the impression that the longer the cigarette smoke stayed in her body, the more stress it washed away. The gradual exhale assured her that there wasn't anything in the closet. And the dream at the stoplight meant nothing.

I probably won't even remember all of it in a week, she thought.

She turned and stepped close enough to the entrance to keep an eye on her phone. At any point, someone else would leave their room and come into the lobby. It wasn't the first time she'd been in a hotel.

Throughout the trip, she lived in motels and lower-end hotels that dotted the area. However, she saw more than one staff member and other guests coming and going in each one. Nighttime wasn't an exception.

No, she dismissed the thought. It was a silly paranoia. No more. She'd see more people in the morning. Driving for as long as she did was only sending her imagination into overdrive. It was because she had been cooped up in that little Chevy for so long.

Jaclyn recalled the trip to Arizona she took with her parents as a little girl. She was just old enough to ride in a car seat at the time, but from what her mother said, they "hardly had a pot to piss in."

They were trapped in an old smart car, little Jaclyn confined to her mother's lap. She remembered being held in place with a pair of strong, yet smooth and slim arms.

The only details she recalled were the oppressive summer heat coupled with a broken air conditioner, a constant thirst, and an oversized camel running from a group of strange machines. It was the first indication of having an overactive imagination: asking why a camel was in the middle of town.

It turned out that not only had the Ellsworths gone to Arizona because of a death in the family—not torture their only daughter—but the so-called *camel* was a mound of soil dug up by local construction to fix the pipes in the area.

Hell of a first memory, she always thought when it resurfaced.

"Maybe what I need is a new car soon," Jaclyn said to herself, looking at the Chevy. "You're probably gonna be shot to shit soon anyway. Maybe a nice Silverado or one of those big Ford pickups. I wouldn't be so cooped up when I'm driving anymore. I can't believe I'm thinking this, but maybe even—" she rolled her eyes and took a drag "—an Eclipse. Probably gonna be the cheapest shit on the market. Always is. But somehow the quality never takes a dive."

She imagined Anthony Charles as an octopus, taller than any building downtown—his oddly handsome face, gelled black hair, glasses, and his white and silver suit. The sleeves multiplied and transformed into tentacles, reaching everything in sight.

"There's nothing that man won't get his hands into, is there?"

It reminded her of Corey playing around on his old desktop computer. That old piece of junk had to have been one of the few computers left on the market that had Windows XP. The odds of finding it at the flea market must have been a miracle.

Jaclyn hadn't brought it up, but still felt like she could've done a lot better since he didn't have a desk to set it up on. The computer itself lay on the apartment floor, a few feet away from the living room couch, where he slept.

Amazing how he never complained, she reflected. *He was probably just happy to have his own computer.*

She remembered the day she brought it home. It took him a minute to attach the monitor, keyboard, and the mouse to the computer. The smile on his face didn't stop shining for the next two weeks.

It was because he printed out all that stuff about web design at the library the day after he got his desktop set up. Jaclyn took another deep drag and thought, *That's what kept him smiling the whole time.*

Someday, he's going be a big shot industrialist in the tech world, just like Anthony Charles. Maybe work for him at some point. Hell, maybe even give him a run for his money and start a company of his own.

If nothing else, one thing was always certain. Someday, he'd make her filthy rich.

12.

After flicking her cigarette butt onto the pavement, Jaclyn stepped back inside. She thought it was ridiculous to imagine someone stealing her phone. But then again, despite the small staff, she wasn't going to put theft past any of them.

Ambiguous thoughts passed through her mind when she remembered telling Corey about housekeepers stealing from customers. It came with an indifferent confession that she'd been one of those thieves herself. She made sure not to do that sort of thing too often at her old cleaning job. But a pearl necklace here and a gold wristwatch there sold at a downtown pawn shop bought her a decent amount of groceries.

The management addressed the complaints with her and her coworkers. The managers looked suspicious looks, to her most of all.

They didn't call any of the staff in their offices for questioning. There wasn't any real evidence to go on. How could anyone prove that one of the maids *stole* something, and the customer didn't lose it themselves? At least, unless they had security cameras.

And even if there had been an interrogation, she felt prepared. All she would've had to do was look management dead in the eye and play dumb.

But the real regret came from finding out that she could've sold the stolen jewelry for a higher price online. Corey reminded her that her ex-husband recommended them cheap internet services.

"It could help him with school," her ex said over the phone. "And nowadays, it's becoming more of a necessity to get a job. He might need it when he gets a little older and wants to find work."

Jaclyn's answer was a hard no. Until she bought her first smartphone, she admitted to not knowing much about the internet. It was a brand-new machine to her. The internet was foreign to her as surgery equipment was to a student on his first day in medical school.

She assumed it was all a matter of pride.

"The less I can associate with some people, the better," she told her parents when they asked why she didn't take the offer. But as she denied it, the regret had already started creeping in.

Walking by Thomas in the lobby, she didn't give him another passing glance. She didn't notice there was still music playing over the speaker system. The sound of Jamie Berry and Octavia Rose playing *Delight* fell on deaf ears.

Her ears were growing accustomed to the composition. She didn't feel excited about it but didn't oppose the cultural shift either. The re-popularization of jazz was a musical revolution coming full circle again. It was a phenomenon that had taken the world by storm.

By this point, every establishment had at least one jazz piece by default. She noticed that people around her were referring to the style simply as *music*, as opposed to any genre.

Now, there were plenty of times when she tuned it out from a mental reflex. For her, the only thing in the universe was the way back to her room.

Jaclyn took her phone off the charger. She walked through the lobby and into the corridor again. The string of mumbling from earlier hadn't stopped, but she didn't make out a single syllable yet. Beneath the music, it all sounded like a cluster of incoherent rubbish.

But it was all coming from Room One Fourteen.

She walked past it without a second thought, but had she pressed her ear against the door, Jaclyn would've heard, "…our offer…"

Then, a weak moan and a tiny *crackle.*

On the way to the elevator, she looked through the hallway to see if there were more people. More so if there were staff aside from Thomas. No such luck.

Hell of a long break, she thought. *And why would they go at the same time?*

Dismissing the thought, she went in the elevator and headed back to the second floor. Approaching her room, Two O Nine, Jaclyn stopped before getting so close to the door. She looked both ways across the hall.

The second-floor hall was emptier than the first. There was no sound up here at all. Jaclyn figured she'd hear a little fraction of the main lobby, but there wasn't even a peep.

It made her wonder if the guests on the first floor heard it at all themselves. There was no way. Otherwise, the complaints would've mounted by now, even with just a few guests.

"You could probably hear a mouse up here," she said to herself, staring down the longer part of the hallway.

Jaclyn considered getting a card key for a different room. But when he asked for the reason, what would she tell him?

"I need a new room because I heard my kid's voice in the closet"?

The more Jaclyn thought about it, the more psychotic it sounded. Any sane man would just give her a strange look and try to dismiss her with as kind yet patronizing tone as possible. He'd act as if he believed her just enough to talk her out of sounding like a lunatic until she left.

She'd need a reason that he could see. But any damage she inflicted would be too obviously be something she caused.

No, the whole idea was insane. There wasn't any voice in her closet, and damaging her room would only get her kicked out.

Her fingertips trembled as she reached for the doorknob. Even though she tried to rationalize the fear away, it still lingered. Jaclyn took a breath, gripping the doorknob.

It'll be fine, she thought. *All I need is some long-overdue sleep and to leave in the morning. I still can't believe I didn't sleep for an entire day.*

Jaclyn unlocked the door, slowly opened it, and stared at the bed. The only thing there was the wrinkled comforter. She took a step inside and looked at the closet.

Finally entering her room and shutting the door, Jaclyn stepped closer to the pair of folding doors. She pulled them open a second time reassuring herself there was nothing inside.

Jaclyn decided to keep them open. She crawled into bed, still wearing her street clothes. She lay under the comforter and sheets with her eyes wide open. Jaclyn had the urge to sit back up and thought about driving just a little further west.

What if he's out there right now? What are the chances? If I just try, maybe I could find him.

It was the beginning of a familiar train of thought, the one that pushed her this far down the path. The one that kept her awake at night.

But I haven't found him. What good's it gonna do not to get any sleep? Probably none at all.

She looked at her phone again, going to the Calls app. Nothing new.

"What if I don't hear back?" she asked. "What if the police don't find anything? Then what?"

Reaching toward the far corner of the nightstand, she came across a group of small controls for the overhead lighting. There was just a power button, two dials to adjust the angle of the lighting, and a brightness control. If she decided to go to a more expensive hotel, chances were, she would've had an option to change the color too.

But it didn't matter. She let the idea go like a torn plastic bag, turned off the lights, and watched the dark for hours afterward.

13.

Harsh rays of light streamed on Jaclyn's face. It turned the pleasant, tranquil darkness around her into a burning red.

The light forced her awake. The sun was glaring in the room though her window. Her eyes were still heavy, but she'd slept enough to get through the day.

After showering and dressing in the same clothes from last night, she got up and went to the door. Embarrassment crawled along her skin from wearing dirty clothes, but it wasn't the first time she did this. It wasn't an issue after doing it so often in the old house, especially when she was on the road.

Ever since Jaclyn had money in her checking account, Corey didn't have to go without shampoo. She also didn't bring alcohol in the house. It saved plenty of money for necessities like doing laundry.

Eyeing the empty closet on the way out, she closed the door behind her. She felt safer and more alone every time she looked at it.

Once she stepped into the hall, it was another long day of driving and praying that the police would call. As Jaclyn had mentioned at the diner, she wasn't the one with training and expertise. But she was desperate enough to search anyway.

They'll call me and they'll say he was found, she thought. *I know they will. I just know they will.*

Cocking her brow, Jaclyn set her eyes on the housekeeper pushing her cart of supplies closer. Just the night before, she was sure the building had been empty. The cheaper motels she stayed at might as well have been ghost towns considering their limited staff. She figured that one person must've been able to maintain the building if it was small enough.

The housekeeper had a distinct sky-blue shirt. Her dark hair was tied back into a ponytail, just long enough to dip down her shoulder.

She was wearing a necklace with a chain as thin as a spider web. The pendant had the same symbol Jaclyn noticed on Thomas. Although the jewelry was rose gold, and glimmered in the overhead light.

Jaclyn wondered if this symbol was more common than she realized. It could've been a Christian sect that adopted a new image for their faith. A living religion did that sort of thing all the time. A slice of the Christian population did that with the Egyptian ankh—reinvent the ancient sign of eternal life and apply it to the savior.

As the housekeeper stopped at the next room a couple doors down, Jaclyn pulled her phone out. She watched the woman grab bottles of cleaning products, opened the Camera app, and pointed her phone at the housekeeper.

When the woman turned toward Jaclyn to grab the paper towels, Jaclyn zoomed in on the necklace for a clear shot and clicked a picture. The image was blurry at first, but it cleared up to create a crisp view of the pendant.

"Man," she said. "Am I really doing this?"

Shame flashed across Jaclyn's face; her increasing curiosity demanded that she go through with it anyway. There wasn't a graceful way to just walk up to someone out of the blue and ask what her necklace meant.

Jaclyn saved the image and opened Bing on her phone. She heard it was easy to query an image into a search engine and find a source for it.

She tapped the option for a reverse image search. Once she uploaded the picture, it took a moment for the results page to load.

It was blank.

"Nothing at all?" Jaclyn muttered under her breath.

She assumed it was one of two things—either it was an image that already appeared on the internet, or informtion about the symbol were being taken down. More than likely, it was the former.

If the internet wouldn't help, she needed someone who already knew the symbol. But who? She pondered this and figured someone in her family could know.

She sent the image to six family members in her contacts. They were also Catholic and had attended the church. Jaclyn figured they knew a few things about spirituality too. She had a vague idea of their work schedules too. Most were day people, except the couple who worked night shifts. Even if it were still early, there was a good chance they'd answer soon.

It didn't take long before one person, her cousin Victoria, replied.

"No," she said. "I don't think I've seen that before. Sorry."

"Damn," Jaclyn said to herself. She texted back, "It's okay," and hit the send button.

Once she sent the reply, it hit her. Out of the people she texted, her cousin Vicky was the one who studied different religions at length. If she already didn't know, it wasn't likely that any of the others would.

But who else was there?

She pulled the folded sheet of paper out of her pocket and opened it. She entered the phone number in her Messages app and typed out a new text.

"Hey Trixie," she entered. "It's Jaclyn. Do you know what this is?"

She attached the image and sent it. Just looking at the time displayed on her touchscreen, she realized there was no way that girl would even be awake. It was only half past six.

But that was a major difference between the young and old. When people were young, they slept the day away. Jaclyn first learned that infants slept twenty hours a day when she was pregnant.

On the other hand, growing older devalued sleep in every sense. The hours spent dreaming every night always decreased with age.

"Trixie's probably still asleep," Jaclyn said, putting the phone back in her pocket.

Of course. She was a bartender, working until two in the morning most nights of the week. The girl was younger too. Jaclyn realized they had enough of an age gap to be mother and daughter.

But Trixie being so much younger meant she wouldn't wake up until at least ten. That was assuming she never stayed up after work.

Trixie also had her whole life in front of her. It wasn't half over yet. She still had every opportunity to grab her life by the throat, tackle it to the ground, and make it hers. Trixie wasn't far enough along her path to see graying hair and old age around the corner. It was a quality Jaclyn envied.

If she wanted, Trixie could pursue higher education again. Or build something huge on her own from the ground up. After all, her parents had money to support her.

On top of that, Jaclyn didn't see a ring on her finger either. Chances were she didn't divorce anyone either. More like, a man she'd been with didn't divorce her for cheating on him. For being impulsive. For not thinking ahead. Not thinking of what lay further ahead than her momentary desires.

Trixie would watch her own drinking—before she made any *real* mistakes. She was just working and paying bills as far as Jaclyn could tell.

It meant Trixie didn't have any family of her own yet. She didn't have to worry about whether she was doing any good for her own kids.

As Jaclyn passed the housekeeper's cart, it made her think about Trixie's position more and how good she really must've had it. Even if she didn't realize it yet.

It was a quality that made her feel a rising jealousy.

14.

Jaclyn walked to the elevator and took it down to the first floor. A gentle moan filled the main lobby. As she walked, Jaclyn couldn't help thinking the sound system was starting to fall apart. She looked behind her, seeing a couple in their early thirties. Despite any logic, she was taken aback to see more guests.

The two of them were smiling and holding hands, sporting t-shirts, shorts and baseball caps like they were on a summer getaway. Why they'd vacation in this part of western Pennsylvania, Jaclyn didn't understand. Aside from the Amish and the Steelers, there weren't many attractions.

Most of their conversation was too low to hear. But even if she were interested in it, most of it was talk of where to eat, and when to meet the woman's relatives at the airport.

At another point in their conservation, Jaclyn heard the phrase, "what happened at midnight."

It could've meant a lot of things, but it stood out anyway. She shrugged it off, walking further down the corridor.

The rooms were even quieter this morning than last night. She figured it was because of a lack of guests and staff. It made her wonder how often the business here was so slow.

It couldn't have been often. This area was near an airport. That was the entirety of Pittsburgh and the towns around it.

As she approached Room One Fourteen, the door was ajar.

It was cracked open, but Jaclyn wanted to peek inside. She didn't know why. The room itself had to have been empty if the door was left open.

There couldn't have been anything going on. Just a set of messy, ruffled bedsheets, a half-used roll of toilet paper, a mostly used tube of shampoo from the hotel, and a handful of used dishes.

It was bad enough that she took someone's picture without consent. Looking into someone else's room was one more mark across her skin—another sin.

What was the point?

As she went around the corner to the lobby, the couple followed, and the *crack* in the door widened. A soft, penetrating creak shot through the corridor.

Jaclyn looked back and watched.

"What the Hell was that?" she murmured.

Her eyes were stuck to Room One Fourteen. She knew she *saw* it open, but there wasn't a sign that a person opened it.

Were her eyes playing tricks? It wouldn't make sense. She actually had sleep under her belt.

Taking slow steps, Jaclyn asked, "Hello? Someone in there?"

She waited, but there was no response.

"Someone in there?" she repeated. "Hello?"

The door kept still. Jaclyn made sure each step was tactful and quiet. She got the image of a guest lying on the floor, injured from an accident nobody else had noticed.

The door quivered as she took another step.

"Hello? Is everything okay?"

One step closer, and a figure emerged from within the room. Its body wasn't in plain sight. Only its head was peeking out from the other side of the door.

It was another housekeeper, her gaze piercing through Jaclyn like an icepick. Her face was young but wrinkled under the eyes. It was like she was forced to stay awake for days on end. Her red hair was wound into a braid so tight that it looked impossible to undo.

Just as she caught a good glimpse of her, the woman *slammed* the door shut.

Jaclyn took a step back, her heart pounding in her throat. She wheezed and gasped.

She looked behind her, making sure other people saw it too. The couple's eyes were wide open, and their brows were cocked.

The lady at the front desk had seen it too. Her dirty blonde hair was tied back, complimenting her black uniform. A pair of brown, square-rimmed glasses perched on the bridge of her nose, highlighting her hazel eyes. She had the same look on her face as the couple.

"Ma'am?" she asked. "Do you need help with something?"

Jaclyn hesitated, looking down. She had the feeling that something strange had just happened but couldn't articulate it. Was it just her imagination? Every establishment had a disgruntled worker.

Finally, she answered, "No. No, I don't think so."

"Well okay," the attendant replied doubtfully. "If you need anything, we'll be happy to help."

She was a new face though. She could've seen Corey, or at least have information that'd help.

Jaclyn went to her Photos app, pulled up the picture, and tremored in retrospect. She recalled the sudden look of confusion and discomfort on Corey's face whenever she'd come home from the bus stop and see a strange man at the dining room table.

It didn't matter how she met the guy. The setting could've been anywhere, though she often meant "a club" when she said it was "at work."

There wasn't a reason for Corey not to believe it. Yet the look on his face told her this was the sign of instant rejection.

Maybe if I prepared you for things a little better, or at all, Jaclyn thought. *It would've been one less reason to run off in the night like that.*

She couldn't help thinking there was a sort of irony. Perhaps he was mimicking her own behavior of acting without warning.

15.

Jaclyn approached the front desk, reading the attendant's nametag. The young woman's name was Sabrina.

But before Jaclyn could say anything, she asked, "Hi, could I help you with something?"

"I hope so." She held up the phone with Corey's picture. "You haven't seen him at all, have you? His name's Corey Archer."

The realization came to the attendant as the perkiness in her face sank. "No, I'm sorry ma'am. I haven't. Is—" She swallowed and asked quietly, “Is that your son?”

“Yeah. He is.”

“But, actually—” Sabrina scratched her chin. “You know, I think there’s something about his face.”

“What do you mean?”

After a minute of thinking, she replied, “I don’t know why, but I feel like maybe I’ve seen him before.” She shook her head and told Jaclyn, “Forget I said it. Did you need me to call the police? Do they know?”

“I’ve already reported it some time ago.” As she said that, Jaclyn wondered if she was getting nowhere after all. “Can’t say I’d complain though.” She gave a weak smile.

“You reported it to the police in *this* area?”

“Not yet,” Jaclyn replied, regretting she didn’t think of that last night. “But I just got in town too.”

“No, I understand. I can find the number for you.”

Right before Sabrina opened a new tab and performed a search on Bing, Jaclyn noticed she just paused a YouTube video. Leaning over the desk, she saw a pair of red wireless earbuds sitting beside the monitor.

The still for the video was titled *Traveling Announcement* and was already viewed by the millions. On a well-lit stage before a crowd of cheering, waving fans was a man who had to have been a towering six foot eight.

He walked with an air of confidence and purpose from the left side of the stage. His hair was pure ebony, well-gelled and combed back. He was wearing circle-rimmed glasses, the frames black as his hair. His facial features were oddly handsome, like someone on the cover of a celebrity magazine.

Anthony Charles. There was no doubt about it. It was a face Jaclyn could recognize anywhere.

Jaclyn started to question what sort of community she wandered into. Were all these people his admirers? Or just a pocket of the population she kept running into?

It must be the latter.

She supposed it could've been the same way in Silicon Valley with its numerous industrialists. That made more sense. Those big personalities were *living* over there. Yet Anthony Charles was something of an icon in western Pennsylvania. He couldn't have lived here. Jaclyn was sure he lived in California with the rest of them.

"So you're a fan?" she asked Sabrina.

Sabrina turned away from her Bing search and replied, "A fan?"

"Yeah. That was Anthony Charles, wasn't it?"

"Oh, yes," Sabrina answered with a smile. "It was. And yeah, I'm a fan, sure. But I think 'follower' is a better word."

"What do you mean?"

"I don't just *like* him. I have a lot of *faith* in him. I've seen what he can do before."

"You've seen him in person?" Jaclyn asked.

"A couple times, yeah. I wanted to take my aunt to see him."

"Your aunt? Why your aunt?"

Sabrina paused, then said, "She hasn't been doing very well."

"Oh. I'm sorry to hear that. If it's okay, what's been going on?"

The attendant's face grew sad as she looked away. The lines around her eyes etched further into her skin. "Coronary artery disease. It's bad."

"*Oh*," Jaclyn replied, trying to string together something meaningful. "That sounds horrible."

"Yeah. She hasn't fainted from it in a while, but she still gets dizzy."

"She's seeing a *doctor*, isn't she?"

"Of course," Sabrina snapped, but regained a somber tone. "He's a good doctor too. But when I get the chance, and I know I will, I want to take her to see Anthony Charles."

Jaclyn was silent at first, then asked, "You think he's gonna help?"

"I *know* he will."

"What was it like seeing him in person?"

"Absolutely incredible. It's an experience of its own seeing what he can do firsthand."

"Like what?"

Sabrina replied, "He turned water to *steam*." Seeing Jaclyn perk her brow, she said, "I know. It sounds *crazy*. But I *swear*, that's what happened. He had this little wooden table he was sitting at to give his talk, right? The only equipment he had was the microphone and a couple speakers. And whenever he finishes his talk with the audience, he picks up his cup of water, takes a drink, sets it back down, and puts his hands on it. The water *bubbles* and it turns to *gas*."

"But he didn't let anyone record?"

16.

"You've seen him too?" Sabrina asked, her face lighting up. "Then you know how unbelievable the man is."

"No," Jaclyn replied. "I haven't."

"Oh." The sudden burst of light disappeared from Sabrina's face. "But no, I guess he doesn't."

"Why is that? You'd figure he wouldn't mind the publicity. I mean, he's a big businessman after all."

"I guess so, but he probably has a good reason. You wouldn't want to be a spectacle to the wrong people, would you?"

"Who are the wrong people?" Jaclyn asked.

"Hecklers. Jokers. The kind of people who refuse to believe what's in front of their faces. The sort that need to be *dealt* with. *Those* kinds of people."

"Oh," Jaclyn replied, feeling as if she were pushed back. "I think I understand. I've had that sort in my life before."

"Really?"

"Yeah. It's like you're trying to explain what's plainly obvious."

The conversation reminded of Jaclyn of a confession Corey made a few months before he ran away. Every day after school, he had a look of gradual distress across his face. At the end of that school week, when she asked what was wrong, he had his head down as he spoke.

"Will you be mad if I tell you?" Corey asked.

A pause, then Jaclyn replied, "What happened?"

It took a minute for him to tell her, but at last he said, "I don't know if I believe in God."

"Whenever Corey told me he didn't think he believed in God," she told Sabrina. "I couldn't believe what I was hearing. Not long before that, he would say how good he felt from going to church every Sunday. I don't know what got into him, but one day, he told me he didn't understand why God let so many people in the world starve."

"Never an easy question to answer."

"I told him that it was all just part of a bigger plan, but you wanna know what the truth was?"

"What's that?"

"I never really knew the answer myself."

"Some things just aren't for us to know," Sabrina replied.

"But you're not always prepared to answer your kid's questions. And when you have a kid, they think you're gonna know everything, right?"

"Sure, you've always been around to guide them."

"Yeah," Jaclyn said, feeling as if she'd just lied. "But I told him that—" her speech faltered "—just because everything in the world's not fair, that doesn't mean He isn't there."

"Well, I don't think that's your fault. It's an awfully big question no matter where you are in life."

"I suppose it is." Jaclyn said.

Jaclyn was questioning what the younger woman had said but didn't want to pose her feelings as a question. There was something about speaking to a younger face that put her on the defensive.

"I think it is. It's part of such a challenging job. It's all part of a sacrifice that's worth the effort, isn't it?"

A pause, and Jaclyn replied, "Yeah. Sacrifice."

Sabrina turned to the computer, used the mouse to scroll down the results, and turned the monitor toward Jaclyn. "I found the number for you."

"Do you have a pen and a piece of paper I could use?"

"Sure, of course." Sabrina answered.

She took one of the pens with the hotel's name engraved down its side and a sheet of notebook paper from her workspace. She handed it to Jaclyn, giving her a weak smile, and reading the phone number off the monitor.

"You don't need me to call them?" Sabrina asked, as if she hadn't heard the answer already.

"No thank you, I'll do it." Jaclyn wrote the information down and slipped the paper into her pocket.

"I hope you find him." The look in the Sabrina's eyes grew colder as she spoke.

"Thanks, I really do too."

"Not to sound inconsiderate, but I'm wondering something since you mentioned Anthony Charles."

"What's that?" Jaclyn asked.

"Were you thinking about seeing him? It's just that you sounded interested."

The idea hadn't occurred to Jaclyn until just now. She considered and replied, "Why do you ask?"

She thought that giving the wrong answer would've offended Sabrina. This was a stranger, but someone who had a degree of power over where she'd sleep.

"It just seemed like you were interested," Sabrina told her. "But I understand how you must've felt, trying to explain something so big to your little boy. I grew up in the church too. Sometimes life tests people, doesn't it?"

"Yeah. Yeah, it really does."

"It can really test your faith, can't it?"

Jaclyn was silent, looking to the floor. "Absolutely," she said.

Sabrina looked somber and replied, "And maybe I don't know you very well. But I think I know one thing."

Jaclyn looked back up and asked, "What's that?"

"That you're amazing person who's been dealt a rough hand, and you deserve a miracle."

"You really think so?"

Sabrina gave a warm smile as to reassure her. "I don't know if you've looked into what's about to happen, but I think there could be one for you just around the corner."

"What do you mean?"

"Of course, you don't *have* to. But if you're interested, he's gonna be going east. Cross country."

"You mean Anthony Charles?"

"That's right," Sabrina answered. "It's not something you'd want to miss. Who knows? You could find the answer you're looking for."

"How would it help me find Corey?"

In a calm, hushed but soothing voice, Sabrina said, "This is someone who brought a blind man on stage and made him see. If someone can do *that*, he's capable of a lot more, don't you think?"

17.

Now that Jaclyn was standing outside with an ultra-light between her fingers, she felt like she had a moment to think.

What Sabrina said sounded crazy. It *was* crazy. Jaclyn felt like she was walking to the front row to an elaborate act. She wondered if people around her were conspiring, as part of a complicated hoax. The sort of thing that ended up in even greater publicity for someone who already extremely wealthy.

It made the most sense. A man with an empire of his own and the gold to show for it only had a few ways to keep moving up. Why would someone who brought himself up this far ever want to stop?

Besides, Jaclyn thought. *The age of miracles was long-over. Who the Hell does this girl think she's fooling?*

But Sabrina wasn't the only one. Trixie told her all about one of his performances—supposedly reversing a disability.

It made Jaclyn wonder, *What were the chances that these two knew each other? What were the chances that they'd conspire together?*

The odds were there. Their workplaces weren't far from each other.

But it didn't mean they knew each other either. They were both talking a celebrity, let alone one she didn't hear a malicious word about. It was something else that made Jaclyn raise her brow in suspicion.

Any other public figure garnered his share of criticism. Even celebrities with the cleanest records.

Jaclyn thought it could've been the outcome of being a tech tycoon who didn't touch social media. She noticed how people who ran platforms that censored people always took the most flak.

But what were the odds of Anthony Charles being the real deal?

There was no way to measure something like that. On one hand, there was a chance that she was being manipulated. She recalled a handful of times where faith healers who broadcasted on television were exposed as frauds.

The first incident that came to mind was Peter Popoff. He claimed to know personal things about his audience through divine revelation. Jaclyn would watch the televised footage of him throwing an older woman's cane onto the stage, as if he'd healed her hips and knees. She remembered her parents giving their full attention to the TV when the woman started dancing.

But Jaclyn, through retired magician James Randi's investigation, found out in the eighties that Popoff wore an earpiece. That was how his wife used to feed the information to him.

Ever since he was first unmasked on the *Tonight Show* as Jaclyn, her parents, and countless others watched, there was one radio transmission she never forgot. It was the words of Popoff's wife:

"Hello Petey, can you hear me? If you can't, you're in trouble."

Jaclyn still remembered turning to her mother at a younger age and seeing the tears well in her eyes. Her father's mouth agape. The television being turned off just as the *Tonight Show* ended.

"I just can't believe it," her mother repeated to herself, muttering, pacing back and forth in the kitchen.

As she was talking to herself, Jaclyn's father just sat on the couch. He leaned forward with his elbows on his knees. He held his temples to cradle his skull. The look on his face was that of Florence Owens Thompson, the mother of seven whose picture was taken during the Great Depression.

But what were the odds that Anthony Charles was another Peter Popoff?

Jaclyn thought that he *could* have been, but something about him was different. Any televangelist would crave to be on broadcast TV. It was in the name of their occupation after all. As she remembered, their supposed *miracles* always worked where the world could see.

Whenever the memories of Popoff resurfaced, so did her father's words:

"The Bible warned us about men like him. Jesus himself warned the apostles when he told them about the destruction of the Jewish temples. All those con men do is prey on people and make us look bad."

Jaclyn hadn't read much of the Bible outside of Mark, Revelations and what the occasional prayer book occasionally referenced. But when her father made the off-hand comments paraphrasing a verse, she'd look it up to make sure he was right, only to discover that he was every time.

This was a man who somehow knew the scripture by heart from cover to cover. The way he spoke about it made each of the books in it sound like common knowledge.

Jaclyn recalled the moment when he condemned Popoff, and she investigated the index in the back of their Bible for false prophets, it was straight from Matthew. Would he say the same about Anthony Charles?

Most likely. Popoff also claimed to heal a paraplegic. It made Jaclyn think Randy could've been onto something. After all, the man in the wheelchair turned out to be an actor.

The man who ran the *Eclipse* empire wasn't the same as the televangelists of the eighties though. He didn't seem to mind publicity—it was how the man got his YouTube promotions. She saw articles about him on Facebook. There were headlines about his latest products over Google and Bing. For whatever reason though, he didn't want to risk some of his events being online.

Even if they were all just parlor tricks, an amateur stage magician would want the exposure. This big tech tycoon wasn't quite part of the same group. She couldn't understand why he wouldn't let anyone film the events.

Would Trixie or Sabrina have known the answer? Jaclyn couldn't confirm, but she didn't get the impression that they knew. If either of them did, there would've been a more concrete answer.

But it was just a hunch she had.

Her thoughts went back to Sabrina—the underlying promise that girl was trying to make. She was implying that this tycoon could—*would* bother to help her. Even if she managed to get his attention, how would he find Corey's whereabouts? It started to sound like a desperate attempt to recruit. A cheap mask that hid a young person's fanaticism.

But on the other hand…

Could Anthony Charles do that? For all she knew, an eccentric man with all the resources in the world could've done things outside the power of local authorities.

She heard stories about celebrities accomplishing things like that. Ashton Kutcher identifying close to six-thousand victims of child trafficking. Elon Musk cleaning up Flint, Michigan's water supply.

And what were the chances that this technology tycoon's stunts weren't parlor tricks at all? Jaclyn thought, *What if there was a new age of miracles?*

She flicked her cigarette butt onto the parking lot and looked up at the falling rain. It had waned into a weak drizzle.

Going back inside, she smiled at Sabrina and asked, "He isn't coming to Pennsylvania at all, is he?"

18.

Sabrina smiled a little as she answered, "Of course. Anthony Charles is actually *from* Pennsylvania." There was a brief pause before her smile widened and she asked, "Did you know that?"

"No," Jaclyn answered. She felt a lump forming in her throat. Her voice was quacking with nervousness as she said, "I didn't know that."

"It's why he comes back to this state every time he travels anywhere in the country. He also does business around the west coast, but at the end of the day, this is his home."

"Right. I can understand that, though I don't think I could move out of the state myself. I've thought about going to Florida or Texas because of the weather. As much as I hate winter up here, I don't know if I could ever leave. Another state may as well be another country to me. Even if I had property down there, is it really where I belong?"

"It's really up to you in the end. It's your life after all. But me? I'd say I shouldn't leave where I belong," Sabrina replied, her lips curling into a deeper smile.

Jaclyn said with an uneasy smirk, "I guess there's just no place like where you grew up, huh?"

"Agreed. There really isn't. Even if you leave the place, it never truly leaves you."

"Yeah. I understand. So, Anthony Charles is coming back to his old hometown then?" Jaclyn mused.

What if he's the real thing? Maybe this one isn't fake, dad. What are the odds?

"Do you know when? Did they release any dates?"

"Whenever he promotes the new line of tech—the dates, times and places get released for *that*. But that's all there is online. Not for the real gatherings," Sabrina replied.

"The real—you mean for the tr—miracles?"

Sabrina gave her a warm grin and replied, "That's an interesting word. You think there's such a thing?"

"Sure. I'm Catholic, you know. And with what's been going on—" she returned the smile "—I *need* to believe."

Maybe Corey will come back soon, and I could fix everything. That'd be the real miracle.

Mimicking Jaclyn's expression, Sabrina said, "That's good to know."

The glass doors swung open. A tall man, at least six foot four, came through the entrance. A pair of black sunglasses hung over the collar of his white dress shirt. He had a light salt and pepper stubble across his chin, cheeks, and upper lip. The man ran his fingertips through his dark, curly hair. He smiled as the overhead light twinkled off his hospital ID card, which hung at the end of a red lanyard around his neck.

Approaching the front desk, the man said "Hey" to Sabrina.

"Hey Doc."

"Think you guys can put me up for another night?"

"Same room?"

"Yes please," he replied, flashing his Visa card.

Sabrina took the card, swiped it, and punched in the information on the hotel's computer software. Once the transaction was approved, she handed his Visa back.

Smiling, she asked, "How was everything last night?"

"Satisfying," he replied, grinning. "Very satisfying."

"Did you want your receipt?"

"Don't I always?"

"That's no problem," Sabrina told him, printing the receipt for Room One Fourteen and handing it to him.

He took the slip of paper and stuffed it into his back pocket.

"Just getting off work?" Sabrina asked.

"No, I actually need to be getting back soon. I'm just on my break. Just wanted to make sure I'm not too late to buy another night here."

"Oh, not at all. You know we wouldn't just throw your stuff onto the sidewalk and tell you to get out. Are you doing okay?"

The smile on his face waned as he replied, "Yeah, I'm fine. There's always a lot to recover when there's a house fire, but I can make it. I always do."

"It's something we can fix," she said.

"Of course." His smile revived as he walked out the front entrance.

"Have a good day at the hospital," Sabrina called out. "Try to *breathe* a little. You're gonna bounce back!"

He waved back at them without turning his head as he walked to his car. It was a white Nissan Altima, its exterior glimmering in the clear sunshine. As the man walked toward his car, the headlights turned on and beamed like a pair of glowing yellow stars.

Jaclyn turned to Sabrina, and then looked down before she asked, "That man lost his home?"

"It's a real shame, isn't it? It happened while he was on the job."

"How?" Jaclyn asked.

"They're not sure yet," Sabrina answered. "But the police chief said it looked a bit like arson."

"*Arson?* But he's a doctor, isn't he? What's he ever done?"

Sabrina looked down to her fingers and responded, "Some people don't like the way of life."

"He seems like a nice enough guy. Maybe a bit anxious. But nice."

"Not everyone's that understanding. People can be judgmental over things that aren't important, you know?"

Jaclyn paused, thinking about her staggering into the court, still hungover from the night before. The days when she used to look in the mirror and see a simple mistake—a matter of bad timing. If her calculations for sobering up had just been a little different, the custody battle wouldn't have started with her tripping over her own feet.

But now that she thought about it again, Jaclyn remembered the looks everyone in the courtroom gave. The numerous strangers who surrounded her had furrowed brows and scowls etched deep into their faces.

Although, after just one stumble on her way in, she found herself able to walk like a sober person. A drunk mastered this skill with enough practice. She'd remember that speaking slowly was key—not only to sound articulate in a time like that, but also to mask the vodka in her digestive tract.

Whether the act was good or not didn't matter. All that mattered was that it'd been just good enough for the judge.

Things that aren't important, Jaclyn thought, frowning. Her eyes grew heavy as she repeated that phrase in her head.

"Right," she said. "Things that aren't important." Looking back up at Sabrina, she asked, "If it's okay for me to ask, what are the dates for Charles' event?"

"You're really that interested?"

"Of course I am."

"*If* you are—" Sabrina paused "—I might be able to get you in."

19.

Pittsburgh. That was further west. As Jaclyn got back in her car, she thought it was convenient that Charles' official tour included the convention center downtown. She thought the location made perfect sense, considering the nearby airport.

Sabrina had offered to add her on Facebook, but she already smiled and declined, lying that she didn't have an account. Instead, Jaclyn said she'd just call the hotel and ask for her when the time came.

She rolled her eyes and breathed easy that at least Sabrina didn't question any of it.

But whatever the magic of Anthony Charles was—*if* it was magic to begin with—it wasn't going to happen during these formally scheduled events. Jaclyn figured the real highlights would be between the gatherings.

She pulled one of the folded sheets of paper from her pocket and saw the phone number of the Dourmsburg police department. She stared at it and lit a cigarette. Jaclyn stuffed the paper back into her pocket after taking the first drag.

She backed up and drove to the edge of the parking lot. Jaclyn looked into her rearview mirror and confirmed nobody was behind her. After pulling her smartphone out, she searched for any mechanics in the area.

Dourmsburg Auto Service was ten miles south from her, with an average customer rating of three out of five stars. Smith and Son was two miles north on the map, getting an average of four out of five. The final option was Carlyle's, six miles northwest, with a four and a half out of five as well.

Even though the latter would've most likely been the best service, she decided on Smith and Son. It was the closest, and Jaclyn hadn't experienced a car problem quite like this before. The Chevy would break down at any minute for all she knew.

She tapped on the option for directions to Smith and Son, and the phone spoke to her in a soothing voice, mimicking the human male, "Welcome back, Miss Ellsworth. Let's start our route to Smith and Son. Turn left onto Jackson Street."

The first time she heard the Directions app speak to her by name, let alone in a human voice—it made her jump. She hadn't entered her name into the smartphone when she first got it. The one she had before this made her enter her name and birthdate to use any of its features.

But this one? It didn't even give her the chance to opt out entirely. Depending on the app, the smartphone would always address her as either "Jaclyn," "Miss Ellsworth," or rarely, "Jackie."

When she first set the phone up, she was strangely relieved she didn't need to enter any personal information. She thought that Silicon Valley started to take the hint about respecting consumer privacy, from all the lawsuits over the past few years.

But after going to her service provider, followed by a few retailers, to do something about the scare, it was already time to give up. She had a bad feeling about getting a replacement for the *Eclipse* she had from the get-go but decided to try anyway. To err was human, and there were times when being wrong was a wonderful thing.

She could've chosen another smartphone that was less intrusive. The tech market was always evolving. She assumed innumerable options were at her fingertips. Jaclyn was even willing to bet there were still a few flip phones on the market somewhere.

"Excuse me," she would tell the employee. "My new phone seems to have my personal information, but I didn't enter it at all. Why is that?"

"Oh? What brand is it?" the employee asked.

"It's an *Eclipse*. Brand-new."

"To be honest, that's probably the reason why. The *Eclipse* phones automatically sync with the information put on your SIM card. Things like cookies for email addresses, social media—all that stuff is bound to be on there."

The revelation set her back the first time around.

"Do you sell any smartphones that don't have that?" Jaclyn enquired.

"To be honest," the employee said. "I don't think so. Most of our smartphones are *Eclipse*."

"What about the other brands?"

"The other ones have the same kind of technology. If I'm not mistaken, *Eclipse* was the company to set that standard."

"How about older models? Do you still carry those old flip phones?" Jaclyn felt hope surging through her as she dared to smile while asking.

"I'm really sorry. We haven't carried those in a long time," the employee replied.

"They're all the same kind of smartphone?"

"Afraid so. If you look online, you might find something being auctioned, but even then, I'm not so sure," the employee said with a frown.

The conversations used to be the same every time. Upon exiting each retailer, she'd look online. She searched for flip phones through Bing and Google's shopping filters. She spelled the term as both one and two words in the hopes of yielding better results.

But they were the same regardless. Nothing but smartphones from the past two years at most. It made her want to throw hers in a ditch and bury the damn thing.

She thought about living without a mobile phone at all. If nobody she knew had an older model stuffed away in their attic. *No*, the thought was absurd. She dismissed it altogether. It was the twenty-first century. Finding anyone without a smartphone nowadays was near impossible.

Jaclyn shook her head at the thought, and driving was another reminder why. Asking for directions sounded obvious to her. It was what people did before mobile devices.

But if she did that, the directions would escape her memory, even if they were well-explained. A Directions app was different though. A visual display better assured that she went the right way.

Besides, verbal directions couldn't re-route her if she ended up taking a wrong turn. This happened more than she ever liked to admit.

Jaclyn sighed, gripping her steering wheel, thinking that the smooth voice on her phone as just something to deal with. As she turned onto Jackson, she wondered if that was the voice everyone got for their directions.

Either that, the voice was what most women got, or—

Jaclyn thought, *Is there an algorithm that figured out what kind of voice* I'd *want to hear? How would software developers be able to figure that out?*

She took a long drag on her cigarette until the ash was long enough to fall off on its own. Thinking back to what she was told about the information on her SIM card, her social media could've been a giveaway.

How often had she posted about the sort of attractive bachelor it'd be fun to sink her teeth into? Now that she thought about it, plenty of them were actors and musicians.

Whoever those nosy geeks in Silicon Valley were, they were damn smart. They took that information and used it as ingredients for an ideal voice. Anything to get people to buy the next product.

"At the end of the road, turn right, Miss Ellsworth."

It made her picture a man in his early forties—blonde with inconspicuous flecks of gray, blue eyes, light facial hair, well-tanned, and a physique sculpted with artistic wonder. She imagined him sitting on the passenger's side in a black, virgin wool Emporio Armani suit. It was the sort of thing a confident yuppie would've worn, as if forgetting he was decades older than the way he was styled.

Jaclyn couldn't believe the mental image that came with a glorified GPS, but how could she help it? It was the quality of the voice. She knew if she heard that voice on the other end of a phone call, there'd be no telling it apart from a real man.

She reached the stop sign at the end of the road and looked both ways. Ritually flicking the ash out of her window, she turned right. Although the town had more gravel and pavement than grass, the buildings weren't close together. Most of them could've fit at least another small shop or two between them.

The grass itself wasn't too green. Most of it around her was a sickly beige, as if it hadn't seen proper nourishment in years.

Occasionally, she passed by an empty, run-down, building with sealed windows and rotting boards. It'd have an uneven space of gravel-coated pavement with a sign offering the rental space in faded letters.

Small clusters of pedestrians were scattered between them. Plenty of them were bent down at the shoulders and oddly pale. If she were out of the car and standing close enough to them, Jaclyn would have seen a few veins protruding on their bodies.

It took her a moment before she realized that most of them were children. They looked back with bulbous eyes at her car, as if they knew whether she had never visited this place before.

20.

"You've arrived. Your destination on the right," the cool male voice said to Jaclyn.

She slowed down, flicked her cigarette butt onto the street, and pulled into the small parking lot. As she parked in one of the outer spaces, Jaclyn examined the building's exterior.

It was a single-storied, canary yellow brick building. The corners had discolored to peanut brown from age. The sign overhead, with a white background and faded black letters, read *Smith and Son* with the establishment's phone number underneath.

As she locked the car door after getting out, she found herself staring up at the sign like it was trying to tell her something. Walking toward the front door, Jaclyn noticed the parking lot was uneven.

It wasn't uneven enough for passersby to think they won't be able to drive on it, like with the abandoned small businesses. But it was on the first steps to that level of disrepair. There were cracks, tiny slopes revealed broken fragments in the asphalt, and handfuls of gravel were lying about the property.

"They're on their way to being like the rest," Jaclyn muttered to herself. "If they don't do something fast."

There were only three other cars in the parking lot. Even the smaller, family-owned garages that she'd visited until then were busier than this one on any regular morning. The one near her house was at the end of an alley, hidden in the suburbs, but it still managed to have a line of cars waiting for repairs. Jaclyn figured it might just be far slower than usual that day.

A gust of wind brushed against her, as if pushing her back. She turned the knob and pushed the door open, ringing the bell just above. As it shut, Jaclyn was overcome by a small coughing fit.

A portly, balding man in his early fifties at the counter opposite the door gave her a wide-eyed look. He had brown hair and a bushy mustache, and wore a navy-blue jumpsuit decorated with gentle smears of oil.

"You okay, miss?" the man asked.

Jaclyn inhaled, cleared her throat and replied, "Yeah, I'm fine."

"Can I help you?"

Approaching the man, she said, "Yeah, I'm having a little issue. Lately, my engine's been making a whistling noise. It'd kick, slow down and go back up to speed again." She read the white nametag stitched onto his jumpsuit, and saw his name was Donnie.

"Is the RPM going up and down?" Donnie asked.

"A bit, yeah."

"Oh dear," he said.

"Why? What does that mean?"

"Well, chances are, that's a bit of transmission work. I don't do that here, but my son does."

"Oh, so that shouldn't be too bad, right?"

"Right," Donnie replied. "As long as you either have a little over a grand to spend or have your car dealer come over and fix it. Either way, it'll be a lot of time and money."

Remembering that she hadn't bothered to sign up for car insurance despite having the money, Jaclyn sighed. She squeezed the bridge of her nose with her thumb and forefinger. Why she still hadn't signed up for it was a matter of putting things off until forgetting them altogether.

She wanted to blame it on force of habit, but regardless, Jaclyn had been driving illegally. Thanking God that she hadn't been pulled over yet was a no-brainer.

"Shit," she said, wanting to smack herself. "How long do you think it'd take?"

"To tell you the truth, we can't say yet. You ever have a transmission problem before?" he asked.

"No, I can't say I have."

"Then you might not like what I'm about to say. Depending on the issue, sometimes it can get done right away or take a little while," Donnie replied.

"There's no way to tell?"

"Well, like I'm saying, we don't know yet. We need to confirm the issue first. Just disassembling takes a lot of labor. Once we get the engine out, *then* we get to the transmission. Just getting to the tranny is usually the bulk of the work."

Jaclyn pondered that for a moment and replied, "I guess I don't have much of a choice. It's either that or no car."

But what about getting something like an Uber or a Lyft? No. There was no way in Hell she'd consider it. It wasn't a matter of money. She could drag Uber drivers all over and pay for the whole thing.

It was the memories of getting an Uber for the first time. They made her swear off paying a complete stranger for driving her around. Two years ago, Corey was at his father's apartment for the weekend, and she had made plans to meet her coworkers at a bar and grille that they had all agreed on.

She told her coworkers in passing that the Chevy needed to stay at the shop for the time being. The mechanic informed her over a call that it needed a new spark plug, oxygen sensor, and it had an issue with coolant loss. Hanging out would've been a distraction from the bill if nothing else.

The trip from her house to the restaurant was estimated to be twenty minutes. Uber showed that the driver's name was Eric: a man her age with neat, combed-back black hair, a clean shave, and a handsome face.

He gave her a friendly smile after pulling up in his Toyota Corolla. She stepped in, and they made small talk about where she planned to go for the evening faltered when his eyes lingered on her purse. Despite being on the freeway, the Corolla slowed down.

Jaclyn watched as other cars passed them and Eric pulled over onto the shoulder of the road. He produced a knife from his pocket as he put the car into park and demanded she give him her purse.

In that moment, her thoughts froze. She screamed incessantly like rainwater down a steep hill. Jaclyn punched him in the nose. She heard a *crack* and withdrawn her fist. Eric covered his bloodied nose as she rushed out of the car.

Standing on the freeway, she ran down its shoulder for a few hundred yards and looked back. She felt light-headed and dizzy.

Jaclyn saw the passenger door being shut and the Corolla driving off. Within seconds, the car blended in with countless others on the freeway.

But as it did, she pulled a pen from her pocket and scratched the license plate number against her forearm. She called the police and charges were pressed. The memory continued to haunt her into the present day. Jaclyn still precisely remembered the sting in her knuckles from breaking that driver's nose.

21.

"I'm really sorry to hear about the trouble, ma'am," Donnie said. "But if it's the transmission, it might take a while."

"Yeah, it's fine," Jaclyn replied as she felt a vibration in her pocket. "I understand."

"I just need your name and phone number," Donnie said, smiling and holding a thin yellow notebook and a pen against the surface of his desk.

"Jaclyn Ellsworth," she said, gave him her phone number. She noticed the lines on his face and the heavy bags under his eyes.

She found herself gazing into a pair of sleepy eyes, wondering if he'd nod off any second. The question in her mind was if the heavy bags were from age, insomnia or something else entirely.

Regardless, she knew one thing about this man. He was a parent like her. However, there was no an indication of him having made the same mistakes as her. She hoped to God that he hadn't. Even if he'd probably look at her with disgust for what she'd done in the past, she sensed a kinship with him.

This man understood the great and unending labor of being a parent. His son was an adult who was perhaps skilled enough to surpass him at his job. But this didn't reduce any of Donnie's responsibility. No matter how old Donnie's son was, he still had a duty toward his son.

Although Jaclyn didn't have any heavy bags under her eyes, she still *felt* them. It may have been an endless labor, but it was never a burden. Her job as a parent had been cut short by Corey running away, she was letting guilt seep into her, like burning gas.

This was the primal duty and she had failed. God only knew where he *was* at this point if he even was anymore.

However real that possibility may be, she couldn't let herself think of it. Corey was alive and out there somewhere. She either had to push the thought out of her mind and keep going or let it gnaw at her brain, one piece at a time until all hope was gone.

The former was the only choice that made any sense.

Better die trying than stop trying, she thought.

"Keys?" Donnie asked. After she handed them over, he said, "Thanks, I'll just get this over to Lloyd and get back to you."

So that's the virtuoso, huh? She smiled at the thought, watching Donnie walk through the wooden door on the right side of the building. *If Lloyd's really the better mechanic, I wonder how his father feels about it. Deep down, is he more proud or resentful?*

It must be like the case of Dan Ryan, the older boy Corey was friends with. When Dan came over, he mentioned how his dad used to play music. It was as if he picked up the guitar by osmosis.

He hadn't just picked it up. If anything, he never put his black Epiphone Les Paul Special II down. Jaclyn had never seen Dan without his Les Paul either in his hand or hanging by its strap on his back. It was like looking at a smaller Jimi Hendrix.

Corey had even confirmed it at one point. The boy even wore his guitar around school and never got in trouble for it. She supposed that the teachers didn't care since he wasn't playing during class.

Outside school grounds was a different story. Any time she saw him sitting down, he used to be playing it. He had even found a way to multitask—picking the strings while maintaining full eye contact during a conversation. His fingering was still slow but it improved a little every time she saw him play.

Despite his progress, Dan mentioned that his dad had told him to do into something else. Music was a waste of time and wouldn't make him much money. It had even escalated to a point where he had suddenly asked to spend the night out because his father threw a fit, pressuring him about getting straight A's and telling him that he wouldn't be that good at playing and songwriting.

She wondered why the boy was getting the third degree so early. He was only twelve, going on thirteen.

Jaclyn agreed to let him stay the night. It was a weekend, so there weren't any worries about getting up on time for school.

She invited Dan to go to church with her and Corey, provided he left the guitar behind until the service was over. It made her thankful that their church was casual—one of the few where people showed up in t-shirts and jeans.

Jaclyn didn't have to worry about something dressy that'd fit Dan. She hardly had the money to get Corey such things, let alone one of his friends.

But a wrench was thrown into her plans when Dan told her that his family was atheist. The boy's tone had been benign, innocent even. The way he told her sounded like he couldn't tell if he was *allowed* to attend or not.

Once she assured him that he could go if he wanted, the boy gave a wide-eyed look and agreed. Jaclyn read curiosity in his face, as if he were about to see a new country. Throughout the Sunday service, she wondered what influence Dan would have on her son and how his parents would react.

The parents, from what she saw, hadn't reacted. But hanging around Dan must've done wonders for Corey. His ambition spiraled upward over time, but what did it have in store for his faith?

Once the two mechanics returned, her eyes were on them. Lloyd walked in first. He was an inch taller than his father.

His hair was styled in a neat combover. He walked in an excellent posture. He only had small wrinkles under his eyes. Lloyd wore a blue jumpsuit with fewer oil streaks and a clean-shaved face. He had piercing eyes that scanned her as if she were being inspected. His eyes stopped at her chest, in a brief cold fascination.

Jaclyn wasn't sure what to make of it. Whenever other men stared at her, the intention was clear. But not here. Lloyd's eyes were closer to a surveillance camera than a person.

He looked her in the eyes and asked, "So, you have issues accelerating?"

"Yeah," she replied, thinking about backing away.

"And the RPM's fluctuating a lot?"

"Yep."

"It's probably the transmission, but it might not be—" Lloyd said. His face was still. "We'll give you a call when we know what's going on. But there's a few people ahead of you, so it might take a little time."

"Yeah—" Jaclyn paused and assured him, "Yeah, that's fine."

"Okay, sounds good," Lloyd said.

He took the keys, turned and walked away through the back door again. Just before shutting the door, he glanced back at Jaclyn once more.

22.

Jaclyn pulled her jacket closed, staring at the back door. She zipped it up all the way, covering her necklace, and looked back at Donnie.

"Is something wrong?" he asked.

She paused and replied, "I think he was staring at my chest."

"Oh," he said in a grim tone, looking at the back door, then at Jaclyn. "I'm really sorry, ma'am."

"Does he do that a lot?" As she asked, she immediately felt regret.

He jerked his thumb at the back door. "*Lloyd?* I mean, he's been a little off, but he's not one to do *that*."

"Off? What do you mean?" she asked.

"Well—" Donnie moved his hand next to his face in little circles "he just hasn't been himself. But I'll settle it out. Nothing that can't be fixed."

"Hasn't been himself how? I still don't understand," Jaclyn persisted.

He looked to the door and back at her before hesitantly saying, "I hope you don't mind me asking something a little personal. Please don't take offense."

"No, of course not."

"How do you feel about this whole—" he swirled his hand again "—Anngology thing?"

Jaclyn gave him a strange look and slowly repeated, "Ann-gology?"

"Yeah." He muttered as if being loud would shatter the building around him. "This whole spiritual thing around the head of *Eclipse*."

"To be honest, I'm not totally sure. I'm curious and I *want* to keep an open mind. But I guess some people around here are *really* into it. I know Anthony Charles is pretty famous, but I didn't know about this stuff before. I guess it's all just a little too strange for me."

"Not a whole lot of people do. But he's been more secluded lately since he got into it. I know I shouldn't judge or anything, but I get worried. That happens when you're a parent, you know? Lloyd's a grown man—he's twenty-six, but he'll always be my kid."

"Yeah. I get that. I've got a boy of my own too."

"Oh," Donnie replied, some of the unease on his face replaced with a friendly warmth. "How old is he?"

Jaclyn paused and told him, "Eleven."

"Hopefully, he's staying out of trouble."

"They can't always."

"Yeah. Not always. So you know what I'm getting at. Sometimes, it feels like if they act a little off, it's because it's part of something a lot bigger than it seems."

Maybe I should've seen it when Corey started locking his door, she thought. "Right." She felt as if a colony of ants was crawling down her face, and then the rest of her body, as this idea coalesced in her mind.. "In a way, worrying is kind of our job."

"It is. But what would you do?" Donnie questioned.

She thought it was a Hell of a question. How do you govern what to do about someone else's son, much less a grown man? He was already independent, his feelings, beliefs and ideas were cemented.

Jaclyn felt it wasn't her business to begin with, yet she had been invited to make it hers. She thought of telling him something solid but minimal at the same time.

She said, "Maybe just talk. See if he's okay. He's a grown man, so he probably knows what he's doing. But a little talk wouldn't hurt." Jaclyn gave him a small, reaffirming smile.

Donnie smiled back and said, "Yeah, it's probably not that big of a deal. We'll give you a call once we find out what's going on."

"Sounds great. Thanks," she replied.

"Did you need anything else?"

"No thanks, just that," Jaclyn replied.

"Have a good one," Donnie said.

As she turned to leave, there was a shadow hidden behind the back door. It blotted out most of the electric light surrounding it.

Once she opened the front door and the bell jingled, there was a set of hushed footsteps in the building. The shadow was gone, and the light it blocked was bleeding into the next room.

Standing outside the building and staring at her Chevy, Jaclyn realized that she hadn't eaten a thing since yesterday evening. She last ate at that little diner by the side of the highway, when the sun cast into gradient of daisy yellow to a bright red, followed by a faded purple.

Yet, she wasn't hungry at all. She found it strange but shrugged it off. She'd eat again later in the afternoon.

Jaclyn started wondering about going back to the diner. What were the chances that the same old woman would be there? More so, what were the odds of her remembering details about where Corey had gone?

She could've wondered the same about Thomas or even Sabrina. But when the old woman spoke, she had a confidence she hadn't heard from anyone else. Everyone else had spoken with a degree of uncertainty.

Then again, what if her visit to the diner had been a one-time thing? It was unlikely. From what she saw, people found it more difficult to fall out of routines as they grew older. Odds were the old woman had a nightly habit.

How could she tell for sure? For all she knew, it was just another shot in the dark. Even if she decided to go, Jaclyn didn't have a car. Uber and Lyft were out of the question, but that didn't mean she couldn't get a ride. Plus, the habit of keeping her taser in the same pocket as her wallet made the idea feel safer.

Jaclyn pulled out her phone and saw there was one new message. It had to have been from one of her family members. They were still the only people she texted that morning who should've been awake this early, and other people didn't have the habit of messaging her first.

But she was startled to see Trixie's name instead. In retrospect, Jaclyn would've been surprised if the girl had even seen the symbol around the housekeeper's neck before.

The bartender had replied, "Yeah, that's the solar eclipse," and ended the message with a smiley face.

Jaclyn texted back, "Can you elaborate?"

She walked to the Chevy, put the smartphone in her pocket, and slid her jacket off. It was still early in the day, but the summer heat was still a bit much for a coat.

Looking at the front door of Smith and Son one more time, she didn't see anyone nearby. It was as if the entire lot had been abandoned.

Once her phone went off again, Jaclyn pulled it out, her eyes were fixed to the little screen. She picked it up to answer, only to find herself staring at the reply.

Trixie replied, "It's the symbol for Anngology. It's kinda how we identify each other."

23.

Jaclyn left the parking lot and walked down the side of the road. She was walking down a patch of crackled pavement meant to be a sidewalk.

It begged the question: was the scattered gravel in the Smith and Son parking lot part of this pavement? Their colors matched.

Every part of the untouched ground was one to two feet long. Jaclyn knelt and took a closer look. Most of the grass wasn't just beige. There were flecks of green, but most of the sickly grass had tiny bits of yellow at its base.

She continued walking, watching her step for more crackled blocks of pavement along the way. She looked up to see a gas station.

The paint—a fire engine red—was starting to chip away with age, but had an air of life that the others didn't. The building wasn't boarded up. Small handfuls of gravel were only on the edges of the parking lot, next to the grass.

She noticed two cars parked around the building. The first one at one of the pumps, but no one was inside. The other car was parked behind the gas station, poking out its front end.

She sighed in relief from seeing another establishment with signs of life and less than excessive decadence.

Jaclyn walked up to the front of the building. She didn't go inside but leaned against the wall adjacent to the entrance. Carrying her faux fur jacket in one hand, she re-read her messages to Trixie.

Trixie's text made her remember a part of her dream. The one she saw on the road, while waiting at the red light last night.

The thick cloud of darkness surrounding her. The hand making its accusatory gesture.

I know you.

The thought dried her throat as she texted, "Oh, I see. Weren't you working until two last night? That's when bars usually close."

"Yeah, I've been up for a little bit. Sorry I missed your text earlier."

"No big deal. Aren't you tired? It's still kinda early."

"Not really," Trixie said. "I don't sleep as much as most people."

"How many hours do you usually get?"

"Maybe five or six."

"You don't usually feel tired in the morning?"

"Nope," Trixie replied. "I'm usually fine."

"If it's okay to ask, how long have you been into Anngology?"

"Not that long to be honest. If I had to guess, maybe just the past year."

Jaclyn asked, "Was that when you first saw Anthony Charles in person?"

"No, a little before that."

"Who got you in that one time?"

"One of my friends. She was in a class I took in college."

"Oh? Which class?"

"History," Trixie replied. "She'd talk about him sometimes when we were out of class."

"Outside of school?"

"No, in school. Usually in the cafeteria. We never really hung out outside of school until I saw Anthony Charles."

"Did your friend ever want to? Aside from that one time?"

"Now that you ask, I don't think so. I didn't think of it until just now. She never really invited me to anything until then. She was probably the only person I really talked to in school."

Jaclyn felt curdling, raisin-colored pity rising within her. *Poor girl,* she thought. *Was she having trouble socializing in college? Maybe even before that too. I bet that came from* some*where.*

"So, were you pretty introverted?" Jaclyn asked.

"I guess. It's more like, I always wanted to make friends like anyone else, but I didn't always know how."

"I'm sorry. I can understand though," Jaclyn replied.

It sounds awfully lonely. No wonder she gave me her phone number so quickly. It was probably the same way with other people coming and going. I bet most of them were put off though. But it's not her fault.

"Not your fault," Trixie replied. "That's life sometimes, right? Haha, c'est la vie."

"I guess so. Maybe we don't see eye to eye on this, but I would've been a little bothered by it myself."

"To be fair, you can't feel strong every minute of your life."

"Nobody does. That's just being a person."

"It is, isn't it?"

"It's nice that you understand."

"I'm a mom," Jaclyn said. "I'm kind of supposed to."

"I guess so."

Jaclyn cocked her brow at the response but decided to drop it for the time being. "Do you know a lot of people who're into Anngology?"

"Not really. I hear it's common in other parts of the country, but I'm the only one I really know about."

"Did you meet anyone when you saw Anthony Charles?"

"Plenty of people, actually. It was a different experience."

"Do you still talk with them?"

"Not really," Trixie said.

"How come?"

"Didn't really exchange phone numbers or social media. Sometimes I kinda regret it though. It feels like a lot of missed opportunities. Plenty of them flew in from all around the country."

Jaclyn asked, "What did it feel like meeting all those people at once?"

"Dopamine. Haha, a little nerve-racking at first, but it was like this big wave of dopamine hitting all at once. It was pretty intense."

"I bet it was. How many people do you think were there?"

"I'm not really sure. If I had to guess, maybe a few hundred?"

"And it was a secret to the public?"

Trixie admitted, "Yeah."

"How'd you pull it off? I'm just intrigued, that's all. To tell you the truth, I was thinking of going to one of these if I get the opportunity." Jaclyn rolled her eyes, sighed and continued texting. "All in all, Anthony Charles sounds amazing. I might be ready to get into this myself."

"A big part of it was moving really late at night. And we had to move quietly," Trixie replied. She sent another message that read, "You really want to join in? I wasn't sure if you were that interested before. You seemed kinda doubtful."

"I definitely do. But before we do any of that, can I ask for a favor?"

24.

"Maybe," Trixie answered. "What is it?"

"I was wondering if I could get a ride somewhere. My car's getting fixed. It's a transmission problem, so I don't want to risk driving it, especially on the highway."

Jaclyn thought that this could be a grave mistake. Trixie may not have been a mugger, but she was still someone Jaclyn didn't know well. Waiting for a response, she slid her hand in her pocket and gripped the taser.

A stream of music was swimming around the gas station out of nowhere. It was seeping into the air, the outside of the building, and the pumps.

The prominent beat of Tape Five covering Bob Marley's *I Shot the Sheriff* came on with a scratchy sound. The tempo was slowed down by several beats per minute and the female vocals had been deepened.

Jaclyn looked at the building, then the pumps and back again. As the song skipped the line, *Sheriff John Brown always hated me, for what I don't know,* her eyes froze while searching the roof for a faulty speaker but didn't find any.

Jaclyn's intrigue was interrupted by her phone buzzing. Trixie asked, "Where?"

"The Ace of Clubs Diner."

"Down the highway from the bar?"

"Yeah," Jaclyn replied. "That one."

"Oh yeah, I know what you're talking about. I used to eat there a lot when I started working that way."

"So what do you say? Can you give me a lift later? I can pay for the gas and the trouble."

Trixie's response was delayed.

Jaclyn began tapping her foot and thought, *Maybe she doesn't have a car. That'd be just my luck. Usually when people take a while to answer a simple question, it means bad news.*

The minutes passed. She flinched at the sudden noise of a shrill beeping next to her. Jaclyn turned and saw a man exiting the gas station.

He was wearing a faded, dark green button-down shirt with a black undershirt. They were all tucked into a pair of worn out jeans speckled with dirt. He was wearing a black baseball cap atop his uneven, dusty, short brown hair. The cap had a Pittsburgh Steelers design at the front. Somehow the design itself had worn off entirely.

The man turned and blankly stared at her with his protruding, bulbous eyes. His mouth was fixed to make his jaw look like a piranha's. It made her think that if he let it hang open, she'd see a hidden row of tiny fangs, sharp as daggers.

A sudden chill crept across her body as he stared, looked away, and slunk toward the car at the pump. It was as if he'd recognized her from somewhere before. It was the same look those strange children had given her earlier.

It made Jaclyn wonder. She couldn't recall a time when she passed through this area. It would've been on the way to downtown Pittsburgh. From what she saw on her phone's GPS, that's where Dourmsburg inevitably led to.

She opened the GPS on her phone again. Initially, the view included numerous cities around her location, including downtown Pittsburgh.

Jaclyn typed "Pittsburgh" in the search bar and confirmed the city center as the specific location for the directions. After loading for a second, the app gave her a set of active directions and the estimated time of arrival. It would take an hour and fifteen minutes of driving.

She would've had to escape the backroads and suburbs for the first half hour. The rest was a matter of powering through the Interstate Three Seventy-Six West.

"Shit," Jaclyn muttered to herself. "Where the Hell did I wander off to?"

Focusing on her location, she closed the current directions. She saw the names of mid-sized suburban towns a small distance away from her, but nothing pointing out Dourmsburg.

She expected this. The GPS wouldn't label any smaller details until Jaclyn zoomed in. This was the first time she'd even done this. Until now, all she did with this app was receive spoken directions.

At first, she didn't quite align her thumbs the right way on the screen. She felt like a fool for struggling to perform such a simple function as getting a closer look on a map. The view remained the same after the first few tries.

If someone younger saw her, they'd snicker at her ineptitude.

She managed to do it on her fifth attempt. Jaclyn didn't understand why it took such a precise movement of the thumbs. She rolled her eyes and zoomed in again but noticed that Dourmsburg still wasn't showing up.

Although the names for highways and streets were showing up. Jaclyn gently swiped in different directions on the map, seeing landmarks like parks and water bodies that were miles from where she stood. But when she returned to the blue arrow on that map which showed her location and the direction she was facing—

There was no label for Dourmsburg on her map at all.

Remembering how *Eclipse* phones were supposed to update, Jaclyn turned the power off, and switched it on after a moment's patience. As the brand logo faded in on a black background, it twinkled like a distant star before the entire screen lit up.

Once her apps appeared, she opened Directions again. Zooming in a few times, the result wasn't any different. Jaclyn was standing on territory that had been unmarked by Anthony Charles and his underlings.

Jaclyn wasn't sure how to interpret this. Was it a sign of freedom, or simply of being unknown to the rest of the digitized world? If the latter were the case, it meant being invisible to the world at large.

The smartphone vibrated with another message from Trixie. "Can we do a video call?"

Rolling her eyes, Jaclyn replied, "Sure."

She didn't just hate calls; she loathed them. It didn't matter if the call was audio or video. Fundamentally, they were the same thing. But considering she was relying on Trixie, it wasn't too much of a price.

Jaclyn answered the incoming video call, remembering that video calls by default were on a three-dimensional setting. It was an innovation of the smartphone industry that Eclipse's competitors were yet to catch up with. Face to face was a live feed of Trixie from the shoulder up as a translucent hologram.

She asked, “Jaclyn? Can you see me okay?”

“Yeah, the call’s working.”

“Good. I’m still learning the holograms on this phone.”

“I know what you mean. I have a little trouble learning this stuff too,” Jaclyn said.

“So what’s the address and what time do you need me there?”

25.

Jaclyn watched the evening sun setting in, drifting down the way a sleeping infant would into his crib. She was sitting at the curb of a nearby convenience store, a trail of thin gray smoke wafted from her lips.

A new pack stopped the ever-growing beast from awakening and rampaging within her. Jaclyn considered the ultra-light as a fast way to lull the beast back to sleep. Better than letting it open its eyes and turn her into a jittering grenade.

She had passing ideas about starving the beast, but thought it was too large at this point. Occasionally, Jaclyn thought back to the moment when she started at seventeen.

Until she smoked, Jaclyn wondered how people could breathe that stuff in, but strangely used to enjoy the smell. Seeing someone else doing it in passing used to make her wonder if it was as refreshing as they made it look.

The moment she started came about when she was trying to think of what to do for her high school senior project. It had to be a project outside of schoolwork, with a mentor who was at least twenty-five. The rules said that she had to find a mentor who was at least that age and unrelated to her, to verify Jaclyn's fifty plus hours of work.

Since freshman year, the project made her feel like a tarantula was creeping up her spine. Once senior year came around, it sank its fangs through Jaclyn's skull, piercing her brain stem. The dripping venom had been potent enough to give her nightmares about getting a failing grade, forcing her to repeat the school year.

Jaclyn thought she couldn't go a waking minute without stressing over it.

You can't graduate if you don't pass your project.

Jaclyn was rambling to a classmate from Algebra II while walking home from school. For once, the subject wasn't whether they should just hang out somewhere or experiment with each other. She didn't have a single idea for the project.

But Nick Hetfield, the tall boy in her math class who played on the basketball team, had produced a pack of Marlboros from his pocket. They were off school grounds and on an adjacent strip mall's parking lot.

Nick had offered her one, saying it could help her relax. The temptation struck her. She wondered if it'd really help. Would she stop at just one, or would it turn into a lifelong habit? But the more she thought about it, the less the question mattered. All that mattered was pulling the spider's fangs out.

She took the cigarette, and they smoked while sitting at the edge of the strip mall.

Jaclyn watched her discarded butt leaving a trail of gray like it was bound to combust. Waiting for Trixie to pull up in her old Ford Fusion, she cleared the bit of phlegm from her throat out of habit. This was another aspect of daily life at this point, so she paid no mind to something this minor.

Checking the time on her phone, she noticed that it was quarter past eight. Trixie hadn't sent another text since telling Jaclyn she was on her way. That was a solid forty minutes ago.

She was tempted to send a message asking if she was okay but decided it wasn't necessary. Jaclyn figured if something had happened, Trixie would have said something.

The woman was insistent on talking through a video chat and kept up a conversation until she said that she left. She wasn't the type to keep people in the dark. But she reflected that this young woman could be someone who wasn't forthcoming.

Jaclyn could've been waiting for nothing this whole time.

"I hope the poor kid's okay," she told herself. "If Trixie can't come, it's not a big deal. She can just say so."

She began to wonder if Trixie was willing to get herself into trouble over this. If this younger woman was considering doing something stupid just to please her. Jaclyn knew it was too soon to infer that.

But it wasn't a farfetched thought.

Mom? I'm sorry I got an F on my report card. You don't still hate me—do you?

She watched the surrounding roads, searching for any cars in the distance. An occasional Ford or Toyota passed her by, but they were a rare sight. It was as if the town of Dourmsburg was always sleepy despite the sun still being out.

Another white Ford rolled down Canton Street toward her. Jaclyn recoiled as it flashed its headlights flashed on and off at her. She strained her eyes, seeing Trixie smiling and waving through the windshield.

Jaclyn blinked in pleasant surprise and nervously returned the gesture.

Trixie pulled over in the parking lot and rolled down her window. "Hey stranger," she cried, waving through the opening. "Get in!"

After getting into the passenger's side and shutting the car door, Jaclyn asked, "Did you get here okay?"

"Yeah, it wasn't an issue," Trixie responded.

"Are you sure? I didn't know it was such a drive."

Trixie rolled her eyes, grinned and replied, "It's not that big of a deal. I like driving anyway. Besides, it's an excuse to get out of the house." She put the transmission into reverse.

As the Ford backed out and drove onto Canton again, Jaclyn said, "Well, I really appreciate it. You're a good kid, Trixie."

"Come on, I'm not a kid," Trixie rebutted.

"*How* old are you?" Jaclyn asked.

"Twenty-one."

"You're still a kid to me, but that's not a bad thing. It just means you have your whole life ahead of you."

"How long do people see you as a kid?" Trixie asked.

"Maybe for a few more years. But it's usually out of affection."

"So why the diner?"

Jaclyn paused and replied, "I'm trying to meet up with someone."

"Who?"

"An old woman. I saw her there last night before I came to the tavern. She tipped me off on something pretty important. I didn't know if I'd see her again, but I figured she'd probably show up again."

"What did she tip you off about?"

Jaclyn hesitated, then answered, "It's—kinda personal. To be honest, I don't know how you'd react if I told you."

I lied to you, you dumbass kid, she thought. And I lied to everyone in the tavern too. My kid isn't home. He's probably fucking dead and it would be what I deserved.

"I'm not judging, but I won't pressure you," Trixie said. "But how do you know she'll be there? Have you seen her there a lot?"

The truth was: Jaclyn hadn't. She only stopped at the Ace of Clubs last night in passing. The old woman was just there by a stroke of luck.

"I only met her the one time, Trix. But if there's a chance she has more to tell me, it's worth taking a chance."

26.

"Do you remember what she looks like?" Trixie asked.

"Yeah," Jaclyn answered. "She had curly gray and white hair, thick glasses, a light blue windbreaker, and a decent amount of jewelry. Mostly earrings, I think."

"You know, that actually sounds familiar," Trixie said.

"Really? You've seen her before?"

"Pretty sure I have," Trixie replied. "I've been to the Ace of Clubs a few times."

Jaclyn gave a smirk and asked, "You didn't try the food, did you?"

"You mean the runny eggs and the undercooked steak on the breakfast menu?"

"Oh *God*, I was thinking about the soggy burger patties."

Trixie asked, "You didn't get food poisoning, did you?"

"No. I took a bite, spat it out, and told them to take it back and cook it right."

"*Then* what?"

"They *did*," Jaclyn answered. "And they tried telling me they had a new cook on staff. Apparently, the woman at the next table had the same issue."

"Color me surprised. So that's how you met this person?"

"Yeah, Hell of a way to bond, huh? She helped me out a bit, and we both ended up getting a free meal as an apology."

"Sounds like a good night overall," Trixie said sincerely. "What was she helping you with?"

A pause. "I've just been looking for something."

"Looking for something? So is *that* why you've been driving through my neck of the woods?" Trixie continued.

Jaclyn's tongue dried at the thought of her lie being caught. "Yeah. That's all."

"It's okay. I don't mean anything by it. I'm just teasing."

"Oh yeah, I know."

"I take it you live in Dourmsburg then?"

"No, I was just passing by."

Trixie was silent at first, then asked, "Then how did you get back to your kid?"

Jaclyn couldn't think of anything to say except "I didn't."

The muscles in the girl's neck twitched and her eyes shot wide open. "Why not? Where is he now?"

"He's been staying with my brother and his wife for the past few days," Jaclyn lied.

Her breath shortened, and her eyes wandered toward whatever lay on the side of the road. The lie spilled out again. She felt like a small, clumsy child trying to drink out of an adult glass. Instead of keeping the lie contained until she thought things out, Jaclyn let it past her lips.

She didn't know if she was ready to fabricate the life of a sibling. Jaclyn was an only child. She had been curious about what it would be like to have a sibling. As a child, she'd ask a few of her classmates and hear short stories about the irreplaceable friendship and terrible rivalry.

Most of all, Trixie didn't deserve to be deceived like that. Jaclyn thought most people didn't, although occasionally, it was necessary.

"*Oh*, okay," the girl told her. "Your brother. What's he like?"

Jaclyn tried to swallow but her mouth was too dry. Her sandpaper-like tongue touched the back of her throat.

She answered, "He's an fireman. Wicked smart. Probably one of the sharpest guys you'd ever meet. He's always had a bit of a passion for physics, but for whatever reason, he didn't choose that as a career. He said the student loan would've been too much, but I think it was just a lack of confidence. He can seem a little too stern sometimes, but deep down, he's got a really big heart. My brother's the kind of person who'd give you the shirt off his back if you ever needed it."

Jaclyn would've used these words to describe her father. The reality was: it *had* been her father, but that was fine. She knew the praise was well-deserved. They were words Jaclyn thought he had deserved at his funeral, if only she had the chance.

But for some reason or another, the funeral home and even the church in her hometown, didn't let the surviving loved ones briefly and warmly reminisce about the dead at the podium. She wandered if it was a Catholic thing but doubted it.

She looked back at Trixie, seeing a pleased look on her face. She was relieved, and her heart rate finally slowed down.

Trixie said, "Sounds like your kid's in good hands."

"Yeah. For sure."

"I guess he knows how long you'll be gone?" Trixie asked.

The Ford hit a small pothole as it approached the highway Jaclyn had exited. It was too shallow to slow the car down but it made them jump in their seats.

"Thank God for shocks," Trixie said.

"It wasn't that big of a pothole. I wouldn't worry."

"I guess. The car's used. It's got a few years on it."

"What year *is* it?" Jaclyn asked.

"It's a twenty-nineteen."

"Yeah, you weren't kidding. But you'll be fine. Trust me, I've had my share of car catastrophes. If there was something wrong with the car, we'd both know by now."

"I guess you're right," Trixie replied. "It's just that this is my first car, so I get worried that something might happen."

"I understand. I used to be nervous about my first car too." Jaclyn reassured her with a warm smile.

"As long as it can get me home and to Pittsburgh, that's all I really care about."

"Pittsburgh… As in, downtown Pittsburgh?" Jaclyn asked.

"Yep, downtown," Trixie answered.

"Why downtown?" Jaclyn knew there were a million reasons for a woman in her early twenties to go there—emerging artists, the music scene, the food and so many events. If she were to search for an event calendar for downtown Pittsburgh, there wouldn't be a day when at least three events listed.

"I guess I forgot to mention this before—it tends to happen when I get excited, but Anthony Charles just came to Pittsburgh this morning," Trixie replied.

"Yeah, I was surprised about that. The lobby attendant at the hotel where I stayed brought it up." *And God, did she ever,* Jaclyn thought. *I probably couldn't even feel unsure about going around Sabrina.* "I guess I wasn't paying much attention to those sorts of events before. But you can't blame me." She gave a blasé shrug and smile. "I've been busy on the road for a little while now."

"No, I really can't."

"You excited for the new tech he's putting out next year?" Jaclyn asked.

"Of *course,*" Trixie said. "But I'm a lot more excited to try and get into the *after*-event. You're still interested in seeing, aren't you?"

27.

"Yeah," Jaclyn replied. "I am."

As she spoke, she didn't know what else to say. What results would a simple *no* have yielded? She didn't feel compelled to refuse. Her curiosity was too strong, and the opportunity too unique.

But what if she refused? Even if Jaclyn was polite about it, she would've expected a soft reply of acceptance Trixie gave off but a much stronger disappointment. Jaclyn would've felt guilty regardless of Trixie's response. Her going meant something to the girl.

Besides, she could choose to leave at any point if the need arose. Jaclyn imagined it being just like the cinema. Somewhere there'd be a small private auditorium bought out for the night—most of the seats would be filled.

Anthony Charles or one of his associates would've paid a hefty amount as hush money to the owners. Unless the party managing the building's affairs was invited to join. Jaclyn imagined that would've been forced to leave. Knowing the value of Charles' company—near a trillion dollars, second place to Apple in the tech industry—a bribe that a white-collar worker could live off of for decades wouldn't be an issue.

"And as long as *I* can get in," Trixie said. "I can get you in too."

"So you need a reference to mingle with this *group*."

"Yeah. You do," Trixie replied.

"Why is that?" Jaclyn asked.

They reached the intersection where the road turned to reach Dourmsburg. Jaclyn was back on that highway again. She wiped her lips with her thumb and forefinger. She hadn't been wearing any makeup that day, so it didn't matter.

It was all stashed away in her glove box, but the napkins were a bigger compromise. Now that Jaclyn thought of it, last night had been the first time in a little while she'd worn makeup. It had to have been a few days at least.

That had been peculiar, she reflected. There was a time in her later twenties, while she was married, when she'd wear it every day. But once the divorce papers had been official, Jaclyn noticed makeup becoming less of a habit.

"Why is that?" Jaclyn repeated her question to Trixie, noticing her question hadn't been answered the first time.

"I don't know," the bartender answered with a disgruntled tone.

"I think it's something worth asking. Don't you?"

But Trixie was silent. Her brow was furrowed; hands gripping the steering wheel as if to choke someone. Jaclyn looked over and noticed all this, yet the car hadn't stopped.

She looked out the window at the lake of wet grass and tiny mud patches. She saw the hills glistening with fresh rain near the horizon. Jaclyn could just make out the distant, aged wooden fences of abandoned properties.

"I wasn't trying to offend you, Trix, if that's how you feel."

No response. Trixie's eyes were fixed straight ahead, her face was still, as if she was a cold rock sculpture.

"Look," Jaclyn turned to her and said with all sincerity. "I'm sorry."

"Yeah. Okay." Trixie's grasp on the steering wheel loosened from a death-grip to a firm hold. "I just don't like arguing all the time. It gets a little old after a while, you know? Like, Randy? He's a nice guy and everything, but I can't get a night at the bar without him starting up something."

Jaclyn rose an eyebrow. "I didn't know he was such a contrarian."

"Yeah, I think it's fine to ask questions and everything but when you constantly start arguments with someone, you're just doing it for the argument's sake. You're not getting anything out of that. It's like you *say* you want to learn and get people to think, but all you're really doing is deconstructing them and trying to invalidate them."

Jaclyn flatly replied, "I suppose so." Paused, then a small spark of interest lit her voice. "So you like driving. I guess it centers you then?"

"Sometimes, yeah," Trixie replied, the aggravation from her voice fading away.

"You typically drive when you travel?"

"Preferably. Either that or by boat, depending on where I'm at."

"You don't fly?" Jaclyn enquired.

Trixie was quiet, her lips were pressed shut, as if a lump rising was in her throat, before she said, "Never."

"How come? It's faster than driving. It's safer too."

"I *know* the statistics. I've heard them before," Trixie replied.

"Then what is it?"

"If the engine in your car fails," Trixie answered. "The car just stops. But in a plane? That's where Hell just begins."

Jaclyn was struck. She wasn't sure how to answer that. Her first thought was the unlikelihood of that happening. But Trixie had already answered that.

I've heard the numbers before.

She swallowed and asked, "Have you ever flown before?"

"No," Trixie answered. "And I don't need to anyway. It wouldn't compare."

"To what?"

"Being on the road or on the ocean. The open air surrounding you. Feeling the road and the water right underneath you. You have an unlimited view around you. What do you get in a plane anyway?

You get crammed in a little seat with a little window to see a little fraction of what you're flying through."

"I don't know. It sounds like sour grapes to me," Jaclyn said.

"Sour grapes?"

"Yeah," Jaclyn said. "It's sour grapes."

"What's that mean?"

"It means putting something down before trying it. It's from *The Fox and the Grapes* from *Aesop's Fables.* A fox sees a vine of ripe grapes hanging down from a branch. He tries jumping up to reach them, but they're too high up. Instead of trying a different way, he just walks away, saying they're sour anyway."

"Oh," Trixie said to herself. She paused, then said, "I've never heard of it before."

"That's okay. I only know it because my dad read Aesop's Fables to me all the time when I was little."

"He read to you?"

"Yeah," Jaclyn answered with a blank look and her brow cocked.

Trixie didn't say anything. Initially, she was motionless but nodded her head as they headed further down the highway.

28.

"Why do you ask?" Jaclyn questioned.

Trixie shrugged.

"It's just an—interesting question," Jaclyn remarked. "I was just wondering, I guess."

"Right," Trixie said.

"So, since you've traveled by boat, I take it you've been to Europe?" Jaclyn asked.

"For a short time, yeah."

"Which countries?"

"First, Ireland, then England, France, and Germany. I travelled the most in Dublin and London though. I could catch a little bit of French and German to get around okay, but it helps when you're actually fluent in the language."

"'Ireland, then England'? Aren't Ireland and England both part of the same country?" Jaclyn enquired.

"I mean," Trixie replied, her sentence faltering. "There definitely are Irishmen who'd beg to differ."

"How were they?"

"The *Irish*men?" Trixie's cheeks turned pink.

"Uh, no, I meant the places you went."

"They were alright."

"Alright?" Jaclyn couldn't believe what she was hearing. How did this girl talk about touring a different continent with such indifference? *That kind of money would've paid the bills for months,* Jaclyn thought. She imagined the thousands of dollars that must've been spent and asked, "Did you go with anyone?"

Trixie shrugged.

"A significant other?"

"Didn't have one."

"Oh. Any friends?"

Trixie paused, then replied, “No.”

“Couldn’t anyone go with you? I guess that’s bound to happen. Once you’re in college, people tend to get busier. I understand. That probably happens to everyone.”

Maybe it’s because they can’t afford it. We can’t all be born with silver spoons up our asses.

Jaclyn realized that if Trixie could go to Europe without a second thought, getting older wouldn’t be a reality if she kept that kind of money rolling in. The prices of some of the new anti-ageing surgeries she’d heard about were more than the annual income of a blue-collar worker, but they were never questioned.

The cheaper ones included the change of one’s natural hair and eye colors. A procedure like that would cost four figures, but the real spending was for restoring physical youth. It was a matter of reversing the combination of proteins throughout the body in multiple sessions, making a wrinkled prune into someone blossoming in their thirties. If Trixie ever did such a thing, she’d have Anthony Charles to thank for the innovation.

“Maybe,” Trixie said as they passed the tavern. “I don’t know.”

“What do you mean?” Jaclyn paused and examined the blank expression on her driver’s face. “Are you alright?”

Trixie was silent at first, but replied, "I don't really want to talk about it."

"Oh—okay. Sorry."

"It's fine. Don't worry about it."

Jaclyn slumped toward the passenger door and looked at Trixie. The girl's face hadn't changed.

There's some kind of wall built around her, Jaclyn thought. *I can feel it.*

A gentle shiver crawled along her skin. She waited to see a tear, a furrow of the brow, a quiver of the lip, anything from Trixie that would've hinted at any feelings.

But there was nothing. Her face was like smooth, pale stone, yet her hands said otherwise. She was gripping the steering wheel again, her thumbs tapping it to an unorganized beat that no one else could hear.

The silence between them was unbroken until the sudden *screech* of the brakes as they pulled into the Ace of Clubs parking lot. Rust decorated the edges of the sign, as if no part of it had been taken down and replaced for years.

The overall design had neon lettering and an arrow that reached around the outside of the sign and down it to point at the restaurant. It wasn't dark out enough for the neon to lights to be on, but once they did, the tall capital A would flicker once a minute.

Trixie put the Ford into park in front of the diner and wordlessly opened her door. Jaclyn got out and followed her to the diner. As the bartender locked her car, she held the door open without saying a word.

As Jaclyn stepped inside, she took another look at Trixie's face for another clue. She noticed a sudden weight in the girl's eyes, despite getting enough sleep. She coldly gazed into the distance. Trixie was looking in Jaclyn's direction, as if to freeze any nearby creature in its tracks.

As they entered, Jaclyn read the sign placed before the front register that read, *Please seat yourself. You will be served shortly.*

A set of double doors next to the register led to the kitchen. If one watched a server go through them with enough care, they'd see the restaurant's back door straight ahead.

They looked at the small rows of tables and booths. Its aesthetic was an overpowering musky green, like fake emeralds. Whatever wasn't this color—just the chair legs—was just bare wood.

The interior was barren of any decor, save the set of windows at the end of the room and a single overhead fan next to it.

As her eyes roved the emptiness of the place, Trixie said, "You know, we got here kinda early. We might have some time before that woman shows up."

They picked a booth in the middle of the room and sat across from each other. Trixie picked up her menu and flipped through it. Jaclyn stared at the double doors that went to the kitchen. She was thinking about getting a glass of water, nothing else.

She was unable to muster up an appetite for dinner. When she listened carefully, she could hear the faint sounds of meat sizzling on a grill.

"I'll pay for it," Trixie said, her nose in the menu.

"Hmm?"

"I said I'll pay for it."

"You sure?" Jaclyn asked.

"Yeah, get whatever you want. It's fine," Trixie replied, dismissively motioning her hand.

Jaclyn put one elbow on the table and rested her head on the back of her hand. Her eyes drifted to the double doors again, but she didn't notice the cluster of shadows lurking underneath.

She looked at Trixie and asked, "Why are you doing all this for me?"

"Hmm?"

"You just met me last night," Jaclyn asserted. "Why are you doing this? You gave me a ride here to find someone, and now you're paying for my food."

Trixie hesitated, then replied, "Because you're my friend. Friends always help each other, right?"

Even with a clear answer, Jaclyn was stunned.

29.

The kitchen doors burst open. A pudgy woman, around five feet tall with deep wrinkles under her eyes walked out. Her ebony hair had the texture of thin metal wire and was tied back tight enough to tear a bit of the skin from the scalp.

She wore a green polo shirt with a snug pair of jeans and black non-slip tennis shoes. Evidently, the uniform of the diner matched the rest of the garish hue of the place. Her name was stitched in golden cursive across her left breast—Brenda.

She was pale enough to pass as a person with albinism—her skin looked like the cheap vinyl plastic. Her eyes were abnormally wide with bright baby blue irises. The ceiling lights reflected and gleamed off them as if they were manufactured from glass.

Her facial features, except her lips, were full like a child's. Her lips were so thin that they might as well have not existed. From a distance, one would look at her and only see a bare outline of her mouth.

She had a small but forced smile. It gave the impression of permanence, like her cheeks had been molded upward, just enough to force the edges of her mouth back. Her expression remained unchanged from the time she exited the kitchen and reached Jaclyn and Trixie's table.

"Hi," she said to them, commanding their attention.

Jaclyn winced, then smiled back. Trixie's menu was already flat on the table, the look in her eyes had altered to a little girl's shivering intimidation.

"My name's Brenda and I'll be serving you this evening. Can I start you off with something to drink?" As the waitress' smile curled and expanded, it felt as though her cheeks would crackle as her mouth moved.

Trixie stared at Jaclyn. The look in her eyes was asking Jaclyn to go first, even begging to—

Please get that woman away from here.

Jaclyn looked back to Brenda and answered, "Uh, just a glass of water, thanks."

The waitress turned to Trixie and asked, "And you?"

Pause. "A rasp—raspberry tea, please."

Brenda hadn't written down anything, but said, "Of course, I'll get those for you right away."

The waitress turned toward the kitchen, and as she did, Jaclyn noticed a black mark on her right wrist. It wasn't shocking at all. Plenty of younger women had a small tattoo on one wrist. It was often a short phrase, a means of deriving inspiration in the face of adversity. The mark of a troubled past beaten in the dust.

But it wasn't the usual cursive writing. It wasn't even writing at all. It was a simple design in plain black ink. Jaclyn realized it was the solar eclipse.

As she walked away, the look of unease faded from Trixie's eyes. "Thank God," she whispered, picking the menu back up.

Jaclyn didn't like hearing that but didn't say anything about it. It was forgivable. She'd already done it often.

She asked, "You okay, Trix?"

"Yeah. Just—that server."

"I know what you mean. She seems *off*, I guess."

Jaclyn just noticed the faint sound hovering under the ceiling of the place. It was the kind of noise you could only notice when there was nobody else around, or if someone paid close attention.

The song was something she hadn't heard before. It was the moaning baritone of Al Bowlly singing *If Anything Happened to You.*

"That's a nice way to put it," Trixie said. "I might be brave after all and try the bacon cheeseburger."

"Really? You sure about that?"

"Yeah, you ate here last night, didn't you?"

"Uh huh, what about it?" Jaclyn asked.

"So you got the *night* cook, right?" Trixie confirmed.

"I guess so," Jaclyn replied.

"So we'd probably have someone else instead. It's a lot earlier in the evening," Trixie pointed out. "You know, I haven't had one in *years*. It'd be a way to treat myself?"

"Over what?"

"You don't know this. A *lot* of people I met after high school don't know this, but I used to be fat."

Jaclyn was taken aback. "*You? Fat?* But *look* at you! You're *tiny*!"

Trixie smiled and rolled her eyes. "Yeah, it was a *lot* of running and a diet of nothing but rabbit food for few years." She sniffled dryly and rubbed her nose.

Lifting her shirt to her ribs, showing a row of faded stretch marks, Trixie said, "Here's the proof." She let go of her shirt and sat back down. "Sometimes *I* still can't believe I did it, but I used to be a big tub of *shit*." She put her hand up as if to stop Jaclyn before she even started to refute her. "I know, I know, I shouldn't say that. But that's how I felt about it. 'You big tub of shit.' That's what I'd think when I looked in the mirror. But it's also what the other girls at school liked to say to me. God, the years of bullying… It was nonstop."

"Wow," Jaclyn was speechless. "I'm really sorry. I know people at school can be little shits." She hadn't experienced bullying like that firsthand, but she witnessed it from a distance and not brought herself to say anything about it.

"For sure. I can't tell you how many times I wanted to hit them. Sometimes I wanted to bash every bone in their snotty little faces—it was *that persistent*. But you know what? As much as they deserved it, I couldn't bring myself to hit them. You know what I did?" Trixie asked.

Jaclyn knew she wouldn't like the answer, but she had to ask anyway. "What?"

"I just went to one of the stalls and cried. I could make up an excuse for being late to class once I had cold water on my eyes. But that's all I could really do. Not long after, I started hitting the treadmill in the weight room. I just got tired of it. Every now and then, the teacher who coached football would worry about how much I ran. But that didn't stop me. Shit, even my dad noticed. For once, I saw him instead of the nanny or one of the maids. One time, he asked me if I was slimming down right before he was heading out to catch his flight. I even got fast enough to join the volleyball team. The other girls snickered, but I didn't think about it. All that mattered was hitting that fucking ball over the net, and you know what? I even accomplished a little goal of mine."

"What was that?" Jaclyn asked.

"I learned how to *spike* that son of a bitch," Trixie answered with a big smile. "And I even nailed one of the girls in the *face*. She was one of the girls who liked to say 'you're a big tub of shit' before we started playing. The volleyball had some of her makeup smeared on it, and by the time she got back up, she looked like a fucking *Picasso*!"

They cackled together in a shared victory, but it died down because they noticed Brenda coming back with their drinks.

After setting them on the table, she loomed over the table, smiling, she asked, "Are you both ready to order?"

30.

Trixie lowered her menu as she looked at Brenda, the apprehension returning to her face from the waitress' Cheshire Cat smile. "Double bacon cheeseburger, please."

"Fries?"

"Yes please." Trixie closed her eyes and looked away, handing her menu to Brenda.

As the waitress took it, she asked Jaclyn, "And you?"

"You know what, I'm not really sure. I might just be good with the water, thanks."

"Alright, I can give you some more time." Brenda looked back at Trixie and said, "And I'll get your order right away."

As the waitress left, Jaclyn muttered, "You know, she didn't write your order. She didn't even have a pen and notebook."

"I noticed."

"You think it's just because there's so few orders at this time of day?" Jaclyn's voice shivered a little as she said, "I guess she just doesn't need it right now."

Trixie tried to sound tough but failed as she replied, "Who cares? Aren't you gonna eat anything?"

Hell of a question, she thought.

It wasn't that Jaclyn found the idea of eating repulsive. It wasn't like having a stomach infection, where the mere mention of food would've made her stomach turn. She simply didn't see the appeal in eating. Jaclyn felt as if she'd eaten a full meal in the past hour.

How long had her appetite been like this? When did it first fade like this? She knew it wasn't all at once. It was a process. As if a slithering worm had come to her when she slept and gradually sucked her appetite away, until her stomach withered like a raisin.

She wasn't sure when it started. Months? No, it hadn't been that long ago. Weeks? Could've been. That made more sense to her. If it had been months, there would've been no denying that she was sick. But it had to have been weeks. The worm sneaking around her stomach hadn't been around when she first got on the road, but snuck in somewhere after that.

"I don't know," Jaclyn answered about eating. "I'm thinking about it."

"Well, it's another reason for that woman to come back."

"Yeah. Yeah, I guess it is."

"Maybe I'll just get something light."

I haven't even eaten anything all day, Jaclyn thought. *I don't want to, but I gotta eat something. Even if I end up forcing something down my throat.*

"I just don't like that waitress," Trixie said.

"I noticed. You know," Jaclyn began, a grin creeping on her face. "We could just get up and leave."

"*No.* We already ordered. We're not gonna dine and ditch, and *I'm* not gonna get arrested. I have a clean record. I plan on keeping it that way."

"Okay, okay, I didn't mean to offend or anything," Jaclyn conceded.

"Besides, we're waiting for that old woman, right? If we just left, what'd be the point in coming in the first place?" Trixie reminded.

Jaclyn paused, then replied, "You know, I didn't think you'd be so eager."

"What do you mean?"

"I didn't think someone I just met would be up for this."

"So hanging out's weird?"

"Well, no, it's not that," Jaclyn replied.

"Then what?" Trixie asked.

Jaclyn cocked her brow and answered, "It's not you. It's just that my friends weren't always this quick about doing something."

Trixie picked up her glass and chugged half the tea. "You sure?" she asked, unconvinced.

"You mentioned something about your dad being on a lot of business trips and having around a lot of nannies," Jaclyn mentioned.

"Yeah." Trixie picked up a smaller ice cube from the glass, popped it in her mouth and sucked it. "What about it?"

"What did he do? It's okay if you don't feel like getting into it."

"He's a bigwig in the automotive industry. He oversaw the sales, so it meant a lot of traveling."

"So, I guess it meant being with your mom a lot?" As Jaclyn asked this, she already knew the answer but hoped she was wrong.

Trixie crunched down on the ice cube and shook her head. "No, a lot of times, she went with him."

"Oh." Jaclyn looked down at her glass of water and swirled it in her hand, watching the ice cubes knock each other. "I'm sorry to hear that."

"Not your fault. There just weren't a lot of kids my age in the neighborhood and acting out probably didn't help my popularity either."

"I guess you connected more with these nannies then?"

"To be honest, not so much. I usually was distanced from them. Whenever I wasn't in trouble, I just ended up watching movies, reading books, and surfing the internet a lot."

Jaclyn asked, "What did you get in trouble for?"

A pause, and Trixie replied, "Theft and vandalism. I was just a dumb kid then—still am, I guess—but when my parents found out, it was probably the longest they've talked to me in a long time."

"What's 'a long time'?"

"Years, maybe. They kept asking why I'd do that, and honestly? I still don't really know, but there was always a rush that came with tagging and stealing. It sounds weird, but getting caught felt good."

"It sounds like maybe you did it *just* to get caught," Jaclyn said.

"No, I wouldn't say that," Trixie replied.

"But then why would it feel good?"

"I don't know. Maybe it has to do with being stuck in a big, empty house with nobody around. Sure, there was always *some*body else in the house, but they might as well not have been there. It was just as empty either way. It gave me a reason to be a spectacle."

"How old were you?" Jaclyn asked.

"Seventeen," Trixie answered. "But I guess something kinda came out of it."

"What was that?" Jaclyn asked.

"Some time later, my parents started mentioning Anthony Charles—how he was so young—not even in his thirties, but had so much going for him. He already had the electronics stuff going on, but that's not what they talked about," Trixie explained. "Apparently, he was also interested in the automobile industry. I think they just talked about the opportunity to meet for a possible design over a video call."

"Yeah," Jaclyn replied. "I heard about the first models when they were in the market. It was pretty hard to believe at first. You don't expect a company that makes phones and computers to start manufacturing cars."

"No, but it still happened. My dad looked the happiest I'd ever seen him. Mom was just as happy, but that's only because *he* was happy. I don't want to sound too harsh—but I could never respect her very much," Trixie said. "From what I saw of her, she always came off as his parrot. Both were ecstatic about the deal, and for the first time, they started being really encouraging to me. They would talk for *days* about how so many opportunities waited for me in college and how I'd do so well in computer science and software engineering."

"Was that a career path you mentioned to them before?" Jaclyn asked.

Trixie snickered and said, "Of course not."

"Did they ever notice it was something you were good at?"

"No, I only learned enough about computers to browse the internet."

"Oh," Jaclyn replied. "I only ask because my boy…" Her sentence trailed off as she felt her head beginning to ache. Jaclyn's head throbbed, making her double over and grasp her forehead.

"Hm? What about him?" Trixie pushed.

Jaclyn paused, rubbing her forehead, and replied, "Never mind. Go ahead, I'm sorry."

"Are you okay?"

"Yeah, I'm fine," Jaclyn answered before drinking her ice water. "What were you saying?"

"Well, whenever I got mom alone and insisted that I didn't want to go to school for computers, she just gave up and asked me to take it up with my dad. I kind of already knew that'd happen, but—I don't know. I wanted to at least *try* and get the message across."

"So, what *did* you want to go to college for?"

Trixie looked at her glass, swirled her glass and smirked with a heavy look in her eyes. "I didn't. I tried to clarify, but my parents didn't want to hear any of it. I really just wanted to join the workforce and start my own life." She shrugged and said, "I don't know. I didn't think of that as such a bad thing.

"But it was still an opportunity, so I got an associate degree in English and found a mixology program on the side. Bars don't usually *require* you to have a certificate, but getting one probably made me stand out to my employer. So, I found a full-time job and got myself an apartment.

"Dad wasn't totally satisfied, I guess. I didn't really like the life of a rich girl, but he mentioned me going back to school at every given opportunity. I don't think he knew about the miracle work, but it was through him that I got to see Anthony Charles."

31.

Did her father even know about that? Jaclyn thought. *I hate to say it, but probably not. To think that he'd be prouder of a younger businessman than his own kid… Can't say I blame her for getting away from that.*

Her train of thought was interrupted by a clanging outside, then a different noise behind the double doors. There was a string of low, muffled grunts. They were abrupt and frantic, like a hysteric trying to form words.

It was drowned out by the sound of a high-pitched shrilling hum. The noise morphed from unintelligible noise to lyrics:

"You are my sunshine, my only sunshine—You make me happy when skies are gray."

Jaclyn leaned to the side, peering closer at the double doors. "Do you hear that?"

Trixie asked, "What?"

"Shh."

They listened together, staring at the kitchen doors with a laser-like focus. They watched it as if someone were about to emerge.

Jaclyn broke the silence, asking, "Do you hear that?"

"Hear what?" Trixie replied.

The singing was difficult to hear, let alone make out over the music in the restaurant.

Jaclyn harshly whispered, "*Listen.*"

Trixie leaned toward the kitchen doors. She looked like she would lose her balance any second.

"You'll never know dear; how much I love you—"

The sound of the muffled grunts stopped. The shrill singing went back to a hum, like a solid creature regressing into primordial ooze.

"You hear that, right?" Jaclyn asked.

Pause, then Trixie answered, "Maybe. I think so. I can just barely hear it."

"What *is* that?"

"I'm not sure. It sounds like someone humming."

"Yeah," Jaclyn said. "I could've sworn I heard somebody else too."

"Like another person singing?" Trixie asked.

"I'm not sure. I think it was deep, like a guy's."

"I'm not hearing it."

"It already stopped,"

"Is it just some lady singing in the back? I can't tell what she's saying," Jaclyn said.

"Yeah, me neither. It sounds like someone older though."

Jaclyn leaned away from the kitchen doors, sitting up straight again. Trixie followed her lead, picking up her menu and flipping through it. "Odd," she muttered to herself.

"A little," Jaclyn said as she looked at the only window in the entire building.

She could just see the sky gloaming. If the old woman was going to show up at all, it'd be soon.

The screech of metal being scraped assaulted their eardrums. Jaclyn and Trixie shook in their seats, adrenaline shot through them.

Trixie muttered, "What the Hell was that?"

"I don't know. It sounded like maybe it was coming from outside," Jaclyn guessed.

As Trixie scooted back in her chair, it produced a bone-rattling *screech*. She stood up, took out her wallet, and left a few one-dollar bills on the table for the drink and a tip. Trixie rushed toward the front entrance, Jaclyn following her.

"Trix, what're you doing!?"

"I just need to see something."

"What? What are you talked about?" Jaclyn asked.

Trixie pushed the front door open and stopped. Her mouth was agape, eyes fixed in astonishment.

Jaclyn paused, then asked with worry in her voice, "Trixie?"

But she said nothing. Trixie just stood there, staring at her car.

Jaclyn stood beside the girl with her eyes glued to the vehicle. "Oh my God…"

Trixie's breathing was slow but heavy. It was just loud enough for Jaclyn to hear. Her face was frozen. She wouldn't even blink.

The car was perfectly intact, except for two things. The hood was standing upright but had been bent at a sharp upward angle. It was as if the culprit had done that performed the feat with sheer strength alone.

Another moment of total stillness, and Trixie walked toward what lay beside the car's front right wheel. She stopped and considered the heap at her feet, near the hood and back again. Her breath grew heavier.

Jaclyn hesitated but followed. She stopped in the front of the car and saw that the insides were half-missing. Several of its parts had been torn out, like a sadistic, amateur autopsy.

She wasn't an automobile expert but knew enough to recognize the parts of an engine. The scrap pile next to the car included all those parts—everything from the oil pan gasket and above.

She took a second look and realized that most of the engine hadn't just been removed, but the engine block itself wasn't with the rest of the parts. It had either been dumped at the other side of the car—or stolen. How someone managed to take it apart in such a short time had to have been impossible.

Then it hit Jaclyn. It may not have been a single person, but a group. The question of whether she or Trixie had been targeted occurred to her. She realized how impossible this was, yet her eyes told an entirely different story.

One of them was a target, which meant someone *knew* they'd be at the Ace of Clubs. This party could've known where either she or Trixie were going *beforehand*. But *how*?

Question of the damn century, she thought as her heart burned with a flickering blue terror.

The terror slowly crept on her like a lion moving toward an alert but still gazelle. It was cooking her heart into charred meat.

If someone was after Trixie, she had money and a family with a Hell of a lot more—if her parents still remembered who she was. If someone was after her, it *would* have been because of her dad and his bank account. But her only way out was Uber, if there were even any around. Jaclyn knew where they were after all. The two of them were standing on the rickety wooden bridge to a godforsaken ghost town.

But God help her if her luck brought about the one in a million chance where she would have to defend herself during the ride. She didn't know Trixie's past too well, but the bartender looked like she'd never been in a fight in her life.

32.

Trixie's breathing wavered with hysteria. She was breathing frantically like a heart on the verge of giving out. Tears were beginning to flow down her face as she turned a deep pink. Her hands were over her mouth.

Trixie was muttering to herself, but as Jaclyn listened, she realized the girl was stuttering.

"F-F-Fuh-FUH— M-hi-MY c-c-c—"

It took her a second, but Jaclyn translated it to *fuck, my car.* She thought that if this girl stuttered so much under her panic, it'd be a chore just to finish her sentence.

But it couldn't be helped. Nobody stuttered on purpose. Jaclyn was a little experienced with people who had a stuttering problem. It wasn't usually due to anxiety, but because of picturing words clearly in one's mind. The people she worked with pictured copies of the same word overlapping each other.

But remedying a panic attack was a different matter. Even if it was the cause of her stutter, they were still two different ailments.

She put a gentle arm around the girl. "Trixie?"

"Oh G-G-Gah-Gah-GOD—"

"*Trix*, take it easy!"

"Eh-eh-I-I c-can-CAN'T." In between sentences, her lungs kept pumping air as if she were a second away from drowning.

"Trixie!" Once the girl looked at her with horror in her glassy eyes, Jaclyn commanded, "Breathe—*slowly*."

"Ah-Ay-I c-cah-HAN'T!"

"Yes—*you*—*can*. You'll only make yourself better if you *believe* you can. I need you to *trust* me." Despite seeing the hesitation in Trixie's eyes, she didn't remark about it. She just instructed, "Now breathe *with* me."

She began to take slow, deep breaths, and gently grasped Trixie's shoulders. The girl tried to follow, and soon her breathing slowed down. It wasn't normal by any means, but it wasn't frantic anymore.

Jaclyn gave her a stern expression, as if to tell her not to give up, or else she'd get a good ass-kicking. But the beating wouldn't come from Jaclyn. It'd come from something inside Trixie that ate at her peace of mind with a slow but satisfying glee.

Jaclyn couldn't help fixating on the look in the girl's eyes. They quivered if you looked close enough. Her eyes were radiating far more than fast, pulsing red terror—but layers of other heated emotions.

From a closer look, Jaclyn read helplessness, and even worse, overpowering isolation. The conviction that nobody in the whole world could help, whether there were people around or not.

She had seen that look before. It was on Corey's face during the nights of her binges before he'd lock his bedroom door. Was he already on the path to struggling with an ailment like this?

"Trix, are you listening to me?"

"Y-y-y…" Trixie squeezed her eyes shut, trying to force the word out.

"*Shh*, don't worry about talking. If it's too much right now, then don't. You're gonna be okay, you got it? *We're* gonna be okay."

Trixie nodded, her eyes still glassy. The tears hadn't stopped—but slowed down like her breathing. Her tears settled down and started building up gradually. They grew ripe on the tips of her eyelashes, and fell to the ground.

Jaclyn gave her a fake but reassuring smile, as if to convince herself. "We'll get a hold of the authorities, and it's all gonna be fine."

"N-n-na-NO ih-it's n-n-nah-NOT," Trixie exclaimed in a burst of panic.

"Don't say that. It *will.* I just need you to trust me." But as she said that, Jaclyn knew Trixie was making more sense between the two of them. "I'll call the authorities."

She knew that if someone was after one of them, they were still being watched by those people. When a lion caught a gazelle, it wouldn't just stop at immobilizing its prey. She chose not to share this with Trixie. God knew the girl was close enough to having a heart attack already.

Producing her phone from her pocket, she looked at the reception. There was just a single bar, gradually flickering on and off. It wasn't much but still worth a try.

Jaclyn dialed the number, pressed the call button and held the phone up to her ear. There was no response. She started to think that the call wouldn't even go through.

But that was a false alarm. It rang once, twice, and then—

An unfazed, middle-aged woman's voice said through the other end, "Nine-one-one, what's your emergency?"

"I need the police *now*. Someone ripped the engine out of the car!"

"Not to worry ma'am. We've got your location—the Ace of Clubs diner between Dourmsburg and Quakerston, is that right?"

Jaclyn hesitated, then replied, "Yeah. Yeah, that's right."

"Are you off the highway, ma'am?"

"Yeah, we're in the parking lot."

"Just stay right there. We're sending an officer to your location right now. Do you need anything else?"

"Er—no, that should be it."

The woman replied with a slow, pleased voice, "It was a pleasure helping you, Miss Ellsworth."

As the stranger hung up, Jaclyn heard the double-beep from her phone, ending the call. She noticed the woman already knew her name. Was it something common with emergency dispatch now?

She hadn't called *that* number in years—*decades*, now that she thought about it. The last time was when she'd just entered her twenties. It was in her art school days, so you weren't expected to get drunk. You were expected to do far more.

She was at a friend's dorm, waiting outside the bathroom. Her bladder was trembling like Hercules when Atlas duped him into holding up the skies on his shoulders. Any second, she would've felt a stream of hot urine trickling down her leg, ruining any chance of meeting people. But the anxiety stopped when she heard a sudden *thud* inside. Her furious knocking didn't elicit a response.

Once she told the host, he managed to unlock the bathroom door from the outside. A boy from the graphic design classes was lying inside. She hadn't met him before. He had slumped onto the floor from the toilet. Shaking him wasn't enough to get a response, but seeing the needle jammed in a fat vein on his forearm was enough for her to call an ambulance. Even then, the dispatch team asked for her name and location.

The kid recovered just fine. The doctors had said that he could have died. But it was better that he ended up disgruntled in a cell instead of a grave. Even then, the sentence only lasted a few days, thanks to the designer's parents. She imagined they were in a sourer mood after paying the bail and threatening to take him out of school.

Jaclyn still remembered overhearing him say, *"Congratulations son, you're a fuckin' felon,"* in the hallway and turning to scowl at her.

She heard that people could fall unconscious from panic attacks too, but it wasn't the same thing. *Fainting* was rare at the most, but was that the absolute worst?

It had to be. You couldn't *die* from having a panic attack. It wasn't anything like a heroin overdose. Jaclyn felt like a damned fool for letting the thought occur to her.

But it could still damage people in a lot of other ways, she remembered. It was the sort of thing that crept in and stole days—even years off your life. Jaclyn may have felt youth was something to envy, but Trixie didn't deserve wrinkles and gray hair in her thirties.

"Listen, Trix," she said with a sunny glow rising in her voice. "They're sending the police over right now. We just need to stay here for a little bit and tell them what happened. Once we do, we can leave, relax, and they'll take care of it. I promise, we won't have to worry about it."

Trixie looked down, then back at Jaclyn with doubt in her eyes.

"And you don't have to worry about speaking right now. Your speech will probably come back soon."

The blonde bartender managed to crack a little smile, wiped her eyes, and nodded.

Jaclyn asked, "And doesn't it usually do that anyway?" It was with enough conviction as if she'd been with Trixie during another panic attack.

Another nod. Then Trixie started typing on her phone. A moment later, she turned it over for Jaclyn to see.

There was a sentence on her Notebook app reading, *"My stutter is usually gone by the next day."*

33.

The shaded colors of the evening were still deepening. The outer fuchsia of the sunset transformed into a flaming red as the sun set. The summery weather began waning for a gentle autumnal chill.

A white Ford Crown Victoria had just pulled into the parking lot and finally turned off its red and blue LED lights. A moment ago, they looked like small, colored explosions that were bright enough to blind those around it. The sides read, *QUAKERSTON POLICE DEPARTMENT,* in black capital letters encased in gold outlines.

The driver's side door opened. Stepping out was a man in a black uniform and matching sunglasses. His salt and pepper hair were trimmed down with a crew cut that was gelled and combed to an obsessive neatness. A thick ebony mustache hid his upper lip. Around that little island of hair, his face had been shaved to an impossible smoothness.

He approached Jaclyn and Trixie, who sat at the edge of the parking lot. Jaclyn was taking the last few drags off an ultra-light with her free hand on the taser, while Trixie glanced at the cigarette butt in silent craving.

"You called the police?" he asked, towering above them.

"Yeah," Jaclyn responded. "That was me."

"You know, you gotta wave us down. Otherwise, we might not see you. It's ucky we knew the location. You called about the car?"

"Yeah. I did." Speaking with a stern tone, she looked up to read his badge number and nametag that read, *Cerny*.

"So what all went down? Tell me from the beginning." The officer knelt to reach Jaclyn and Trixie's eye level. "You came to the Ace of Clubs or a bite to eat?"

Jaclyn turned to face the diner again, as if there were a set of windows behind her. Yet she imagined somebody standing behind her, on the other side of the wall.

She turned back to the officer and replied, "Yeah, we were just hanging out."

"Yeah, and then what?" he asked.

"There were a few strange noises coming from the parking lot while we were waiting for our order, and we came out and saw *that*." Jaclyn pointed to the car. "The engine was torn out, but the engine block was *gone*."

"*Gone*?" Officer Cerny scratched his chin and said doubtfully, "Awfully strange that someone would wanna steal an engine block."

A flame shot from Jaclyn's tongue as she replied, "You're telling *me*!"

"Take it easy, ma'am. I'll talk to the staff inside. There's a chance they might have the incident on video."

"Video?"

"Of course. Chances are, they have surveillance cameras keeping an eye on the parking lot. Just about every establishment does." Officer Cerny asked, "Maybe you both want to go inside though? You know the temperature's dropping."

"I guess. We'll be okay out here."

"You sure?"

Jaclyn hesitated, as if to step away from Officer Cerny. "Yeah, we'll be fine."

"I guess. It'll get pretty chilly though," he persisted.

"We're *fine*," Jaclyn asserted.

He paused, then took slow footsteps toward the diner entrance. They locked eyes as he walked. The policeman was scanning her body over as if he were a machine. It was the laser-fine look Lloyd gave her—a set of jagged icicles digging into her eyes.

A he turned his head away, Jaclyn peered at the back of his neck. He had a simple tattoo there—the same design on Brenda's wrist.

She listened, leaning toward the front entrance. There was a graveyard quiet crawling between the front door and the walls.

Jaclyn squeezed her taser tighter as she heard a voice within say, "It's not up to us now. Let them decide what to do with her."

She imagined it'd be Brenda, but the voice was unknown. It was a man's—a rough and heavy baritone. The raspy sound was that of a malformed voice box, a legion of rusty nails moving down the cold flesh of her arms.

The period after that was silence. She looked at Trixie and smiled. "You doing okay over there, Trix?"

Trixie looked at her, shrugged and looked back down at her feet.

"You didn't hear what they said inside at all, did you?"

Looking back at Jaclyn, Trixie shook her head, raising an inquisitive eyebrow.

"I didn't catch a whole lot, but it was something like 'let them decide.' What do you think that might mean?"

Trixie gave a nervous look and shrugged again. Her eyes sank as if to apologize.

"If it really helps you—" Jaclyn placed a hand on the girl's shoulder "—you can keep using your Notepad app. I don't mind."

Trixie smiled hesitantly, her head was still tilted toward the pavement. She produced her phone and started typing.

Jaclyn peered over and once the phone was turned her way, she read, *"Thank you. I appreciate that you understand."*

Officer Cerny stepped back out and piercingly glared at Jaclyn and Trixie. He stuck his thumbs in his pockets and grinned. As Jaclyn looked up, she pictured the man's teeth becoming narrow and sharp like sewing needles.

"Is there a phone number we can reach you at? Is there a tow coming?"

"There is," Jaclyn answered, reluctantly telling him her number.

She wanted to hand over a fake one but couldn't think of something on the spot. What if she refused to give any number at all? If nothing else, it would've meant never hearing back about the culprit at all.

"How long ago did you call the tow?"

"Right before calling the police."

Officer Cerny smirked and grunted before turning away from them. He started walking back to the police cruiser before telling them, "Well, we'll be in touch." In a mocking tone, he muttered, "Keep your eyes out, and say hi to Anthony Charles. You're both very lucky."

Jaclyn and Trixie watched him as he got in the car, slammed the door shut and backed up toward them. The sudden zero to forty made Jaclyn jump back. The car was inches from running her down—

But then it came to a loud, abrupt stop. The engine purred like a satisfied cat before moving forward again and leaving the parking lot.

34.

Jaclyn was clenching her chest with one hand as if to prevent her heart from stopping. Her throat was drier than burning sand. Her tongue had retracted like a threatened snail hiding in its shell.

I might go mute just like poor Trix here, she thought. Lord, what did I just get myself into? She looked up at the clouds, then at Trixie.

"Hey Trix?"

The blonde looked back with her eyes wide open.

Jaclyn took a deep breath and felt a small pain in her chest. She wouldn't tell Trixie about it—whatever the cause was, the girl didn't need to know. She already had enough on her plate to render her silent.

"I'm sorry."

Trixie cocked an eyebrow, beginning to tilt her head.

"You were the one who wanted to do me a favor. You did something generous and look where it got us. Look where it got you."

I'm so sorry, Jaclyn thought. *But I didn't deserve the help. I know I asked, but you should've just said no. Even if the reason why you wouldn't come was a lie, I'd understand. I'm the one who owes you now.*

Trixie held up her index finger, gesturing to wait. She wiped her eyes and typed on her phone. She turned it to Jaclyn, the message read, *"Did you destroy the car?"*

"Well—no, of course not."

The text was backspaced and replaced with another saying, *"Then it's not your fault. It's better to think about what to do next."*

Jaclyn paused and then said, "I guess you're right. Do you want to wait for the tow—"

Trixie interrupted, shaking her head vigorously. She typed another message for Jaclyn: *"Please, I really want to get out of here."*

"Oh—did you want to get a ride?" Jaclyn's throat constricted at the thought. Would it be Uber again? She couldn't help wondering what if she'd need to fight off a second attack.

A shake of the head. *"No. If I'm not driving, I don't feel safe. Is it okay to walk?"*

"You sure, Trix?"

Pause, then a nod before she typed, *"Yeah. I'll tell you later. I'm sorry."*

Relief came over Jaclyn as she replied, "No, it's fine." She stood up and said, "I don't mind."

She offered a hand and a smile to Trixie. She returned the grin, and Jaclyn pulled the girl up onto her feet.

Jaclyn asked, "Do you need to stop somewhere at all, or would you rather just relax?"

Trixie smiled and held up two fingers.

"Just relax for tonight?"

Trixie nodded.

"You sure you don't want to eat first?"

The girl just smiled and shrugged.

She isn't saying no, Jaclyn thought. *She's probably hungry but feels guilty about asking to eat. She just ordered food not too long ago. Better to wait until she's in the hotel room.*

"Ready to get going, Trix?"

She nodded, and they started walking down the side of the road. Jaclyn looked back, as if the old woman's car was about to show up any second.

What about the black Cadillac? she thought. *What were the chances of seeing that? The old woman didn't make that up, did she? I hope she didn't make a mistake.*

Jaclyn turned around to see Trixie was already far ahead of her. If this highway weren't a straight shot, Jaclyn knew she would've lost the girl.

She trotted down the shoulder of the road, shouting, "*Trixie*! Trixie, wait up!"

A moment later, Trixie turned around and looked as if she'd just seen a unicorn crossing the street. It made Jaclyn wonder if she got her attention just through the sound of her shoes against the pavement.

"Didn't you hear me, Trix?"

She looked down, slightly embarrassment etched into her face, glanced back up into Jaclyn's eyes and shook her head. Grabbing her phone, she typed out another message.

"I guess now. I'm sorry. I kinda daydream sometimes."

"Well, I don't want to lose you, okay?"

Trixie smiled and nodded.

As they continued, Jaclyn walked beside her, wiped her lips and asked, "A daydreamer, huh? So I guess you're one of the creative types?"

A shrug and a pause before Trixie typed, *"I guess I've written my share of poetry."*

"Oh, how long have you been doing this?" Jaclyn asked.

Trixie cocked her brow. *"During school."*

"Was it just when you were in college?"

"No. Since the end of elementary school," Trixie typed.

"What did you write about?" Jaclyn asked with a smile.

"Mostly nature. Sometimes it was just my mood or even an occasional crush."

A silence fell between them, the question on Jaclyn's mind made her feel like she was walking across a pool of wet cement. "You said you *used* to, right?"

Trixie nodded.

"How come you stopped?"

"It wasn't gonna make any money and I was never that good," Trixie explained.

"Who said that?"

The question went unanswered. Trixie kept her head down, her gaze turning icy and distant. Her face grew hard and stiff, as if she'd stared into the eyes of Medusa. A cold breeze swept down the highway and past Jaclyn. It brushed through Trixie's hair, sweeping it in front of her eyes.

As she held her bangs away, Trixie stopped, shutting her eyes tight. She looked like a cloud of dust had been thrown in her face.

Jaclyn stopped in her tracks and asked, "Hey—Trix? You okay?"

There was no response at first, but she gradually opened her eyes, nodded and stormed forward.

"*Hey,*" Jaclyn exclaimed, sprinting after her. "Wait!" After catching up, she said, "You know, I'd appreciate it if you'd quit doing that."

Trixie slowed down and her face lost its stony hardness. She typed, *"I'm sorry. I shouldn't get upset so easily. I guess some things are a little touchy for me."*

"It's fine. Just—don't leave me behind. There's a reason we're going *together,*" Jaclyn said.

She nodded wordlessly.

Another silence. Jaclyn wasn't sure what to say. Even if there was an understanding between them, she felt a wall of cold steel between them. She didn't *insult* the girl or say anything wrong but managed to provoke this new unspoken distance anyway.

As the sign pointing to Dourmsburg and Quakerston came into view, she said, "Trix?"

No reply.

"I wouldn't force you, but if you ever wanted me to see them, I'm sure I'd love your poems," Jaclyn said.

Trixie didn't say anything, but a hint of color returned to her cheeks.

35.

The silence between them was still tough as a diamond. Trixie hadn't said anything since she apologized for storming off and Jaclyn didn't want to press any wrong buttons. Asking more questions might've provoked her to run off again, and this time without stopping.

The night hadn't settled in completely. There was enough daylight to kiss the green and beige of the grass where cows would've once grazed.

Jaclyn looked closer at the grass, surprised that she hadn't noticed the amount of creamy light brown patches when she first drove through these parts.

That could've been an illusion created on by the darkness last night. She'd only seen little details aside from the silhouettes of her surroundings. She noticed colors, but only dimmed, solid hues. The night hid any details of decay last night.

Nonetheless, the hints of light brown looked brand-new. She'd only seen them after being closer to town. It was as if this plot of withering grass had an outward ripple, brought on by a strange spell cast on the land.

The chill of the night was stronger now, intense enough to bite their skin. Goosebumps were crawling across Jaclyn's flesh, even with her faux-fur coat on.

Trixie was still in a t-shirt and jeans, as if the sunshine were still glimmering across the landscape. Jaclyn couldn't believe that girl was walking with the same energy as ever, without the slightest attempt to keep herself warm.

How is she doing it? she thought. *I've lived in Pennsylvania all my life and didn't go without a jacket in this weather. And she's skinnier than me too. I guess you'd have to really be used to the cold.*

The sign up ahead was clearer now. They were close enough to see the distinct white lettering against a green background. At the end of the road, it forked off to Quakerston on the right and Dourmsburg on the left.

"Trixie?" Jaclyn asked, beginning to feel breathless.

No answer.

"Hey, *Trixie*."

She turned around and faced Jaclyn, giving a sharp exclamation demanding just what in the Hell she wanted. The look struck Jaclyn like a slap to the face. It took her aback. There was even a faint but pulsing jab, like a bee and stung her neck.

But she still asked Trixie, "Aren't you cold?"

The look on Trixie's face lost its bitter edge. It changed to a curious gaze, like someone had asked her a question in a language she never heard before. She looked down and shrugged. Then she faced ahead again and kept walking as if the question hadn't been asked.

Jaclyn groaned and muttered, "Stubborn girl."

She unzipped her coat and slid it down her arms. Once it was off her body, she opened it wide behind Trixie like an owl swooping down to ensnare its prey.

Jaclyn wrapped it around her body and felt Trixie twitch as if she was rejecting it. But the girl eased and even held the teeth of the zipper together.

"You're acting like you never wore a coat when it was cold out," Jaclyn said jokingly. But her smirk drifted off her face since Trixie didn't respond. Her face grew sad when she realized what she said. "Look Trix, I know you had a rough time back then, but you don't have to act like you're too tough to accept someone's help."

Trixie jerked her head around, glaring at Jaclyn. She looked like a tiger, roaring at an unknown predator to keep away from its young.

A pause. "You helped *me*, didn't you? You were the one who gave me a lift. It's not gonna hurt to let someone show some kindness in return."

Trixie's face remained tense, but not for long. As it softened, she looked toward the sign again, pulling the jacket tighter around her as if in an embrace.

They were twenty yards from the sign before Jaclyn slowed down and asked, "Hey Trix, you mind if we slow down? I'm just a little winded."

She looked and noticed that nobody was next to her. She looked to her other side and behind her. She noticed Trixie was already a few feet behind.

The girl must have stopped between Jaclyn's sentences. Jaclyn couldn't think of another explanation that she could think of.

Trixie's brow was furrowed—not in foul disdain—and eased into a look of unadmitted concern.

"It's fine," Jaclyn insisted, gesturing her to keep moving. "I just need to slow down for a minute."

Trixie caught up, walking at a slower pace and giving her the same look at her.

"Trix? Why are you looking at me like that?"

Trixie cocked her brow and slowly looked away.

"What?" Jaclyn asked with some agitation.

Trixie looked back, her eyes turning somber.

"I *told* you, it's fine, okay?" Jaclyn put an arm around her. "I might not be old per se, but I'm older. I'm sure as Hell not in my twenties like *you* anymore." She gave Trixie a friendly smirk. "I can't always keep up so easily, and my body's starting to let me know that."

Trixie furrowed her brow again.

"It'll be okay. That's just what happens when you get older," Jaclyn explained.

Trixie typed on her smartphone, *"Getting tired from walking still can't be good though."*

Jaclyn paused, shrugged, and replied, "I guess so."

Trixie didn't say a thing after that. She was looking at her feet until they reached the end of the road.

Jaclyn found herself gazing at the sign from across the street. The choice was either Dourmsburg or Quakerston. They didn't have a way to just go back.

Trixie was the most responsive of everyone she texted earlier, and her family didn't speak to her much. Picking her up would've been like taking in a stranger at this point. Most of the people she reached out to hadn't even responded at this point.

And who could Trixie get a hold of? Jaclyn knew she had to have been the most company that girl had had in years.

She also had an idea of what Dourmsburg was like. The town had an air that turned her blood to ice water and made her nauseated. Quakerston couldn't have been any different, but the police force was about kiss them with a pair of rear tires.

One of the two had to be the place to sleep at night. Jaclyn took her smartphone out of her pocket and went to Bing. The Maps function should've told the walking distance for each.

Dourmsburg wasn't much of a drive from this intersection, but what about Quakerston? If nothing else, it could've been a shorter walk. To her left, she could see a vague cluster of lights through the thickening darkness. Down the road to Quakerston though, it was harder to make out any signs of business. The distance to a warm bed was anyone's guess.

36.

The Maps app revealed that the distance to Dourmsburg was less than half a mile. There was no doubt that the lights down the road to Jaclyn's right were houses. But that didn't mean it was too far a walk from any businesses, much less a motel.

A place to stay in Quakerston could've been concealed by whatever lay in the distance—vegetation, other houses, or anything else the town had in store. If there *was* a motel around in that area, the lights on the front sign might not have been on. It wouldn't have been the first time Jaclyn noticed a vacant place to sleep with such a minor dilemma.

She cleared her search and entered Quakerston. The reception out here was no better than before. She had one bar, just enough for any calls or internet signals to go through. Trixie leaned in to see how long a walk it'd be.

The result popped up. Jaclyn and Trixie both gave the screen a wide-eyed look. Nine and a half miles.

Jaclyn repeated the distance to herself. It was another nine and a half miles on top of this. Her feet were already sore, and her short breath had the better of her.

And there was Trixie. She had more energy, but to make her walk another *nine and a half miles?* All the girl wanted to do was rest, even if she had a bit more fight left in her.

That distance was just getting to the *town*. That wasn't counting the closest place where they could sleep for the night. It could've been a few miles to get to a warm bed.

"I guess," Jaclyn said with a touch of regret. "Dourmsburg it is then." Her head hung down as she turned left, and Trixie followed. "Trix?"

The girl faced her with an attentive look.

"Are you sure you don't want a ride? I can just go back myself."

Trixie raised her eyebrows, and her eyes began wandering as if searching for an answer. After a moment's consideration, she shook her head and started typing.

Jaclyn watched her thumbs move across the touchscreen like the fingers of a skilled pianist. *If it was still an occupation, that girl would've been a* Hell *of a typist. If she was doing that instead of bartending, she might not be in this mess.*

Trixie turned her phone over to Jaclyn with the answer: *"I can't be in the car unless I'm the one driving. It's kind of a phobia. Even if it's someone I trust behind the wheel, I just can't do it. Whenever I started driving, I let a close friend get behind the wheel. It was the middle of winter, and he skidded across the highway on a patch of black ice and smashed into a tree."*

Jaclyn was taken aback. "Wow. That's horrible. I'm really sorry that happened."

Trixie shook her head.

"What happened after that if you don't mind me asking? Did your friend make it out okay?"

Trixie shut her eyes for a moment, took a deep breath and slipped her phone back into her pocket. She didn't respond again.

Jaclyn felt another hurdle being erected between them. How did you find the right words to comfort someone after an incident like that? And what about the after-effects it had? There wasn't a way to just persuade someone out of a phobia.

As they walked, Trixie was fast enough to put distance between them. Centimeters became feet and turned into yards.

"Trix," Jaclyn called.

She stopped and turned.

"Don't get ahead of me. I'll end up losing you," Jaclyn said.

Trixie nodded and they continued into the town. The Cozy Moon was awaiting them. Its lights pierced through the gathering night. They stared at Jaclyn and Trixie like a cluster of rats' eyes.

It couldn't have been the only place to stay. Even in a small, run-down area like Dourmsburg, hotels had competition.

Jaclyn took out her *Eclipse* again, searching for other hotels and motels in the area. She was right. There *were* other places in town.

The town had Frankie's Lodge, Motel 6 and the Dourmsburg Inn. They were all in different parts of town, but Jaclyn supposed she could walk a few more miles if need be. Trixie would be okay with resting a little more on the way.

Jaclyn checked their information on Bing's search results—

They were all closed.

"Closed?" Jaclyn muttered to herself in disbelief. "How are they *closed*?" Her voice grew fiery, each sentence laid a brick in her wall of frustration and anger. "It's not a holiday! Even if it was, hotels are still *open*!"

She called each of them, from the closest to her location to the farthest. The Motel 6 and Dourmsburg Inn responded with an automated voice message. Each stated that they would be closed for the remainder of today, and the two days after.

"Unbelievable," she whispered, disconnecting the phone.

The last number was to Frankie's Lodge. It was a three-mile walk, but the online information about them being closed could be a mistake.

A human voice answered the phone. It was a man's lax baritone. "Hi, you've reached Frankie's."

"*Hi*," Jaclyn said, "I was wondering if—"

"I'm sorry, but we're temporarily closed," the voice said. "If you need to book a room, please leave your name, number, and message after the tone. We'll get back to you as soon as possible."

The shrill *beep* sounded in Jaclyn's ear and she ended the call.

"I don't believe it," she said, her voice quieting to a low flame. "They really *are* closed."

She looked back at the Cozy Moon. That building claimed to be closed too, yet the lights were on and the parking lot full. The thought of—God forbid—sleeping on a cold parking lot passed her mind, but there was a chance that they wouldn't have to.

If the lights were on inside, that meant there were people. It also meant she'd get answers as to what was going on in Dourmsburg tonight.

She felt like a vacuum was crawling through her gut as she approached the Cozy Moon. She wiped her lips as Trixie followed her to the front entrance.

She peered through the glass doors and tugged at them. Nothing. It was locked. Another peek, and as she looked toward the front desk—

There was Sabrina, typing away at the computer with a grin.

Jaclyn pounded her fist against the door. Sabrina looked over to them, got up, and walked to the entrance. She cracked the door open as if to sneak outside.

"Miss Ellsworth?" she asked. "It's a pleasure seeing you again." She looked over to Trixie and said, "And you have a friend, I see. "Miss—" Sabrina swirled her hand in the air, piecing her words together. "*Trixie Carter,* is that right?"

Trixie nodded.

"You both need a room tonight, don't you?"

"Yeah," Jaclyn answered. "We do."

A pause, then Sabrina's grin widened. "I could squeeze you in—you came at the most opportune time."

37.

"We still have a room with two beds open," Sabrina said to them when they reached the front desk. "Will that do?" She was grinning, as if she were hiding something behind her back.

"Yeah," Jaclyn replied, picking up one of the hotel pens and handing over her card. "That should be fine."

Sabrina swiped the card and held her hand up to chest. "No need to sign anything, Miss Ellsworth."

Jaclyn cocked an eyebrow. "Really? Are you sure?"

"Of course," Sabrina answered, handing her card back. "We already have all your information."

They stared at each other. "All our information?"

"Go rest. You must be exhausted. Your feet are probably sore." She handed Jaclyn two keys to their room. "Your room number is One-Fifteen."

"Okay," Jaclyn said meekly. "Thanks."

She and Trixie walked through the main lobby to the corridor. She hadn't noticed the sound from the speaker system at first. The volume was too low to pick up right away, but when listened closely, she heard Caravan Palace's *Lone Digger* playing.

Jaclyn hadn't heard this song before, but it wasn't playing at a normal quality. The tempo had been slowed down, giving the horns and female vocals a far deeper sound. It sounded like a groaning, blasphemous murmur from inside the earth.

The corridor was quiet, more so than the first night Jaclyn stayed. There wasn't even an occasional murmur from the nearby rooms.

Jaclyn and Trixie walked slowly, like they were tiptoeing around a sleeping minotaur. Each breath one of them took was as silent as the hallway itself. There was a long pause, a gentle inhale, followed by a weak puff of thin, warm air brushing against the back of her neck.

"Trixie?" Jaclyn asked and looked back. "Have you ever met her before?"

She looked up at the ceiling, pondering. Then she shook her head, clenching her eyes shut.

"Are you sure? It seemed like she knew you."

Trixie nodded. "Y-*yeah*," she said, balling her hands into fists. "I'm sh-sh-*sure*."

"You don't need to strain yourself, you know."

"Eh-it's okh-*okay*. It's h-ha-*happened* bef-f-*fore*."

"Well," Jaclyn replied as they reached room One-Fifteen. "If you need a little more time to recover, that's okay."

"I'll b-be f-f-fuh-*fine*. M-m-maybe I m-met her at th-thah-*the*¬ *ev-event* I told you ab-b-*bout*."

"Maybe," Jaclyn replied opening the door with her key. "But honestly, I'm really not so sure."

She held the door open for Trixie, and as she closed the door, Jaclyn realized something. Sabrina was right. There was a dull, pounding pain in her feet, though she hadn't noticed it until now. It was like the ache repressed itself until now.

But how did Sabrina know? She hadn't mentioned a long walk before. Did she know that Jaclyn had driven here the last time? Did she hear Jaclyn panting at the front desk?

She couldn't have. Even when she was out of breath, she wasn't loud. It brought her thoughts back to what Sabrina said at the front desk.

We already have all your information.

Then there was the voice—the one she heard in her dreams. It was the one Jaclyn *thought* she heard upstairs.

I know you.

This was the last place of them all that she wanted to sleep in. Jaclyn couldn't help thinking that she was led back to this place. A ridiculous, paranoid thought. Nothing in the world was keeping her there. Even if there was, who would have the power to arrange everything? Nobody.

But what about Trixie? Her family's wealth was knowledge open to the public through the internet.

Being let in at *all* was nothing short of a stroke of luck. Had she never socialized with Sabrina, she and Trixie would have been on the street. Jaclyn shivered at the thought of lying on the concrete, at the mercy of anyone passing by.

Letting Corey sleep in the car without a working heater when they had moved houses had been one too many mistakes. She couldn't add Trixie not having a bed to sleep to that list.

Jaclyn wasn't her parent. She knew that. But all her father's money wouldn't buy companionship. It wouldn't bribe people into caring. Loneliness must have been as natural as gravity.

If I can't do anything else, Jaclyn thought. *I at least want to change that for her. None of this is her fault.*

As Trixie sat down on her bed, Jaclyn noticed the flatscreen television high up on the wall opposite the two mattresses. The volume had almost been muted. The remote was on the nightstand between their beds.

It was livestreaming an event. All the cameras were focused on a stage engulfed by shadows. A lone spotlight pierced the shadows. Trixie instantly grabbed the remote and turned up the volume.

"Thank you so much," the television blared through the deafening silence of the room. "I'd like to begin by saying that I don't just see a customer base—I see the staff here, the people working tirelessly with *Eclipse*, and all of you as—*family*."

A lone man of six foot eight stood on stage. His pure black hair was combed back with utmost precision. A pair of circular glasses were perched on the bridge of his nose, augmenting his air of wisdom. The only thing exceeding that was an aura of unending bravado.

His midnight black hair and glasses were contrasted by his ghostly pale complexion and white suit. Inside the ivory exterior was a graphite dress shirt with a pattern of black crescents on the collar corners.

Just before he raised his left hand to silence the adoring crowd surrounding him, Jaclyn caught a kind of anomaly. She wasn't sure, but she noticed deep scar tissue on the back of his hand.

Jaclyn felt a momentary déjà vu but couldn't say why. She tried to remember if she had seen anyone else with that kind of mark across their hand before.

Had the man on the screen met with an accident? Was it a birthmark? It was impossible to say for sure, but Jaclyn thought the former was more likely. From what little of it she saw, the scar tissue was more pronounced than a typical birthmark.

"*Wow,*" Trixie said with delight and wonder in her voice. "I c-ca-can't believe we m-m-*missed* it. All those p-puh-people are suh-so l-lucky. B-b-But at luh-least we s-s-saw it *this* e-eh-early."

Jaclyn paused, fixated by Anthony Charles' smile. It looked closer to a mouth full of tiny knives. "Wouldn't someone post it online though?"

"*Yeah*, but it wouldn't buh-be at the s-s-suh-*same.*"

"I guess so," Jaclyn said under her breath, almost automatically.

She thought that acting surprised at Trixie's tone would've been stupid. She could've foreseen it from the moment she first heard the girl say the name *Anthony Charles*. From the conversations in the tavern and those in the car to now, it was as predictable as night following day.

Nonetheless, she thought it was just as unusual a sight.

It made her wonder how Trixie may have reacted to being out on the street. Not just being subjected to the cold and lack of a bedding—but missing this broadcast.

Doubtlessly, she had known about the show and the precise time it would start. It must have been on her mind as they walked toward Dourmsburg that evening. Jaclyn thought it could've been another reason why she had been so eager to get ahead.

But what would've happened if Trixie had missed it? Jaclyn pictured the chance of her falling into an even deeper panic with that pile of lumber thrown atop the blazing fire of her panic.

"I guess he has a sort of charisma, doesn't he?" Jaclyn asked.

"He ruh-really *does.* Ev-everything he d-d-does is am-*mazing.* I duh-don't know ha-*how* he duh-does so m-*much.*"

"And he's eating up all the love from the cameras, huh?"

"Wuh-what do yah-you m-m-*mean?*"

Jaclyn looked down and back at the screen. "Nothing, I suppose."

38.

Trixie raised an eyebrow and turned back to the screen. The smile reappeared on her face as Anthony Charles continued his speech.

"Gaming," he said. "It's one of the largest industries among the tech industry—a multi-billion dollar one—and for an excellent reason. It doesn't simply entertain us. It brings us *together.* It binds us together as a *community*, and it's time to keep improving it.

"I believe that as a business, Eclipse *owes* the countless gamers in the world the same dedication to innovation that we've given mobile, desktop *and* laptop users everywhere. Over the past few years, we've *continued* to improve technology across the board, our dedicated staff has taken it upon themselves to venture into the worlds of console and PC gaming."

A massive light flashed in the room like an atomic bomb, and the audience gasped. Even Trixie joined in, knowing her cue by heart. The look on her face was that of unmitigated admiration, like she was hearing a piece of sacred music.

The image of a long, black rectangular box was projected against the wall behind Charles. A little set of flat rings emitting a sickly green glow was at its center.

The insidious grin on his face widened as he said, "I give the world the revolution in virtual reality—the *Luna*." Once the unified applause had settled down, Trixie's included, he continued. "Not *only* is it the next step in at-home gaming, but it's activated by a laser retinal scan, unique to each individual user. The ultimate privacy protection."

As Trixie lay on her stomach, kicking her feet, as if she was swimming through a placid lake, Charles pointed up toward the console's glowing rings. His gesture was swift and precise, knowing exactly where to guide his hand. He never took his eyes off the crowd.

The set of flat rings on the console looked like an immovable eye, frozen in place. It looked more like an alien surveillance camera than anything else.

The cheering from the crowd was even louder than before. Trixie hadn't joined in the screaming and clapping, but the look in her eyes was that of pure awe.

And everyone's eating it all up, Jaclyn thought. *No doubt this'll make him even bigger in the industry.*

As the cheers died down, she was overcome by a coughing fit. It was minor as first but choked her enough to make her lean forward. She bent her knees, resting the weight of her torso on her hands.

Although it couldn't be helped, yet she still felt like an ill-mannered child.

Trixie turned and faced her. She paused and then said, "Jaclyn? Ah-are y-you ok-k-kay?"

Covering her mouth, she nodded and stood upright. The coughing continued as Jaclyn found her way to the bathroom. A thick, moist substance shot up to the back of her throat, like a bullet shrouded in thick smoke, and finally was expelled at the rear edge of her tongue.

It had a startling taste. She couldn't identify it. It was something thin, warm and *metallic*, even.

She swallowed the substance. When Jaclyn reached the bathroom sink and turned on the faucet, she stared at her reflection. Her face had grown clammy and pale, there were dark circles under her eyes.

God, what's happening to me? she thought. *Is that really my face?*

It was like Jaclyn saw her own face after days of going without. This had to have been a trick of the lights. There was no other way the sudden paleness, the crow's feet, and the bags under her eyes would've gone unnoticed.

Just as she caught a glimpse of herself, Jaclyn kept coughing. Doubling over again, she covered her mouth.

The fluid shot up again and splattered against her hands. Jaclyn couldn't stop herself. Whenever the hacking subsided, she withdrew her hands.

Jaclyn's eyes froze with terror. The evidence before her eyes could've had a hundred different reasons.

There was a knock on the bathroom door.

"J-Jaclyn?" Trixie's voice called out. "Ah-Are you ok-k-k-kay in there?"

"*Yeah*, I'm fine." Was she going to tell Trixie anything?

She wasn't a medical expert but knew it was a possible sign of an infection. It could've been anything from flu to bronchitis, or worse.

Bronchitis could be a likely culprit. She was a smoker, which made her susceptible to that. But until now, her palms had never been speckled with fresh blood.

39.

As Jaclyn finished cleaning her hands, the presentation ended with a final roaring applause. Trixie lay face down on her bed. Her feet were near the pillows with her, sneakers still on.

Jaclyn whispered, "Where have I seen that before?"

She felt a small, fluttering pain in her abdomen as Trixie began to snore. She couldn't tell if the ailment was getting worse or if it'd been like this for some time. Jaclyn had felt pain and been breathless before, but nothing quite like this.

The pain wasn't less or more than before, that she could tell. From what she knew, it was something different this time. Instead of being caused by sprinting too far at once, a hectic coughing fit had caused it.

How had I ignored it this long? The driving didn't let me notice it. But I can't tell Trixie, she thought.

Sitting on the other bed, Jaclyn felt the weight of her fatigue pull her body. She pulled her shoes off and heard a faint sound. Turning to Trixie, she listened closer.

"A sleep-talker?" Jaclyn asked herself.

Trixie was murmuring, *"Sah…Mee…"*

"What the—" Jaclyn leaned closer, trying to guess what the girl was saying.

"Son—Meat—" She was softly rasping the phrase in her sleep. This was the first stage in a long cycle. First a light snore. Then an exhale. Next, a lighter snore than the first. A pause after that, and then—

"Son—Meat—"

Jaclyn recoiled, with a strange look on her face.

What the Hell does that mean? she thought. *It was probably because she hadn't eaten anything. Poor girl. I should've gotten her something along the way. But it's too late now. She's dead asleep. My feet are killing me—*

She looked down at her shoes.

But the least I can do is get her something for whenever she wakes up. Who knows when she even ate last?

Jaclyn sighed and slipped her shoes back on. Her feet were still throbbing from the trip earlier, but she figured the exercise would be good for her.

"After this," she told herself. "I'm finally gonna hit the hay." She looked back at Trixie. "I better get a thank you in the morning."

Jaclyn got up and left the hotel room. She slowly walked down the now familiar corridor. She glanced up at the bronze numbers that marked Room One-Fourteen, not quite making out the low sounds just penetrating the door.

Jaclyn wasn't too sure, but she assumed that the noise was someone mumbling in secret. She kept walking, brushing it off. It was late after all. The occupants knew other people were trying to sleep.

As she passed Room One-Fourteen, Jaclyn heard a faint *squish* and a *rip*.

Even though the hotel was almost full, she thought the other guests were all in bed rather early. She looked at the time on her phone. It was a few minutes past ten.

But then it hit her. If all the hotels in the area were reportedly closed, wouldn't everything else be closed too? Hotels may be open all night, but most businesses would have shut down for the night by now, especially in a small town.

After she thought about this, Jaclyn realized that the lights in those establishments were still on too. But that didn't mean a thing. She figured they might be closing and finishing their nightly cleanup.

Jaclyn went to her Maps app. She felt stupid for even considering it. Thinking back to when she first arrived, Jaclyn hadn't seen much business around the pizza joints some distance away from the Cozy Moon or anywhere else in the area.

Then again, she had only witnessed a passing glance of Dourmsburg—and who would judge her for just asking a question?

She searched for restaurants in the area and waited for the results to load. It was just another reminder of the God-awful reception. A couple of minutes passed, and finally, she had an answer. Jaclyn saw several different eateries appear throughout the area.

And they were all open.

Jaclyn flinched at what she saw. Why would they all be open this late? It didn't make any sense, but she decided to accept her good luck.

The nearest option was a sandwich shop just over a mile away. It was called Cooper's Cuts. She decided that its average four out of five-star rating would make it her last stop for the night. It was worth it, even if her feet were bruised by the time she got back.

As she walked, the cool breeze grew stronger, like a crying voice. Looking at the still empty, cracked roads, Jaclyn felt the whispers of the wind intensify to a strained howl against her ears.

Jaclyn's arms were shivering inside her coat. The cold managed to find its way through the ends of her sleeves to sink its fangs into her skin.

She managed to distract herself. Nothing could entirely occupy her from the surrounding chill, but the Trixie's question kept her train of thought. Did her sleep-talking mean anything?

Jaclyn pondered, clutching her upper arms and sinking her face into her jacket collar. The mentions of meat were obvious, sure—but what was the other part?

Something about the sun? Could be. The entire sensation around the *Eclipse* brand and its symbolism for Anthony Charles' followers would make sense. Or was it *son*, like a child or a young man?

Was it about the talk of searching for Corey? Jaclyn thought Trixie could've gotten fixated with this issue through something like osmosis. She was the one who drove them to try and see that old woman.

That strange old woman, Jaclyn thought. *The one who mentioned a black car—what kind was it again? The old woman who wore… She wore… What exactly was she wearing that night? She wore a set of earrings, didn't she?*

The questions repeated in her mind on a cycle, spiraling like a small whirlpool. She looked away from the empty road and faced straight ahead.

"Earrings," Jaclyn said to herself. "They were all different colors, I think." She thought about it and mentioned, "Yeah, that's right. Red, pearl, green, gold…But was it pearl or gold…?"

She remembered there as something about one of those earrings that had captured her attention as the old woman spoke about the black car she saw Corey in.

She felt breathless breath again. But that was fine for now, she decided. Too late to quit walking. She could rest once she got inside Cooper's anyway.

Jaclyn hadn't looked at their menu but had an idea of what'd make Trixie smile in delight. The girl was craving for a reward for her strict diet for God knows how long. Something layered with cheese, a little grease and a hearty pile of meat would do perfectly.

As Jaclyn approached Cooper's, she was beginning to hear a faint but consistent sound in the distance.

40.

Cooper's was a single-storied building with a bone-colored exterior. A glowing sign with a neon green outline and cursive lettering was hung out front. It glowed bright enough to singe the retinas.

The front door sat askew in its frame, tilted by a loose top hinge. Its frame was rusted iron, the rest flimsy glass.

A set of long, narrow, paper-white fingers were pushing it open. The door made a whining *screech* that could've peeled the skin off her ears. Jaclyn flinched as her eyes met with the young man on his way out.

His deep, icy gaze made it seem as if he'd been staring at her since she left the Cozy Moon. His eyes were orbs protruding from their sockets, glistening in the burning, bright light. The lips were thin, almost non-existent. They were tilted downward into a permanent scowl. His jaw hung enough to show his teeth—small with an unusual distance between them and sharp enough to look like those of a shark.

He was six feet tall with broad shoulders, a wiry build and a small pot belly. He had a small hunch at the top of his spine, making him arch like a cane. Little uneven strands of hair poked out of his flesh, making him look like an overgrown rat, shaved by a giddy, sadistic child.

Jaclyn noticed the wrinkles under his eyes as he pushed his bicycle out. Its frame had been beaten within an inch of its life. The tires were ill-fitted and the chain looked much too loose to stay in place. A small basket hung from the handlebars, filled to the top with bagged orders.

If it weren't for his lack of gray hair, Jaclyn thought. *I would've thought this kid was as old man.*

His eyes swere fixed on her as he pushed the bicycle onto the street. Even after he got on and started pedaling, he never said a word. It was only when he was riding up the way she came that he took his eyes off her.

She watched him swerve around a manhole cover on the street. It occurred to her that it must've been taken off its designated hole that led down into the sewage system. Jaclyn stared at it, wondering how she hadn't noticed it before. She must've been focusing on Cooper's and that faint sound in the distance.

At first, she couldn't identify it, but after listening closer, Jaclyn realized the noise was human. She couldn't have called it *singing*, though it had a musical quality. It was a *group* of people rhythmically crying and shrieking together.

Looking around, Jaclyn couldn't determine *where* it was coming from. It was like the sound was emanating from several directions at once, yet she didn't see what was *making* it. She was paralyzed, feeling an invisible cluster of flies climbing on her body.

Jaclyn's calves trembled. The sound deepened the swirling cold around her like a cursed incantation. The chill was spreading from her arms to her torso, and then everything below, despite Jaclyn's clothing shielding her. She felt like pure ice water had flooded around her ankles and frozen her voice with a strangling grip.

She was forced to take a step back toward the lopsided glass door. It was like an invisible string tugging her heel. Her calves shook violently as she paused, and one leg was tugged back another step.

She turned and the door was close to her face. Jaclyn stepped back and pulled it open, forcefully enough to make the top hinge looser than before. She stepped inside and pulled the door shut more carefully.

Nothing outside was coming in Jaclyn's direction. She didn't see anything on the street, yet she watched through the glass.

A voice behind her asked, "Can I help you, ma'am?"

Jaclyn's breath was already short from the walk but hearing that only made her heart jump. She looked back, seeing the man at the counter giving her a slight grin. His figure was like an egg, with a black combover to cover his clear baldness. He had to have been in his early forties, but the front half of his scalp was already claimed.

His skin was pale, exactly like the delivery boy on the bicycle. His eyes were a deep black and his irises so dark that they were consumed by his pupils. The corneas were jaundiced to a canary yellow. She was forced into silence, as if the howls of the wind took away her voice.

A ceiling fan hung over them, spinning with a weary slowness. It made a small squeak with every spin.

Finally, she muttered, "That sound…"

"Hmm?" the man asked, cocking his brow. "What sound?"

"The one *outside*—do you *hear* that?" Jaclyn's body withdrew into itself as she spoke. She wrapped her arms around her torso.

"Hear what?" As the man walked around the counter, he furrowed his eyebrows. He went to the door, pushed it open and poked his head out. Silence, then he smiled and said, "Oh, *that*."

As he walked back in and pulled the door shut behind him, Jaclyn asked in a hushed voice, "You heard it?"

The man got behind the counter again and replied, "That's not something to be *concerned* about. I take it you're not from around here. I don't know if I've seen you—" he narrowed his eyes, taking a closer look "—although maybe you do look a little familiar."

Jaclyn felt her heart beating in her mouth. The grip on her ankles was tightening and freezing them.

"No," she replied. "I've never been around Dourmsburg before. At least I don't think so. Not until last night anyway."

"Perhaps you haven't. Then you're not familiar with the little traditions started here some time back."

"I can't say I am," Jaclyn replied.

"It's just the start of the little—*festivals* we have."

"What kind of festivals?"

"It's more of a—" he tapped his yellowed, uneven fingernails on the counter "—*spiritual* kind of gathering. I'm sure you've heard about what's going on in downtown Pittsburgh though."

Jaclyn was silent at first, but replied, "A lot of things happen there almost every day."

"Nothing compared to this. He's coming *back*, you know," he said.

The words flashed across her mind again. *I know you.*

"You mean—Anthony Charles?"

The man nodded. "It's just that there's been quite a lot of excitement about it. Whenever you're not just a businessman and a big entrepreneur, but also the anchor of your hometown, everyone waits for you to come back home. Because of him, we're about to enter an age of incredible wealth."

41.

Jaclyn's eyes widened. Her mouth was slightly agape. She looked down at the floor, unable to gather the right words.

"So, there's a bit of business around these times," the man said. "But what can I get you, ma'am?"

Jaclyn felt the fingers of the wind creep against her ankle. Her thoughts were reduced to a static.

"I don't know," she said in a hapless monotone. "A friend of mine's celebrating how well she did with her diet. Just something with plenty of meat. Surprise me."

A moment of pure silence passed between them.

The man grinned as if he was thinking of a cruel lie and said, "That's no problem. The kitchen's been going non-stop today. I'm sure you can smell it."

He was right. She hadn't realized at first, but it was much like the smell at the Ace of Clubs. Now that she thought about it, the scent from the grills wasn't beef at all. She couldn't identify it, but the odor was something closer to pork.

He grabbed a small notebook from behind the counter and scratched against it with a black pen. The shadows under his eyes widened as he tore the sheet of paper off, walked through the narrow corridor and turned left into the hidden kitchen.

There was a moment of the man whispering back and forth with someone who was in the middle of cooking the orders. Jaclyn couldn't make out most of the conversation but picked up bits of it.

"Does He know that she's here?"

"Of course. He has every means to find out."

The conversation continued as she found a lone wooden chair at the other side of the room. Watching the corridor, she picked up the chair and tried to lift. It was heavier than she expected. Jaclyn began to question whether it had a dense, metal skeleton within. Her shortness of breath returned as she decided to drag it toward the entrance. Setting it against the door, she realized the chair was wobbling.

It was hand-crafted. She could tell by the back's uneven design was the work of an amateur. Jaclyn figured it could've been something the owner had dabbled in himself, but there was no way to prove it. It wasn't the sort of thing one asked about. She wasn't about to get herself thrown out over a piece of shoddy craftsmanship.

But it was just enough to sit on and try to catch her breath. The chair didn't feel like it was about to collapse, so Jaclyn figured it was safe. She decided to hold it against the door as a kind of silent alarm if anyone tried to enter.

For all she knew, the delivery boy or one of the townsfolk crying in the distance could've been sneaking around to watch her. The cold air was still gently brushing against her neck. If it felt any warmer, that would've been her cue. The lopsided glass door wasn't much protection, but it was still a barrier.

A part of her mind still couldn't decide if she was just paranoid. Despite the attack on Trixie's car, there was no reason to attack Jaclyn.

And what about the girl staying in the hotel room on her own? Jaclyn checked her phone. No new messages. No missed calls. Nothing. She figured if Trixie found anything amiss, there'd be an immediate text about it. If nothing else, she'd ask something about where she ran off to without even leaving a note.

Jaclyn couldn't help wondering if someone could've done something to her. No—it was a ridiculous idea. Even with her stutter at its worst, she would've made an explosive ruckus.

Besides, she was one of them. Trixie was one of these so-called Anngologists. If her name was already on file, so was that.

She would've been known on some level. After all, Sabrina seemed to recognize her face.

She didn't think it'd make sense for them to attack someone for no reason, let alone one of their own. There were conflicts between different sects from time to time. Why would one *want* to attack someone in his own clan?

Jaclyn thought, *But then again—*

She remembered her parents' hollow expressions and their dead tones when they brought up the allegations about Jonestown. They told her it was the worst mass suicides in American history. Her father didn't go into further detail, but she had ideas of what he meant by *abuse.* Jaclyn never asked because she already knew.

Dad? I guess it's pretty silly, but sometimes I'm afraid of being right.

She pictured him the way she saw him as a child—the ten-foot giant with strong, callused hands who carried her around with ease. The image of him bending down to reach her level, smiling and looking at her through his thin glasses formed in her mind.

As the image came, her breath normalized. Her heart slowed down, having sunk back down to her chest again.

The image said like he always did, *It's okay, baby doll. Everyone gets scared. It's just part of being human, but we all have to face the truth. Sometimes that's the scariest thing of all.*

"Ma'am?"

Jaclyn winced in her seat, as if the chill had whispered straight against her eardrum. She turned to see the man at the counter. He was holding up a cheap plastic bag. Its contents were something beginning to bleed a reddish-brown through its paper wrapping.

"Your order's done," he told her.

Jaclyn froze but she pushed herself to stand back up. Her ankles were reduced to jelly. She looked into his yellowed eyes and his gaze gripped her entire view. As she approached him, his body didn't move an inch. He began to look like a stone idol, gesturing her to run.

She took the bag and asked, "What do I owe you?"

His face hadn't changed, but he put his palm up, gesturing her to stop. "There's no charge, ma'am."

Jaclyn furrowed her brow. "No charge?" A pause, and she asked, "Why not?"

"It's been paid for."

The wind was creeping in through the door, brushing itself against her ankles. "You mean it's on the house?"

"Not quite. Someone was kind enough to pick up the bill for you."

"Oh," Jaclyn replied, trying to summon the strength to step back. "I see." She failed to move, her ankles shivering. "Who was it?"

"That's no concern of yours. At least not right now," he replied.

Jaclyn looked down, then back at him. "No. I think I'd like to know who's paying for this."

The man smiled and said, "Eat up. Enjoy your night, Jaclyn. Someone your age oughtta be resting."

42.

She stood there, stunned, her mouth agape. "How do you know my…"

Her eyes were still locked with the man's as her sentence faltered. Jaclyn stepped back. Her heart exploded like a cluster of fireworks.

The man's smile widened, displaying his array of crooked teeth. "*Eat*, Jaclyn. I'm sure you and your friend are tired."

Jaclyn's back was just touching the door. She paused and asked, "How do you know my name?"

"Your *name*?" The man's grin turned more devious.

"*Yes*—my *name*. How did you know it? How did you know it was Jaclyn?" she demanded.

His smile turned to a blank look of indifference, as if he was reading statistics aloud. "An old face I thought I recognized—" he scanned her over "I guess. It was from a long time ago. Maybe twenty years or so."

As she moved further back, Jaclyn began to push the door open. "That *is*—" she paused as a breath of cold, dusty air licked her skin "—a really long time ago."

"People don't always forget the past," he said.

"No. I guess not."

She stepped out of the building, continuing to watch him. Her knees weakened, trembling like a flimsy sheet of metal. Jaclyn was paralyzed in confusion and awe. The idea that this stranger could have known her left Jaclyn thunderstruck as she turned to face the cold, swirling wind again.

Maybe twenty years or so, she thought. *Impossible.*

She listened for any noise behind her. God only knew if he was planning on sneaking up on her. Jaclyn was ready to feel even the smallest hint of a foul breath brushing the little hairs off her neck. The moment that stench reached her nostrils, she'd spin back around and smash her knuckles into the bridge of his nose.

It'd be just like the Uber driver—only if he didn't know how to hold her into submission.

The wind grew wet, clinging to her hands and ankles as she started walking. The howls and shrieks morphed together, harmonizing like a ghoulish symphony that microwaved her ears.

Jaclyn's heart shook as she started panting. She didn't have any more than a fleeting moment to sit. Her instincts were screaming at her to *run*—faster than *lightning*!

But her legs didn't have the strength. Any time she tried to sprint or even jog, Jaclyn's lungs filled with liquid lead. The strength had drained from her legs like water did in a narrow pipe.

The smell of rotting leaves and decaying flesh grew pungent as she approached the open manhole. It stung her nostrils and sucked any remaining drops of strength out of her. Jaclyn edged near it and her foot slipped—

"SHIT, SHIT!" she called into the hollow night.

Her foot slid through a shallow puddle of dark, viscous, reddish-brown liquid. Before she could jerk it back, it was already halfway in.

A sudden, fiery jolt of pain struck her ankle. Jaclyn thought that she might not be able to move it. She saw deep into the manhole when she looked down. It was a short distance between the surface and the thick shadows. Deeper down, she could see the outlines of a ladder. Below that was pure darkness.

Despite the groaning and the shrieking around her, Jaclyn heard a faint sound from the manhole. It was a low gurgle, as if something was rising from the waters. There was a sharp *splash* at the bottom, followed by a scream that bubbled up to the surface.

Jaclyn didn't recognize it at first but thought the sound couldn't have been just any sewer vermin. It was a different kind of animal.

She pulled her foot out. Another small burst of pain shot through her ankle, as if the bones were beginning to melt. She had either twisted or sprained it, but she didn't have the time to look.

She heard a croak out from the bottom of the manhole. As she walked past it and felt another shot of flames in her right ankle, Jaclyn stopped. She looked back at the hole. She felt a vague familiarity with the noise.

Jaclyn listened closer, taking a step toward the underground tunnel. She couldn't help holding her breath when she heard the croaking again.

The noise was intelligible. Jaclyn couldn't believe what she was hearing. The noises were *words.*

"Hal…Hel…" the voice called.

"Hello?" Jaclyn said. "Who's there?"

She heard an adult male. It wasn't the voice of a child, but it had to be her mind playing tricks on her. The sound couldn't be real. Neither the faraway, rhythmic shrieks encircling her, nor this.

The voice cried out from the manhole, *"HELP! HELP!"*

Jaclyn held her chest and squeezed. She stepped back in disbelief. It was just another hallucination like the voice from the closet.

But in the closet and over the phone, the sounds Jaclyn thought she heard had been fleeting. Even her dreams never lasted this long.

"HEEELP!" the voice cried again. *"HERE! I'M DOWN HERE!"*

No, she wasn't hallucinating this time. The voice she heard was *responding* to her. Jaclyn took another step and grunted in pain.

"IS SOMEONE UP THERE?" the voice screamed again.

Jaclyn tried to tell him, *yes*, but she couldn't. Her voice was stuck in her throat. Gazing down the manhole, she thought she saw a shape moving at the bottom. She couldn't tell if it was even human or not.

Whatever the reason, she figured somebody wanted Trixie and her to be in Dourmsburg. There was a reason these people knew her name.

With Trixie, there was an obvious reason for wanting her here. From what Jaclyn knew about cults, money was always a target. She recalled news articles about how members were pressured into paying thousands to rise within their ranks in the cult, Nexium. Then there were the stories of the Rulaizong, and how its ninety-thousand followers in Taiwan were bullied into handing over large parts of their wages.

But why Jaclyn? Trixie's money may have been public knowledge, but hers wasn't. It could've been just because they were traveling together now.

What were the chances of this man being a trap?

"SOMEBODY HELP ME! I—"

Whatever lay at the bottom of the manhole, it gave a monstrous scream. It abruptly ended with the sound of metal plunging into flesh.

43.

The sound of rusted iron penetrating skin and muscle burst into the darkness *again*, and *again*, until at last—

It overpowered the voice and overtook the night. The man's voice, whosever it was, eroded away like sand on a beach.

Jaclyn's body turned stone cold as she heard a sudden *splash*. It echoed even louder than the sound of the plunging metal. There was no doubt in her mind. Whatever had risen from the water collapsed back into it. She wouldn't hear it again.

Jaclyn didn't want to believe that it was a person down there, but how could she convince herself?

The manhole was silent again. Jaclyn's foot jerked back, as if the muscles in her heels were pulling her away. An incredible heat throbbed and pulsed in her brain, like white fires cooking it from its center.

She felt like she was levitating. Her cranium was foggy. Jaclyn couldn't believe what she'd heard.

She turned around and tried to take off, but red-hot pain struck her ankle again. In a burst of panic, Jaclyn forgot about her injury.

"You dirty bitch," Jaclyn gruntled as she stumbled and hunched over.

Everything in front of her looked like it was drifting away. As she continued limping, Jaclyn heard a gentle clang below her.

She couldn't tell if the thing that lurked down the manhole was tracking her. Jaclyn shouted back to the man who cried out to her for help, didn't she? As much as Jaclyn wanted to, she couldn't deny that there really was someone down there—

And something else that wanted the man to stay down in the sewer.

Trying to ignore the burning pain in her ankle, Jaclyn realized this—if that stranger heard her, so did whatever kept him from returning to the surface.

The howling wind settled, making way for the lunatic shrieking. Easing into a thick mist, the air curled around her legs like a pair of hands trying to hold her feet to the pavement.

Holding her breath, she thought an Uber was her only way back to the Cozy Moon. Her ankle was getting worse by the minute. She produced her phone and opened her Uber app. The cost would be six dollars and some change; she repeatedly hit the accept button as if that would improve her reception.

The fear of a strange driver didn't matter. That incident wouldn't happen again. Jaclyn figured it was still a one in a million chance anyway. All that mattered was getting back to the one place in town she *knew* was safe.

The odor near her toes was turning sharper. It was like a barrage of tiny needles jabbing into her nose.

Despite the maddening noise around her, she heard a dull *clang* from the manhole. She had no reason to turn around. It would only slow her down even more.

Looking from her phone to the road and back again, Jaclyn watched the status of her ride. The string of black letters on her screen told her that Uber was looking for any available drivers. The period at the end of the sentence was turning into an ellipsis and then a period again on an endless loop.

She was moving, but it wouldn't have stopped a car from picking her up. Any car in town with her location could've easily caught up with her.

But no cars were showing up on the mapped area on her app. The only moving presence was the blue dot spotting her location.

Another few seconds, and the text on her phone changed to:

There are no available drivers in your area.

A cold sweat formed on her palms and forehead. Her vision started blurring. The pain in her ankle worsened. A scream of agony almost escaped Jaclyn, but she held it back.

Any unnecessary sounds would only make her more noticeable. The more she stood out, the more of a target she could become.

Jaclyn stopped. A cold wave swept across her body at the sound behind her. She held her breath and struggled to take the next step forward. A string of *clangs* emanated from the manhole.

There was a pause, and a faint but deep snarl on the surface. Jaclyn heard it clearer than a morning church bell. The sound was beastly, like that of a hungry wolf. She looked at her peripheral vision but didn't dare to turn her head. If she did, the presence behind her would strike.

Struggling to limp any faster up the street, she caught a glimpse of the waning moon. It was at its final phase—crimson and bloodshot. The moon was peeking out from under a cluster of charcoal clouds like a beast behind a child's closet doors.

Jaclyn kept her eyes on the road. Another hungry snarl, louder and clearer than before, moved up the road. The sound made her ears burn.

The heavy footsteps made a low *squish*. They were slow at first but grew louder each time. Jaclyn heard them following her.

She increased speed but not much. The agony in her ankle moved to the bottom of her calf.

A thin, raspy voice behind her said, *"Jaclyn… Jaclyn…"*

It didn't sound like human to her. It was nothing more than a poor imitation of a person. The voice had another deeper layer, as it continued calling her name. Somehow, it was a whispering tenor and a guttural bass at the same time.

"Jaclyn…"

The footsteps behind her were faster—light trot.

Jaclyn couldn't believe it, but she *saw* the Cozy Moon now. Good God, how had she not noticed it before? It wasn't much farther now. The small hotel was close enough to look like the size of a baseball from where she was. Just a bit more, and she would be home free.

"JACLYN…"

The terrible whisper behind her sounded desperate. The squishing trail the thing's steps made became a jog. Its wetness was beginning to dissipate. Soon, the footsteps were a dry *clacking* against the rough pavement.

She extended her free arm as if to reach for another person's hand. When she was close to the parking lot, she even started jogging. Her eyes watered, but it didn't matter. All that mattered was being home free.

"JACLYN—" A set of long, ice-cold fingers reached for her shoulder, freezing it to the bone. *"I KNOW YOU—"*

44.

Finally, she turned around, purely from instinct. She imagined the thing behind her to be vaguely human, with exaggerated Dourmsburg features. It'd have enormous glassy eyes that never shut, a lipless orifice that imitated the human mouth, and a set of teeth with gaps that could tear through living flesh.

As she tried to face the thing, Jaclyn already let the pointed edges of its grimy fingers tear through her coat and into her skin. It would drag Jaclyn through the empty street, screaming for her life, and pull her into the manhole. It would pull her deep into the sewers and eat her piece by piece while she was still conscious.

And all Jaclyn would see the dark, and the face of that *thing* until she passed out from the pain.

She saw the silhouette of something vaguely human before her. The sight made her eyes dry up and burn. Jaclyn reached in her pocket and squeezed the taser.

But she didn't scream. There was only one thing Jaclyn hoped for, and she wished it with all her willpower. She mustered a single word under her breath before shutting her eyes and letting go of the taser.

"Corey?"

Her voice was a mere whisper, weaker than a tranquil breeze. Nobody would've heard Jaclyn, not even someone standing right in front of her.

She opened her eyes again. Jaclyn winced, feeling the long fingers wrapping around her throat, fingernails piercing into her flesh.

But despite the whispers scorching her ears and sensing someone gripping her shoulder—Jaclyn didn't see anyone. There wasn't a physical form of flesh and bone, but she still thought someone was standing there.

She stepped back and stared into the space in front of her. The few streetlights in the town didn't reveal much. Their glow was dim, like the wiring hadn't been maintained in decades. They only shone through a short, straight path.

Jaclyn stood still, cloaked by the cold. The lunatic shrieking in the surrounding distance was simmering down. It settled down, and became a peaceful quiet, as if it had been a wordless command.

The graveyard silence was overpowering. She felt the lingering presence fade but couldn't help thinking there were still countless pairs of eyes hidden beyond the dim lights.

Jaclyn turned and headed to the outer edges of the parking lot. Listening for any noise around her, she thought it was time to grab the car and get the Hell out.

It didn't matter if she couldn't risk the Chevy on the highway. It was at least drivable. She'd take Trixie and go through the backroads. If driving for most of her life taught her anything, it was that there was always a different route.

She'd go back to that mechanic in the morning and get the Chevy back. The car hadn't already broken down, so Jaclyn knew there was a *little* time before it did. She hated doing this to her car, but what other choice did she have?

All she had to do was leave town, and she and Trixie were golden. Depending on the distance to another mechanic, she'd get Trixie back home whenever it was possible. Only problem was, her job was on the middle of the interstate. It'd be a daunting task finding another path that doesn't go through Dourmsburg.

It's okay, she thought. *There was always another route. Hell, it might even be closer than I think.*

But how far did this cult reach? For all she knew, these Anngologists could be in the next town—or several towns after that. She knew that they had a presence on the highway adjacent to this town, and perhaps an even larger one in Quakerston.

"That cop had a tattoo for God's sake," she muttered.

As Jaclyn approached the Cozy Moon, she realized how hard she had been rubbing her lips. She drew her forefinger away and found it smeared with deep burgundy lipstick.

"And all this over some takeout."

She stopped at the front entrance, remembering that the establishment wasn't taking anyone else in tonight. A faint, gentle moan seeped into the air and sailed across the Dourmsburg sky. Gripping the door, she decided to tug anyway.

Jaclyn expected it to be locked—that she'd have to bang on the door and persuade the front lobby to open, or just find another place to sleep. What would become of her for the night was one thing, but at least Trixie had a warm bed.

But this time, the door wasn't locked at all. It opened with ease despite it being locked earlier that evening.

Jaclyn looked at the front desk. Sabrina was there, grinning and watching her. The attendant's eyes were shadowed underneath, as if her sockets had hollowed out. She stared with wild intensity, like she never had lids to keep her eyes moist.

She raised one hand and wiggled her fingertips as Jaclyn entered. "Staying in for the night, Miss Ellsworth? You came back sooner than we expected."

Jaclyn stopped in her tracks. She tried to avoid eye contact but couldn't help gazing into the dark pair of irises. Until now, she didn't notice just how straight and narrow Sabrina's teeth were. By the looks of it, that young woman had to have more than the proper amount.

"Yeah," Jaclyn replied. "I think so."

The words automatically slipped out of her. She didn't want to spend another second here but felt there wasn't a choice. It was either this, or drag Trixie out of bed and try her luck miles away at another hotel with a hurt ankle—and go back to the lingering presence in the empty street.

She looked away from Sabrina, going back to her room. As she walked, Jaclyn felt an icy chill running down her neck. Sabrina never took her eyes off her. She may not have *seen* it, but had no doubt about it.

Going back inside her room, she saw Trixie. The girl was on top of the covers, facing the wall next to her, curled into the fetal position. She hadn't even turned the lights off before falling asleep.

Jaclyn didn't see her face, but curiously watched her and thought, *Does she always sleep like that? She'll wake up freezing in the middle of the night.*

After putting the take-out in the fridge and her taser on the nightstand, she turned off the lights. Jaclyn got in her bed and crawled under the blanket. The throbbing ache in her feet and the burning in her ankle, wouldn't let her fall asleep at first.

It took several minutes, but the pain reduced. Jaclyn breathed in relief and resisted the urge to cough. If she had an affliction, she knew holding it in wouldn't change anything. It was the simple reminder that she was trying to avoid the inevitable.

As the clock struck midnight, she closed her eyes and heard a weakened, muffled groan from the adjacent room.

45.

When morning came, the sunlight was dim, like a defeated daybreak. It didn't pierce through the layers of shadows shrouding the hotel room. The sun had a faint, sickly glow.

As Jaclyn woke up, she thought luck was the only reason she could see any natural light in her room at all. She sat up and felt a dull headache and a heaviness in her eyes.

Glancing over at the other bed, she saw Trixie sitting at its foot. The girl was hugging her knees to her chest and facing away from Jaclyn.

A pause. "Trixie? What's wrong?"

Trixie's complexion was paler than the night before. She had goosebumps that looked like developing smallpox. She had a thin layer of cold sweat on her skin and shivered on and off.

"Trixie?" Jaclyn asked again. "Are you sick?"

A deep, cold silence followed. She felt as if there was a growing distance between her and Trixie again. Whenever the girl became silent, Jaclyn thought it was like trying to speak to a ghost—an aimless, drifting spirit who couldn't hear no matter how loud the real-world voices around her were.

Trixie's voice was raspy at first, but it cleared as she spoke. "D-did you hear that?"

"No? Hear what?"

"It was fr-from the other side of the w-wall last night."

Jaclyn didn't recall much from that point. After coming in and closing her eyes, anything else was too fuzzy. She couldn't remember if something else happened. Jaclyn wasn't sure if she even got a good look at Trixie.

Trixie *was there* when she came back, right? Yeah—of course she was.

After a second's thought, she started to remember hearing a couple odd, muffled groans from the room next to them. Jaclyn thought about it more, realizing it could've been a multitude of things.

People tossed and turned in bed all the time. Not to mention, it was a hotel. It occurred that the noise could be a couple staying the night.

"I heard a couple groans maybe," she said. "Nothing that weird. You get that at hotels sometimes."

"I kn-*know that.* I wasn't talking about *that.*"

Jaclyn was taken aback. She hesitated at first, but asked, "Then what? I didn't hear anything else."

"I heard wh-what people in the other r-room were saying."

"You were eavesdropping?"

Trixie shot her a glare with a laser-like focus. "Not on p-*purpose.*"

Jaclyn winced on seeing her face. She wanted to ask just what in the Hell happened to her last night but kept quiet anyway. She figured it'd only distress the poor girl even more. It sounded absurd to her, but Jaclyn still wondered if Trixie needed medical attention.

Trixie's hair looked matted and oily throughout. Her eyes had a twitchy, glazed look about them. Clusters of tiny red blood vessels surrounded her pupils. Thin layers of mucous were clotted near her eyes. Dark rings formed around them.

Despite the rising tension in her gut, Jaclyn asked, "Then what happened? What did you hear?"

If she looks like this, Jaclyn thought. *Chances are, she probably hasn't slept in days. She might be paranoid from it, but with the place we're in? It could be a Hell of a lot more going on in these parts.*

"It was a group of people. They were saying 'midnight, midnight' and then they were chanting some kind of weird jargon. You *know* I've traveled all over the world—and it wasn't any language I've heard before. They weren't really *speaking* it. They were *chanting* it in a strange rhythm."

Jaclyn paused with her eyes wide open and replied, "Are you sure you weren't just dreaming?"

"God, I have no idea. I remember hearing that and a horrible, muffled *screaming* as I was just dozing off. I couldn't sleep after that, and it's been a few days too."

"A few days since what?"

"Since I slept last," Trixie snapped.

The girl's response swept Jaclyn's mind back to last night. She wondered if the two of them were sharing the same experience, witnessing a—

MURDER

—vivid hallucination. That's what last night had to have been. The things she and Trixie had heard didn't happen in real life. She saw something that was only possible in a dream. The more Jaclyn recalled the fear from last night that she still felt in her gut, the stronger her conviction grew. It was fear that crawled across her mind once she closed her eyes.

There was nothing *possible* about it all. The rhythmic, lunatic shrieking emanating from the dilapidated buildings. The dim scarlet moon. The voice from the sewer, and whatever put a sudden end to it.

None of it was any different from the voice in the closet. But the effect it all had on her and Trixie was different.

"You haven't slept in *days?*" Jaclyn asked.

Trixie was still but eventually shook her head.

"You think maybe that's the reason why?" Jaclyn's question trailed off.

No response.

Jaclyn looked down, then back at the girl. "Well, it's happened to me before."

"When?" Trixie asked.

A cold silence followed. Jaclyn balled her fists and imagined Trixie as a tall, thin priest with white hair and skin like old leather. She pictured a metal screen between them. She thought of herself in the dark skirts and button-down shirts of her youth. A lump suddenly formed in her throat, as if she were summoning the courage to talk about the times with those boys behind the stage in her high school auditorium.

"It was a long time ago," Jaclyn said. "You're gonna think I'm a terrible person after I tell you this, but I probably deserve it anyway." She paused and kept her eyes away from Trixie. "Remember how in the bar, I only came in for a glass of water?"

"Yeah. What about that?" Trixie asked.

"Well, the truth is I'm a bit of an alcoholic. No, that's a load of bullshit, Trix. I *am* an alcoholic, and this whole trip's been a major test for me. There's a reason I had to stop drinking. It probably cost me one of the most valuable things in my life, but I had to stop before it took even more. It *almost* took even more. Have you ever been in the car with a drunk at the wheel?"

Trixie didn't say anything but scrunched her brow and kept her gaze focused on Jaclyn.

"It's probably one of the scariest things in the world. I only use the word *probably* because I was the one driving. I remember my kid repeatedly asking me not to drive. I think he was eight or nine at the time. He walked to the bar I was drinking at that night. It was pretty late—maybe past one—and I remember he kept asking me not to drive. I don't know if *he* was taught anything about drunk driving at school yet, but he saw me stumbling at home enough to figure out by himself that it was a bad idea.

"He was asking me to walk home instead and our home wasn't that far away. Maybe a ten-minute drive. Probably less. And that's what I told him as I turned the ignition, 'We're not far from home, Corey. We'll be okay. You shouldn't be out like that anyway. Do you have any idea what time it is? What if somebody'—"

Jaclyn's eyes stung as if she had been prodded with a hot needle. She suddenly teared up, and an unbearable hot flash hit her face. Her jaw shook like an engine that was about to fall to pieces, but she continued anyway.

"'What if somebody grabs you?'" She sniffled and sobbed. "'Don't you *ever* do that again, *understand*?'" Jaclyn's hands were trembling, one of them pointing and wagging a finger accusatorily. "'You don't have *any business* being out after dark.'" I saw his face in the rearview mirror. He was in the back with tears streaming going down his face. I don't think scolding him made any difference. That wasn't the reason for the wide look in his eyes.

"And as luck had it, we were living in a really run-down area at the time. So, there was a bit of a drug problem too. It's the kind of thing that happens when the people living there don't have anything to hope for or look forward to.

"The neighborhood spirals into this sort of degeneracy—and there were more patrols in the streets, but nothing else. A Band-Aid on an open wound if you ask me. But as you can imagine, there were more cops patrolling the area at night." Jaclyn snickered and said, "Shit, some of them just circled the same couple blocks over and over. And *just as luck would have it*, one of them flashed his lights and pulled me over." She paused and forced a fake laugh. "There aren't many things in this world more embarrassing than being arrested in front of your kid. *That* should've taught me. But it didn't. It didn't really stop until…" As Jaclyn's speech faltered, she looked to the floor.

At last, Trixie interjected. "Un-Until what?"

The silence was colder than ever.

"Jaclyn? What happened?"

There wasn't any response at first. Jaclyn kept her eyes down, as if she hadn't heard Trixie. The shadows under her eyes widened and dimmed.

"I guess I have a confession."

46.

"W-What?" Trixie asked, raising her brow and leaning forward.

Jaclyn looked into her eyes, wanting to back away. She had the choice to say *nevermind* and end it right there. The agenda for the day would've stayed the same:

Get the Chevy, take Trixie to a comfortable area if not her own home, and see a doctor. Once the doctor gave his verdict, just remedy the problem herself. Nobody else needed to know about the problem, whatever it was.

And Trixie didn't need to know the sentence in Jaclyn's head either—*My son's been missing for God knows how long and I'm actually trying to find him.* Her reaction wasn't anything more than guesswork.

This person now in Jaclyn's care would hate her. She'd curse her, leave, and never come back. The confession would be their last moment together.

Trixie—the second child failed.

But who was Jaclyn kidding? This was just some *kid* she met a couple nights ago. She was a *stranger*. The second they went their own ways, that'd be the end of it. They'd never see each other again, let alone speak.

Trixie couldn't have seen it any other way either. Even if this girl didn't have friends, unlikely as that was, she'd move onto the next step in her life. Jaclyn knew how dramatic people that age were. Jaclyn had been age at one point.

She remembered being twenty-one. One of the first things that came to mind was claiming to be friendless—

Yet having an address book halfway full of phone numbers next to her bed. She even had her own landline phone—and was chastised for using it when her mother needed to make a call. These were people from high school who she talked to most days of the week—

What were their names again? Before she even turned thirty, Jaclyn wasn't sure anymore. Chances were, they thought the same of her: a faint, pleasant memory that no longer had a name.

But what if Trixie understood why she lied? Most people wouldn't have driven Jaclyn to try and find the old woman who tipped her off. Someone who'd do a favor like that could forgive her too.

It was just a stupid, compulsive lie. Hell, it wasn't even a lie that Jaclyn planned. The lie was something that just slipped out. It was a reflex. Back at the bar, it felt better to twist the truth than be judged.

And who better to understand that than Trixie? Jaclyn thought it only made sense to tell her. Even if she decided to continue lying, Trixie would find out at some point. It was only a matter of time before the girl started asking questions.

W-Why haven't you t-talked to your boy? How do you kn-know he's ok-k-k-kay?

"J-Jaclyn? What ih-is it?"

"Trix, would you do something for me?"

"W-what?"

Jaclyn's mouth was dry as she answered, "I need you to be understanding."

"Of c-course," Trixie replied.

As she was about to respond to Trixie, her eyes and heart felt heavier. Remember what I said to you back at the bar? About my son?"

"Uh-Uh huh."

Jaclyn forced the answer out. "I lied to you."

Trixie muttered when she asked, "Y-You l-lied to me?"

A pause. "Yeah. I'm sorry, but you deserve to know. The truth is, I haven't talked to him in a long time. I'm not even sure how long it's been. He doesn't even know I'm here."

Trixie's eyes turned cold and harsh enough to make her shiver as she asked, "He doesn't? Why not?"

Jaclyn hated the answer she was about to give. The thought of the truth made her think of the punishments and ostracization she deserved. She even began to think that lashes across the back were better than confessing.

She breathed in some dry air and replied, "Because I don't know where he is."

Jaclyn's heart dropped to her stomach when she admitted this. It was like admitting to failing at her most crucial job.

"*Why* don't you know where he is?" There was a sudden confidence and righteous cruelty in Trixie's voice that struck Jaclyn between the eyes like a hammer.

"Because he's been missing," Jaclyn responded.

"Why?" Trixie's voice grew more commanding with each question.

Her tone made Jaclyn feel ever smaller. The size and power of this *young girl* had grown to that of a giant. Being confronted by her voice was like having her bones pulverized to dust.

"Because…" Jaclyn sounded as if she'd continue but her sentence collapsed right there.

"Because…?"

Jaclyn's voice was weak as she answered, "Because he ran away."

"WHY—DID HE—RUN—AWAY?" Trixie demanded.

The room was overwhelmed by a terrible silence. Jaclyn kept her gaze away from Trixie by staring at the floor. She couldn't look the girl in the face—it was holding onto dry ice.

It occurred that she could lie to Trixie again. The right story could steer the conversation in a new direction. It'd be a shield against every drop of righteous fury racing through Trixie's veins.

Jaclyn knew there was a soft formula for lying to most people. The lie needed to be short and simple. Anything more than that, and it wouldn't have been believable. Was it enough to simply say, *I don't know?*

No, it never was. When she was a child and that answer was the honest truth of God, it still wasn't acceptable. It wasn't adequate for a *lie*, let alone one about something this dire.

Her mind raced like lightning but remained blank. The only thing that she could up with was four words, and inevitably the truth the spilled from her lips.

"I wouldn't stop drinking."

Jaclyn didn't turn her head, but heard Trixie stand up from her mattress and leave the room, slamming the door behind her.

47.

Five minutes passed, and Jaclyn finally looked at the other bed. She looked at the impression left in the mattress, as if it was a full person speaking to her. Despite getting the silent treatment, she stared anyway.

Jaclyn couldn't discern why she'd been paralyzed until now. She couldn't even make herself stand up. Her legs were stiff. Her heart was dissolving in a thick black oil dripping down her brain.

Trixie was the one person who had been by her side in all this—now she was gone as well. First her ex, then Corey, and now her. The one real difference with Trixie, without a doubt, was that she was in the middle of Dourmsburg. For a moment, she was the easiest to reach. She was also out in the open, an unknowing prey.

Jaclyn pulled her phone out and didn't see any calls. No surprise that Trixie hadn't called in the past few minutes, but there was nothing from her ex or the police either.

No new leads and no new threats to drag her off to court. For whatever reason, both parties seemed to have given up—how long ago or why, she couldn't say. She couldn't even remember the last time either of them got a hold of her. Jaclyn never received any calls, but she couldn't see her ex or even the cops in her recent history.

Going into her text messages, she returned to the earlier conversation with Trixie. Her eyes and hands were stuck as she wondered if sending a message would only make things worse. No, it was better to act now than later.

Waiting was what I did with Corey, Jaclyn thought. *And look what happened. He's still gone. I can't make the mistake of waiting anymore.*

"Trixie," she typed. "I'm sorry I lied to you before. Will you please forgive me? Where are you?"

Jaclyn sent the message and pushed herself to stand up again. Approaching the door, she heard the growing chatter outside her room. It wasn't loud enough to decipher any words, but the tone sounded as if these people were planning something together.

It was either her imagination, paranoia, or this festival. The *festival*, she reflected. The return of Anthony Charles. The so-called healer. He would be in Dourmsburg that night, and if he was—

Trixie would be there too. Missing such a thing would drive her mad. There was no way she didn't know it was that night. And if the cult was in the hotel, there was a chance that she hadn't left the building yet.

Despite her stomach clenching, she opened the door. A legion of elongated shadows was waiting in the hall, opposite the door. They lingered and stretched from neighboring rooms to the ceiling, like wiry scarecrows.

They didn't move from their open doorways. The silhouettes had a quiet stillness, as if they were anticipating the next movement. What struck her was their similarity to one another. Each body was an elongated torso, no wider than a baseball. The head was more of a narrow bulb. Every silhouette didn't show signs of hair or even facial features.

One of the figures right next to Jaclyn stretched its long, narrow arm and closed its door. Just as it slammed shut, the other shadows followed.

As the last door closed, she found herself holding her breath. Realizing she was squeezing her room's front doorknob; Jaclyn took a deep breath. She tried to stop her hands from shaking but failed.

Another breath and she stepped out into the hallway. The only sounds were that of the collective muttering from the lobby.

"Trixie?" she asked in the empty corridor. "Trixie, are you there?"

She was answered when she called of the girl's name. It wasn't Trixie's voice at all. The answer was a small hush of the crowd in the lobby. They were still speaking amongst each other but only in whispers.

Jaclyn felt the sound tickle her ears like the edge of a rusty nail brushing against one's skin, she stepped into the lobby. An immediate, collective hush settled over the room like a cloud of poison gas.

A group of faces she hadn't seen before was in the lobby. Their shared complexion was sickly pale with thinned and furrowed eyebrows. Their pupils were dilated and fixed on her as she stood there.

Her chest was caught in an icy grip. Jaclyn noticed the features of those in the crowd. They were identical to last night's delivery boy. The only difference was that the skin on their faces was pulled back tight enough for it to tear like paper. She couldn't be sure, but Jaclyn suspected that they had the same lineage.

Inbreeding? she thought.

Jaclyn shuddered, picturing the possible timeline in her mind. The legion of bulging, unblinking eyes watched as she approached the entrance. She tried to look like she didn't notice but couldn't help looking back at them. They followed her, even after she stepped outside and looked away from the gathered crowd.

There was no outrunning them. Her ankle was a pulsing, flaming reminder. She didn't turn around, not hearing any sound behind her. Ignoring the pain, she limped to the parking lot and wondered what those people had on their laps.

"What *were* those red things?" she muttered to herself.

Each of them was holding a mass of scarlet silk on their laps. At first, Jaclyn registered them as blankets or quilts perhaps, but she couldn't say what they were for.

No, they had to have been something else. If these were anything like prayer mats, they would've been used out in the open by now.

Taking the phone from her pocket, Jaclyn noticed her battery—sixteen percent. She still needed to use the Directions app.

Looking at the map, Jaclyn remembered that the route was simple. She just had to turn left after exiting the parking lot, turn right at the end of the road, and then it was a straight road. But simple or not, it was the distance that made her stomach cold.

Two miles, and on a hurt ankle too.

Jackson Street looked empty to her. There were no cars. Looking at the cracks and small depressions throughout the pavement, she was amazed that Trixie had managed to pull off the drive earlier.

But the festival didn't mean that people wouldn't be around. Maybe the persistent shrieking last night wasn't a hallucination, and maybe—

Despite what she tried to tell herself before, the underground hadn't been there either.

Jaclyn knew Smith and Son would be closed, but that didn't matter. All that mattered was getting the Chevy back anyway, finding Trixie, and Corey most of all.

48.

Jaclyn's phone buzzed in her pocket. There was a chance that it'd be one of her family members who hadn't answered yesterday, or it could be Trixie. She wasn't praying that it was Trixie, but she had hinted at some level of forgiveness.

Jaclyn couldn't think of another way to get out of Dourmsburg, except *finding* her. She whipped out her smartphone. It *was* a new message—from Trixie.

"The lie," she had written to Jaclyn, "Isn't why I left."

The text message eliminated any other possibility from Jaclyn's mind. There was only one other reason she would have stormed out of the room. She felt stupid for thinking it had been the lie to begin with.

Telling Trixie any of that was a mistake. The girl would've caught on at some point. She wasn't stupid, but Jaclyn knew she could've had another story to cover her ass. Any detail of the truth felt like too much to give away, but Trixie would've known either way.

It was almost a blessing that Jaclyn only mentioned the drinking and the running away and not any other details. There was a low and pathetic murmur inside her head.

I'm sorry I was out after dark. I was just playing video games at my friend's house. You're not gonna hit me again, are you?

No, Jaclyn decided, shaking her head. She wouldn't do it ever again. After declaring a new sober lifestyle, that she promised to begin practicing the moment she found Corey.

The stabbing in her ankle made her clench her teeth, trying to hold in the groans that wanted to escape her lips. Jaclyn couldn't find a reason to be quiet because she was avoiding the pavement after crossing the parking lot and staying on the grass. She didn't see any groups of people outside. Occasionally, a child was playing or a piranha-faced townsperson who was watching her from inside his house. But there was no business in the streets. It was a ghost town. Nonetheless, grunting in pain would've been a sign of weakness.

"Jaclyn," her father would've said to her. "You're not a little girl no more. You're gonna have to grow up."

She'd never been sure if the comment was about the tears—or the reasons for them. Often, Jaclyn would have gotten into a fight with one of her friends when she cried as a teenager. What if her parents had been around to know about their only grandson going missing? What would they say if they saw her cry about it?

Her mother would've been silent. She always was when her father scolded her. Now that she thought about it, this could've been the one time when her father wouldn't have said anything at all.

A childhood memory resurfaced. Her father had learned over the phone that one of his teammates had stayed behind when they rushed to a flaming, collapsing building. Inside was a child who sat on the floor, crying hysterically.

Her father just stood there with the landline against his ear and a stunned look on his face. After an hour of trying, her mother had finally got him to speak and explain what happened.

But that was just a co-worker, not his family.

She wondered about the idea of a dead relative being present around the living. Jaclyn never felt sure about it but heard about it plenty of times from her Catholic family—more at funerals than anywhere else.

And she was certain there were such things as spirits. The idea of Heaven meant that spirits *must* exist. So, a spirit could observe—*visit* the living, even though the surviving loved ones often didn't notice that.

In her family, rumor had it that this was the reason a spirit chose to visit people in their dreams sometimes. Since her parents' passing at the hands of a now-*convicted* drunk driver, she hadn't dreamt of them at all. A few family members claimed otherwise. Part of her thought that they were lying, but they didn't have a good reason to make that up. On the other hand, it did always get them a moment of awe-struck attention.

But maybe they didn't visit her at all. After her parents had died, they could've known all about the drinking that she insisted Corey should never tell anyone about.

The more she thought about a prolonged silent treatment, the more she felt like an overgrown child herself. It was enough reason to earn such a silent treatment. After all, she'd failed to do what her parents wanted her to achieve more than anything—growing up. And what was a greater test to see if a child had grown up than raising one herself?

The question made her heart sink into a lake of murky oil. Her ankle stung a little as she reached the end of the road. It occurred that the manhole on Jackson that she tripped on must've been covered back up again. She was standing at a three-way intersection, and finally learned the name of that perpendicular street. Jaclyn crossed Jackson and limped her way down Handerson Street.

"I'm sorry," Jaclyn typed. "And I mean it. Where are you? We'll talk it out. Besides, it's not safe to be out alone like this."

Quiet and unintelligible whispers crawled around her. As she listened, her ears grew cold despite the bright afternoon daylight, as if the voices were right next to her. It was a sound from the run-down, boarded up houses. She couldn't pinpoint why, but a quiet sense of familiarity crept up her spine from walking down Handerson.

It wasn't the sound of the conspiring voices but the old buildings. She thought she was in this spot before. Jaclyn dismissed it, seeing Smith and Son just up ahead.

As she suspected, a flimsy sign saying the business was closed hung on the front entrance. Even when she reached the parking lot, the Chevy wasn't anywhere in sight. She figured it could be sitting somewhere at the back of the building.

It made sense. The establishment didn't have much garage room. With a closer look, she noticed a few other cars sitting on the other side. One of them must have been hers.

Her ankle hurt worse as she limped to the back of the building. Jaclyn couldn't deny her ankle was swollen by now. Once she got to the car, she could sit down again and feel sweet relief.

She stopped at the back of the lot, staring at the cars. There was a Toyota, three Fords and a Mazda, but no Chevy in sight.

Jaclyn hunched down, clenched her knees and coughed into her fist. After wiping it on her pants, she limped to the front again. She could only guess if the door would open. If not, she still had the chance to rest—a few moments away from the cabal in the hotel before her next move.

Either way, Jaclyn was closer to finding Trixie.

As she reached the front, her phone went off again.

"How can I be alone?" Trixie replied. "I'm with people who want me and won't leave or hurt me."

Dear Lord, she thought. *I don't know what these people are up to, but neither does Trixie. Whatever they're planning, it's gonna kill the both of us. But how do I make her see that?*

As she considered her words, Jaclyn felt the lock holding the front door shut. She sighed and felt a twinge in her forehead. Cursing under her breath, she shook the door by the handle as if trying to strangle it.

The lock snapped. Jaclyn stumbled as the door swung open.

She stood still, looking inside to see an empty lobby. The gentle buzz from the dimmed ceiling lights filled the room. A pair of black flies were pacing on the front desk.

"Is anyone here?" Jaclyn called.

The wind groaned as it rushed down Handerson, brushing against her. Nobody called back to her, but half of the lights nearest to the entrance blinked. She winced and took a step back as the flies paced faster on the desk. They buzzed in a harsh agitation, flying and landing back on its surface in a repeated circular pattern.

"Mr. Smith?" There was a gentle echo as she called again. Jaclyn stepped forward, looking to the door that led to the back. "Mr. Smith? Are you there?"

She limped to the back of the desk and saw that its top drawer was ajar. The end of a thin silver chain was peeking out like the head of a snake. Glistening in the light above, the silver twinkled, almost winking at Jaclyn and whispering her name.

She gripped the steel drawer handle, feeling a thin film of cold perspiration on her palms. There was a firm resistance as she pulled, but Jaclyn managed to yank it open.

It opened with a booming *thud.* Jaclyn flinched at the sight first, but then she bent down and took a closer look. The object twinkled in front of her eyes.

The innermost end of the drawer was shrouded in shadows, hiding a small dim object next to the broken link. She peered closer but failed to get a better look. Reaching inside, Jaclyn grasped it, feeling its rough surface. Imagining that the object would be rusted, she held it in the deficient light.

On closer inspection, Jaclyn realized that it was a roughened cheap metal—pure tin. It was a pendant, no wider than a quarter, with the sign of the solar eclipse. It had a loop on top through which the chain would snake through and wrap around someone's neck. She noticed that the loop was broken, as if the wearer had pulled it from the chain with brute force.

It couldn't have been Lloyd's. He wouldn't have snapped it off his neck. She thought it had to have been Donnie's instead—possibly joining the cult with his son—and leaving. Between all the cults she read about, abandoning the faith was the unforgivable sin. If this one was like the others, Donnie was shunned out of town by now.

Jaclyn put the pendant back and closed the drawer while keeping an eye on the back door. The pair of flies hung onto it, their wings fluttering in a placid, tantalizing hum. Their frantic pacing had stopped. Their bodies were still except for the wings.

"Mr. Smith?" she said again, limping to the door. Her voice quivered as she continued. "I'm sorry I'm here. I know you're closed, but I need to pick up the Chevy. It's really urgent."

Opening the back door, Jaclyn found the corner of a hallway that suddenly turned left. Jaclyn whipped out her phone and opened the Flashlight app. Her battery was already down to twelve percent. If Jaclyn didn't find another light source, she'd have no communication outside the Cozy Moon.

"Mr. Smith?" She stepped into the dark narrow hallway. It was just spacious enough to fit someone with slightly broader shoulders than hers.

When she flashed her light down the end of the hallway, Jaclyn saw the end a hundred feet away. The door there was the only one in the corridor, but it wasn't what made her jaw drop.

Jaclyn's eyes watered and her stomach churned. The walls and ceiling were covered by a still swarm of black flies. They were scattered around, buzzing in place like the ones on the door behind her.

The flies scrutinized her but didn't move as she walked. Jaclyn kept glancing between the door and the flies. The legion of insects was in a flawless calm.

Jaclyn could feel the walls brushing against her shoulders as she touched the doorknob. The flies hadn't any made physical contact but didn't move from their spots either.

"Mr. Smith?" she asked, gripping the knob. "I'm picking up the Chevy."

The doorknob *creaked* as she pulled it opened. A single light bulb dangled from the ceiling on a metal cord, filling the center of the room with a dull glow. A small group of cars in various states of repair was scattered around the garage.

Jaclyn couldn't get her eyes off the middle of the room. An icy shiver ran down her digestive tract. She let out an ear-piercing shriek and stumbled back. Tripping, she fell on the smooth concrete floor. Sporadic pain shot up her tailbone as she landed. She was still leaning away from seeing what was laying at the center of the room, as if it'd stand upright again.

The owner was lying on his back next to a faint pair of tire tracks. Donnie Smith's eyes had rolled back into his head. Only the whites and the thin blood vessels beneath them were visible. His mouth hung open at a wide angle, like it had been undone. The color had disappeared from his face, but the blood was fresh.

The bits that had soaked through his clothes and stained the concrete were just beginning to clot. A small pool of crimson settled on his neck.

Although her hands were shaking, Jaclyn edged forward to look closer. His throat had been torn straight out without any precision. The wound was wide-open with rough edges. Jaclyn snuck closer one slow step at a time, as if Donnie would spring up onto his feet and tear her to ribbons.

Judging from the edges of the wound, they were nearly human bite marks.

49.

Jaclyn backed away. There was only one question racing through her mind: where was Lloyd?

She remembered his natural glare when they first met. There was a mechanical cruelty in them.

Jaclyn examined the room. She wondered what Lloyd looked like when he curled his lips back. No other type of human teeth was able to tear living flesh with such ease. Only what or *whoever* she had seen in Dourmsburg could have done this.

Jaclyn's thoughts flashed back to the question of inbreeding. That was possible, but the chances of an entire town with the same lineage were damned near zero. Nonetheless, no known defect shaped the teeth that way.

She started wheezing and gripping her chest. Jaclyn's heart was pounding through her rib cage. Jaclyn knelt and kept her mouth closed as she fell in a small coughing spell. Speckles of warm metallic liquid sprang up to the back of her tongue. She swallowed, making herself forget about it.

Mucous, Jaclyn thought. *Funny-tasting mucous. That's all. It's nothing that serious. Especially when a doctor confirms it.*

Trying not to think of the drops of blood on her palms in the hotel bathroom, she examined the room. It was a garage, for God's sake. There had to have been a library of blunt metal objects around here.

And God only knew where Lloyd was. If he was still in the building, Lloyd knew where she was.

Jaclyn hobbled over to the work bench, opposite the back door. Being quiet was near impossible. Even when she tried, Jaclyn still heard the scuffle of her shoes against the concrete floor.

She crept up to the workbench, searched it and the area above. Nothing. Jaclyn cursed under her breath, seeing no tools or anything else.

"Crazy bastard," she said.

She bent down under the workbench and her eyes twinkled. Jaclyn got on her knees and crawled. There was a dull wrench next to the wall, blending with the shadows. She grabbed the dust-covered instrument, clung to it for life itself, and shuffled back.

Her shoes *squeaked* as she was getting out from under the workbench. Standing back up was agonizing enough to make Jaclyn scream. She clenched her teeth, and the muscles in her neck strained as she got back up.

Jaclyn looked at the garage door behind her. There wasn't a way to tell if she could lift the thick, rusted iron door on her own, let alone quietly. Despite the decay, she noticed a new onyx keypad next to it. The *Eclipse* branding was embossed in gold lettering.

It had to have been a lock or an alarm system—probably both. Most warehouses had them. She remembered a vague memory of articles promoting this line of gadgetry.

Jaclyn's ankle made her forget that she hadn't eat in days, but her stomach brutally gnawed on itself. It burrowed its way up to her liver. The hunger gave way to nausea.

The overall feeling sent a wave of noxious fumes through her eye sockets, as she limped to the back door. It pulled her eyelids down, as if staying awake was a feat of strength.

She crouched at the corner near the back door. Jaclyn curled into a fetal position and leaned in close enough to touch her ear against the cold surface.

A dull, rhythmic sound could be heard outside the room, but she couldn't tell where it was coming from. The one thing Jaclyn knew was far away. But all her efforts weren't enough to keep her from falling asleep as the muffled thumping drew closer.

50.

Jaclyn sprang awake, clutching at a piece of metal. She pictured being gagged, her hands pressed against part of a steel contraption that kept her bound, and Lloyd standing opposite her with his icy gaze.

She looked around the room. Jaclyn anticipated the blunt sting of teeth against her flesh—

But nobody else was around. She was still in the garage. The only thing keeping her company was Donnie Smith's body. A small cluster of flies hovered around him, waiting him to decompose. She could barely make them in the dark.

She checked her battery while turning her Flashlight app on. Three percent. The moment she shone the light on Donnie, the flies scattered.

Jaclyn looked into his blank eyes, thinking how the look across his screaming face wouldn't change. Not until someone else changed it for him.

Jaclyn stood up, ignoring the pain and the sound outside. She reached the body, knelt next to it, and closed his mouth. She gently touched the man's eyes.

She felt the acid in her stomach regurgitate when she glanced down at his neck. Jaclyn covered her mouth to protect herself against the flies. She stood up and crept to the back door. She'd make a burial spot for him when it was safe.

With a deep breath, she squeezed the wrench harder than ever. There was no way to know if anyone was in the building. Jaclyn braced herself for the moment she'd swing the wrench and crack the bastard's skull at the temple. But if he managed to take his own father down—

Jaclyn squeezed the doorknob and twisted it. She stopped, her hand twitching. She knew it'd creak when it opened. The building didn't have a second floor. If Lloyd was still here, he'd be in the hall or the lobby. He had no place to hide in the dark unless there was a hidden door somewhere in the building.

She turned off her flashlight, stuck the phone back in her pocket, and slammed the door open. Jaclyn rushed into the hallway, her arm cocked back, ready to swing the wrench.

Looking down the empty hallway leading to the lobby and the end where she imagined Lloyd could've been hiding, she breathed in relief.

Nobody was there, not even the legion of black flies. The countless footsteps outside echoed across the room.

She squeezed her temples with one hand, wheezing lightly as she caught her breath. A solitary tear trickled down her cheek. It made its way to her chin, grew pregnant, and fell, turning invisible as it hit the floor.

Realizing that she already received a new message, Jaclyn grabbed her phone and opened it. Trixie had sent her something else.

"And they feed me," it said.

She shoved the phone back into her pocket. Her wheezing deepened. Jaclyn was beginning to gasp. She couldn't begin to calm herself until she wiped her mouth.

It took her a moment, but she forced herself to continue to the front door. The sound outside surrounded her, yet it didn't come any closer than a short distance away. It was constant, as if able to drone on for hours without slowing down.

She slid the wrench in one of the pockets inside the coat. As she zipped it up, the bar of cold metal touched her racing heart.

Swallowing, she opened the front door. Jaclyn realized just how long she slept. The red moon scowled at her from the night sky. She stepped back out of the dim moonlight and watched in speechless awe.

Cultists were marching together in droves, coming down Handerson with a purpose. All of them were wearing a long crimson robe that brushed the pavement. Its sleeves went past their fingertips and hoods draped over their foreheads. The shadows covered their faces better than any mask.

The group reached the horizon and beyond. They were travelling in the same direction that Jaclyn had gone last night, as if the crowd was a single organism.

However, one of the crimson figures stopped and turned to face her. It weaved through the rest of the crowd with ease. Its concealed face never drew away from hers.

As it approached her, Jaclyn's stomach turned. Her pulse ran faster than a racehorse. She felt her arms stiffen and abdomen tighten. Her legs turned into freshly dried cement. Jaclyn tried to scream, but her vocal cords wouldn't move.

The figure began to pull its hood back. A wide smile was twisted across its pale face, as if signaling Jaclyn—

And the grimace was *familiar*.

A pair of twitching hazel irises stared from underneath the figure's hood with a cold concentration. As it fell around the person's neck, Jaclyn saw the face of a woman. It was Sabrina, though she wasn't wearing her glasses.

The sight made Jaclyn wince. Clusters of centipedes were crawling in her stomach when she saw the change.

Her skin had an abnormal pus-like yellow hue. It was thin enough for Jaclyn to see traces of salmon-colored blood vessels bulging through. The overall texture of her skin looked like it had been pulled back, making her eyes jut out of their sockets.

Her pupils had enlarged, and the irises were narrow as paper. Her corneas were no longer a natural white. They had a sickly pale green swirl.

"Miss Ellsworth," she said in a low voice.

Jaclyn couldn't respond properly. She stood there, stammering, unable to form a single word.

"That's right, Miss Ellsworth. It's me. It's Sabrina. I've changed."

"H-*How*?"

"It's *progress*. It's proof of my *ascension*."

After a long, cold pause, Jaclyn asked, "Ascension?"

"That's what the solar eclipse *is*, Miss Ellsworth. A sign of *change*. New beginnings. Before we found this, each of us was going nowhere in life—miserable and lost. *Now*, we each have the chance to progress, and you'll experience it *with* us."

Jaclyn's heartbeat was irregular. She wanted to shriek a deafening *NO*. Her instinct was telling her to bolt as fast as she could—to run and never look back. To Hell with everything else. To Hell with her ankle. It could snap clean off but even that wouldn't stop her from hobbling up the highway.

To Hell with Trixie and Core—

No, she wouldn't allow herself to finish that thought. Not ever again. A jolt of shame slapped her across the face and brought her back down to reality.

If Jaclyn refused, she'd be revealed as an outsider. Sabrina wouldn't just unmask her as a non-believer. Jaclyn would be labelled things far worse than that. An apostate. A traitor. A deceiver. Someone who knew about their meetings and turned against them. Another person to end like Donnie Smith had.

She had to remind herself that the one response she could give was "Of course."

Sabrina's grin widened, revealing drying ruby-colored flecks. She grabbed Jaclyn's wrist and squeezed, cutting off all circulation. Jaclyn looked down at the woman's jaundiced hand. It was riddled with small, green blood vessels. Rough, brown nails extended from her fingers.

Jaclyn tried jerking her hand back. It was no use. Sabrina's grip was too strong. The woman tugged and pulled her toward the crowd. She couldn't believe someone so much younger had overpowered her with such ease.

Proof of my ascension.

The words rang loud and clear in Jaclyn's head again as they entered the crimson river. Sabrina lifted the red hood back over her head, and the surrounding members turned to them. Jaclyn's brow twitched as she raised it.

She saw the outlines of their faces but little else. All the details were hidden beneath the shadows cast by their hoods, even after a closer look. They looked down at Sabrina's hand, the jaundice covered by her sleeve and the night. The other members around them saw how her hand squeezed Jaclyn's wrist.

They faced forward again and kept walking.

"Sabrina," Jaclyn said in a frantic, raspy voice. Her mouth was drier than sun-bleached bones. The taste of cigarette ashes was overpowering. "Where are you taking me?"

There were no words. Just a tighter squeeze around Jaclyn's wrist. Her hand was beginning to go numb.

At first, she only saw the river of people stopping further down Handerson. They formed a large circle. They were mostly still, watching those who shifted to the center and sank beneath the asphalt surface.

For a fraction of a second, she looked further up the street. There was a silhouette that piqued her interest just as much. It wasn't another member of the cult, but the shape of an abandoned black limousine. She couldn't see anything else about the car. Not even the *Cadillac* sign on the front.

51.

Jaclyn tried to remember the kind of car the old woman at the diner had described. It *could* fit the description, but was that a limousine? No, that was impossible. What were the odds that Corey had been taken in by some rich family—

One that belonged to the cult of Dourmsburg.

She looked back at the shifting circle of crimson hoods. Jaclyn caught a glimpse of one other person who wasn't covered with a robe at the center. It was a young woman with blonde hair and a freckled face. The girl wasn't moving at first, hesitating, but then she sank below the pavement.

Jaclyn's eyes were wide open. Out of blind hope, only one person came to mind. "Trixie?" She paused, then shouted, *"Trixie?"*

But there was no answer. The crowd didn't even look back at Jaclyn. They continued to descend without any distraction.

Her eyes wandered further down Handerson. Cooper's was a little further ahead. The sign flickered as Sabrina tugged her wrist harder. She felt a dull pain throbbing in her abdomen again. As fast as she limped, there was no way for Jaclyn to keep up, even by force.

She and Sabrina stopped when they reached the circle. Jaclyn looked around. She was surrounded. If she couldn't catch up with Sabrina, she knew there was no way of outrunning a mob like that. When Jaclyn strained her eyes, she realized that the crowd had reached beyond the horizon.

Getting Trixie meant waiting for the entire crowd to clear off the street. Wherever she was led, the one thing Jaclyn had was her memory. Forgetting the path down under meant no way out.

Jaclyn never thought of being below a city before. She had never glimpsed the way underground systems were laid out. If it were the sewer system, most of the walkways would look the same. Memorizing the small details of each turn and every corridor—

It was an impossible task. The perpetual fatigue in Jaclyn's eyes and her throbbing stomach feeding on her body stopped her. The two things keeping her awake were Sabrina's unrelenting grip and her inflamed ankle.

Jaclyn felt her arm being released. Blood flowed back into her hand and fingers again. She looked at the center of the circle again, finding herself at the manhole. It was the same one she hurt herself on. Seeing her toes over the opening again, and the cover next to it, Jaclyn jerked her foot back.

She stared down into the narrow abyss, watching the top of Sabrina's covered head descend. Jaclyn wasn't sure, but thought she saw a flicker of dim light at the bottom.

"Hurry," someone behind her hissed. It sounded like the person's voice box was eroded, and all that remained was a forced whisper. The sound blended in with the moaning wind as it started up again.

"Go!"

'Move!"

"Hurry!"

The howling voices were rough as sandpaper. Getting down on the first step of the ladder, Jaclyn couldn't distinguish male voices from female ones amongst the crowd. They were one with the wind, spewing tiny bits of arid dirt at her.

Jaclyn felt a burst of pain when she stepped down. It felt like bones grinding against each other. The metal was icy to the touch. A clear slimy liquid coated it, like chemical rain. The pungent odor of sewage and rotting flesh rose from the abyss and invaded her nostrils.

Her hands trembled. She was about to slip and fall to the bottom. Her feet trembled uncontrollably. Jaclyn couldn't tell how far down the ladder she had gone. She only knew that sliding off and slamming against concrete meant breaking her spine.

She lowered one foot and placed it on the next step. She released her breath. Jaclyn felt as if she achieved the improbable. Each step was easier. Even the pain wasn't as harsh.

Jaclyn looked up. One of the crimson-robed cultists looked down at her. She caught a glimpse underneath the hood and faced back down at the ladder. Black fear rushed through her.

"God in Heaven," she whispered. "Was that even human?"

"Keep moving!" someone on the surface called.

She wondered if Trixie saw under any of their hoods tonight. There was no way she could've. Aside from Sabrina, Jaclyn didn't get much of a look herself. But the person watching her from the surface—the part of *his* face that was visible—

She thought if Trixie saw *any* of that, her brittle nerves would've snapped immediately. A glowing engine light was enough to trigger a panic attack. Seeing Sabrina or that man would've made her catatonic.

The thought of seeing the lower part of the man's face from the ladder made her nauseous. Her skin was coated in goosebumps and sweat as she reached the last step.

She couldn't tell if that *thing* was walking right above her head. Jaclyn tried not to think about it. But it was impossible to do so—his filthy shoes were about to dribble mud on her scalp. She moved just fast enough to avoid being stepped on and got off the ladder.

An old dim light shone through the walkway in front of her. She couldn't see how far away the next light was. It was enough to see the cracks in the aged pipes, and follow the figures surrounding her.

The smell punctured her lungs and burned the little hair in her nostrils. It was a struggle to keep the stomach acid down. She started wheezing again and covered her mouth and nose. Jaclyn couldn't help noticing that nobody around her was doing the same.

The nearest footsteps behind her moved closer. A gentle, audible breath brushed her neck and shoulders. It was chilling like the metal ladder. She took her hand away and breathed through her mouth again. Jaclyn wouldn't look back, only straight ahead at the group.

As she walked, Jaclyn recalled what she saw of that man's face, *Skin yellow as butter, peeling and scaly—jaw unhinged and hanging down—tongue black and bigger than a cow's, dangling and dripping saliva to the ground—Yea, though I walk through the valley of the shadow of death, I will fear no evil: for thou art with me; thy rod and thy staff, they comfort me.*

Yet her heartbeat was more unsteady than ever.

52.

Being awake was more of a burden despite everything. The lingering dimness throughout the tunnels further drained Jaclyn's energy. She thought about holding her eyelids open like she was in school. But now that the presence behind her had taken a step back, she had more reasons not to fall asleep. Jaclyn's limp already made her stand out. Doing anything else suspicious would've increased that.

As they turned right, she tried remembering any small details but started dozing off. She strained her eyes observing the crowd in front of her. Jaclyn was looking for any kind of map between them. It didn't matter if it was over a mobile device or a print map. It would've been something to steal if she didn't have any other choice.

But no, none of those she could see were holding either.

A shrill *squeal* echoed behind her. Jaclyn winced and looked down and to her left. A small black shadow scurried past the crowd. It was a fat, elongated oval running down the damp corridor like an electric current.

The crowd shifted around her as she tried to identify the thing. A glimpse at its long, thick tail, and there was no mistaking it—

A *rat*! An enormous *sewer rat!*

It stopped in the middle of the tunnel and stared back at Jaclyn. It stared at her with a pair of bulbous eyes that glowed dull green, like those of a cat in the dark. The rodent put its grubby hands up to its mouth. It smacked its lips, showing a pair of uneven, chipped incisors. The rat glanced at the cultists and ran further down the path.

When she started following them again, Jaclyn noticed several of them watching her. She couldn't even see their eyes but felt their suspicion. Jaclyn faced straight ahead with the others, pretending not to be monitored.

After a moment, the people who were looking at her turned away. They faced forward like the rest of the group.

What Jaclyn needed was to coax information out of them. Anything that would lead her to Trixie and perhaps even Corey. She didn't see any child, but a pre-teen boy could've been hidden in a different part of the crowd. Jaclyn knew that it was a shot in the dark at best—

But the car up at the surface could've been the car that woman at the diner had seen. She knew how ridiculous it sounded in her head. Jaclyn knew the odds were a billion to one.

It didn't matter though. Jaclyn didn't see another way to find him while she was in Dourmsburg, and a slim chance of finding Corey was still a chance.

She was tempted to cut through the crowd. The pain in her brain grew to a low, charring headache. The red presence was dominating. The group dictated that silence, so Jaclyn had no choice.

As they turned right again and took an immediate left, Jaclyn pondered about how people in the area already knew her name. The people in the Cozy Moon. The man in Cooper's—

Not just people in Dourmsburg. There was the emergency dispatch agent too. They didn't just speak to her by name when she didn't give anything to identify herself. These people also called her by name more than they did Trixie.

But why would they be more interested in Jaclyn? She couldn't make sense of the idea. It had to have been a coincidence. Jaclyn was just the person keeping the rich girl company.

It took all her strength to keep her eyes open. They had encountered two four-way intersections in the tunnels so far. At each left turn, the lead pipes had greater white discoloration caused by age and negligence. Tiny fragments on the walls had stained and chipped away, their dust lay on the floor.

It stuck to the bottoms of her shoes. The man-made pebbles sent tiny pins up her ankle. She tried to shake them off, but a stinking, wet substance stuck them to her soles. Jaclyn looked at her feet. She saw a group of small, brown roaches gnawing at a clump of greasy hair.

A wave of sickness swept over her. Turning her head away, Jaclyn couldn't push the realization away, that the hair was too long to be any animal's.

The silence behind her finally broke.

"Don't be afraid, Miss Ellsworth," someone said in a low, whispery drone. "The decay is a barrier we all have to pass."

Jaclyn was quiet, but after mustering the courage, she asked, "How much longer until we do? Will we see him soon?"

The voice behind wasn't a source of comfort. It only made the spiders crawling through her intestines multiply from dozens to hundreds.

It's the man with the unhinged jaw and the dangling black tongue, Jaclyn thought. *But how is he even speaking? How can he talk with his mouth like that?*

"Sooner than you think, Miss Ellsworth. You'll find what you've been needing."

"And what's that?"

A pause. The slow, cold breath moved down Jaclyn's neck again. It grew moist, like a cool, sticky mist. She didn't realize it, but the sensation made her wipe her mouth against her hand.

The voice said, "You've been lost. There's someone *missing,* Miss Ellsworth."

Jaclyn shivered and asked, "Do you know who Trixie Carter is?"

"Of course. But it's not her. She wasn't the one you've been looking for."

"What do you know about her?"

"That she has a world of potential before her. Still only twenty-one on the correct path, thanks to her father. She was but a lost little moth, but lucky enough to find us. She found the light she had needed for *years*."

"Years?" Even when Jaclyn repeated it, the implication astounded her. *Years*, not Trixie's entire life. "What was she like before then?"

"Solitary. Suicidal. She never told anyone though. It's something you can piece together when you see someone break, *often* enough."

The word hung over her like a thick black oil. *Suicidal.* Did Trixie ever attempt it? Jaclyn didn't want to ask, even if the answer was already out there. She was starting to believe these people had *watched* her at some point. The confidence in the voice behind her was all too real.

And Jaclyn didn't want to ask if Trixie had attempted suicide, fearing that she already knew the answer. "Did you know she'd come to this group?"

"Yes," the voice said.

"How?"

"We've been watching for a long time, Miss Ellsworth."

53.

Jaclyn would've stopped if she didn't have to keep up with the group. Her knees had stiffened and bowels had liquified. Despite the fatigue, her eyes were wide open, and her mouth was agape. The natural color had faded out of her skin.

"How long?" Jaclyn asked the voice.

The voice answered, "Ever since she started to blossom into an adult."

"Why then?" Jaclyn asked.

"It was the best time to intervene."

Jaclyn was fixating on the end of the tunnel straight ahead. It was a hundred yards away, but clearer than a cloudless day. There was a one-foot thick, old rusted iron door that stood at seven feet tall. It was ajar, welcoming the group as it streamed in.

A faint slow melody of chimes and piano floated in the air as Jaclyn limped toward it. The rhythm was irregular without any semblance of a beat. The tune was a cacophony of broken chords, and a strange ethereal echo. The sound was violating the eardrums.

Jaclyn felt the tiny hairs on her skin stand up from static electricity. She felt the cartilage in her joints pressing against her bones.

As she approached the iron door, Jaclyn saw people in front of her descend again. She thought about the possible size of the Anngologist cult. The realization that there were probably too many to count was a colorful explosion. If Dourmsburg had gatherings in the sewer system, what about other towns?

The idea made her organs churn. Since she had been in Smith and Son, Jaclyn was aware of a continuous mass presence. She glanced behind to see that the numbers extended beyond her field of vision.

It made her think of the trains that still went by these days. She virtually never saw them anymore, even on the road. When Jaclyn did, there was a habit of counting the cars. The hundred or so that usually passed by made her feel as if she'd have to wait at the railroad crossing the whole day.

"Why then?" Jaclyn asked.

"The young and capable are the most vital," the voice answered.

"Where were you watching?"

"We were right beside her. We always were."

"Did she know?" Jaclyn asked.

The voice was silent at first, but then he said, "She never needed to, Miss Ellsworth."

Jaclyn felt the heat from her skull rush out when she heard that, but she had to think of lies of her own. "A way to be by her even when she didn't know it—it was only necessary."

"That's right," the voice replied, pleased at what it heard.

"Were we there personally?"

"We?"

Jaclyn's throat froze. She was a mouse stuck in the corner, surrounded by a legion of hungry cats. She spoke with unusual confidence. "Of course, 'we.' I wouldn't be here if I didn't follow Anthony Charles."

"There are *outsiders* who would interfere, who'd infiltrate."

"Naturally, there would be," Jaclyn replied. "And it's more important than almost anything to identify them and get rid of them. They're the enemies of our progress. Our *ascension.*"

The voice remained silent. Jaclyn wondered why he hadn't reacted. Several people were listening to her conversation. If a single cell identified her as an intruder, the rest of the cells in the artery would flush her out.

Looking at her feet, Jaclyn noticed that she had been walking over small puddles of viscous, whitish saliva, splattered with globules of yellowed mucous. She recoiled in disgust but kept moving. Passing through the iron door, Jaclyn noticed a faint glow and a weak odor of smoke. It was almost too dark to see, but she began moving down the stone corridor.

It led to a spiral stairway with narrow steps. The blocks of stone she stepped on were oddly smooth. The minimal mortar between each brick was hardly visible, even with adequate lighting.

Jaclyn descended the steps with care, and began to see bits of flickering light in the distance. The smoke gently trailed throughout the corridor and smelled of burning wax and hair.

She jumped when the voice behind her spoke again.

"You speak of our ascension, Miss Ellsworth."

Another cold pause.

Jaclyn's body clenched up in the little room she had. She slouched and her shoulders hunched closer together, just to put an inch of distance between her and from the voice.

Did Trixie get this far and stay calm? Jaclyn doubted it. There was no way the girl hadn't fallen into a sheer panic attack by now—

But there were no sounds of someone being frantic. The crowd ahead of her kept to themselves. The other cultists were silent except for their droning footsteps.

Jaclyn realized that Trixie must've been coerced into the cult somehow. Knowing their rituals and degeneracy, she thought there wasn't anything they weren't willing to do. Everything was a game if it was for one of their strange rites.

She noticed the corridor ceiling. It had deep cracks extending as far as she could see. She realized that they were deliberate carvings when she looked closer. It was an ongoing abstract pattern of intertwined spirals and crescents.

"It's not something you'd know about," the voice told her. "You haven't had the time or attended the rites to show yourself capable."

But neither has Trixie, she thought. She only talked about the so-called 'miracles' of Anthony Charles.

"Do the ascensions always happen underground?"

"Of course not. They only do when there are hundreds of us at once."

"What about down *here?*"

"Almost never."

"How much has Trixie seen?"

"Little more than you, Miss Ellsworth."

"Has she ascended too?"

The voice was quiet as they reached the end of the staircase and walked down a level hallway. The source of the light was visible now. Jaclyn strained her eyes and saw that there were flickering candles further down, on either side of the hall.

Each had a malformed, sunken shape. They were each wrapped together within their own thin wicks. The closer she drew, the more she realized that the smell wasn't wax. The scent lingering throughout the passageway was akin to burning fat. But it wasn't like any animal she smelled before.

"Not in a way that she's aware of," the voice answered. "But *you* might have already gone far."

Jaclyn's body pulsated with shock at the statement. The truth had just been a premonition when the first text appeared on her phone—

But the truth was fully realized now.

Jaclyn didn't have the nerve to speak. As they approached the heart of the tunnel through the open doorway, she finally asked the question on her mind.

"Then why is it down here *now?*"

"Because of *you*, Miss Ellsworth."

54.

As they entered the next room, Jaclyn spoke in a dazed voice. "Me? Because of *me*?"

But there was no answer. Jaclyn stood there with a stunned look on her face and turned around. People were already splitting off on their own. She turned back and took in her surroundings.

The room was dwarfing her. The ethereal sounds lingered and pervaded the sewer's corridors like a thin mist. She was an ant under a magnifying glass. The area was four times the size of any church she'd been to. Jaclyn was at a loss for words at the architectural design.

She felt as if she were standing in a degraded European cathedral. Every side of the room had an array of asymmetrical, tall, gray stone pillars. They were bent and uneven like crumbling spines afflicted by scoliosis. There were connecting arches between them. They formed a second floor for more of the crimson cultists to gather.

The entire room was lit by malformed candles. They encircled each pillar and made their own long columns against the walls. The candles hung on top of one another above the second floor. The smell of the sewer had vanished—the odor of burning hair and fat dominated.

The walls and pillars had abstract patterns, identical to the ones carved throughout the corridors. The design was etched in wider patterns to the side of the room opposite the door.

The sides had thicker lines which seemed to be characters of a language without a Latin, African, or Asian origin. It was an alphabet Jaclyn had never seen before, without any traditional separation of words. Each of the letters had numerous harsh angles and roughened edges. They were all strung together like a mockery of cursive writing. Jaclyn realized that it had to have been a language of its own—something new and hidden from the rest of the world. Their arrangement made Jaclyn think they were an incantation to some strange spell.

There was an empty stage made from smooth obsidian under the thicker carvings. The sea of red robed figures stood a short distance from the stage. It was like an invisible border that no one dared to cross had been painted across the floor.

There was a large cluster of misshapen candles above the stage. They were packed closer together than any other cluster in the room. They were also the only unlit ones. A long black velvet curtain with splotches of fungus was hung from the ceiling to each side of the stage.

"Miss Ellsworth," another serpentine voice called.

As Jaclyn looked around, the red swarm slowed down and closed in around her. Seconds ago, a shifting circle of distance was between her and the cultists. Now the charcoal-colored circle of empty floor around her was shrinking. The red hoods were a legion of antibodies surrounding a pathogen.

"Miss Ellsworth," the voice hissed to her again like a creeping, frozen wind.

She tried to find where it was coming from but failed. Jaclyn realized the entity in the crowd that decided to speak to her was female.

She felt something wrap around her left hand and *squeeze*. The thing grasping her was cold and boney with a rough, prickly hide like a withering cactus. Jaclyn looked down at it, furrowed her brow and tried to scream.

At first, her mouth just hung agape. Her scream couldn't leave her throat, as if something hanging in the room had held her vocal cords still.

A crimson sleeve extended from the edge of the crowd around her. An inhuman appendage emerged. Its general outline was like a person's hand gripping hers.

Human biology began crumbling everywhere else. The fingernails piercing into Jaclyn's skin had an uneven gradient of dull grays, with the texture of graphite. The skin was a deep, murky yellow, beginning to darken into a dull golden. It was dotted with tiny spots of dried, maroon blood.

The cultist's arm had lost any trace of smoothness and natural hair. It turned into a hide of reptilian scales halfway, each with a brittle burgundy outline.

Jaclyn repeatedly jerked her hand back to escape its slimy touch.

"Miss Ellsworth," the entity called.

She pulled using her legs but didn't budge.

"Miss Ellsworth—I was *right.* Your boy…"

Jaclyn managed to sputter, "My-My *boy? Corey?"*

"Yes, the black Cadillac. Don't you remember?"

"What do you know about Corey?" As Jaclyn asked, she couldn't help thinking that this *thing* and its comrades had locked her child away somewhere. Once that thing gave her the word, she'd grab the wrench in her jacket and—

"I don't believe you recognize me, Miss Ellsworth. Please, let me re-introduce myself. I knew you'd be here. A *lot* of us did."

"Who-Who are you? How do you know about my son?" A blizzard cold went across Jaclyn's body as the entity's voice sounded more familiar.

"Miss Ellsworth, do you remember being told that Corey was seen going in a black Cadillac before you came to Dourmsburg?"

Jaclyn paused and answered, *"Yes—"*

"And do you know where it went?"

"No, I'm not sure."

"The limousine, Miss Ellsworth. The one up on the surface. It's here, with us. Don't you remember? I told you it would be."

She repeated the words back, reeling from the absurdity, *"Told—me?"*

"It wasn't long ago. You *do* know who I am. There's no way you don't."

Jaclyn wanted to blurt out the answer that lay deep in her stomach, but said, "No."

With its free hand, the entity grabbed the edge of its hood. "Of course, you do. We met in the Ace of Clubs, and I know you and Miss Carter were trying to see me again. I know because the rest of us know." It pulled back its hood.

Intense disbelief burst through her mind like a bomb, but she couldn't deny what was before her eyes. She couldn't deny this person's *ascension.* Jaclyn couldn't deny that she recognized the face.

"We know," the entity said. "Because we watch and listen from your pocket, Miss Ellsworth."

55.

"From my pocket," Jaclyn repeated in a total stupor.

She was stunned, captured in a thick, oozing vortex of speechless fear. When Jaclyn looked the entity in the face, she recognized the weak cheekbones, round and soft jawline, thin lips, narrow brow, and even the *earrings*! She had the *earrings* Jaclyn remembered from the Ace of Clubs too.

For a split second, the earrings had drawn her attention again. They had a hypnotic quality, even back at the diner. A portion of the jewels beneath their surface glimmered non-stop. The dull lighting surrounding them didn't change that.

The familiar drawing, the all *too* knowable sigil in the earrings like a coveted gem. It was the symbol of the solar eclipse, twinkling like it was trying to draw Jaclyn's eyes closer. Panic rose in her as she looked into the entity's eyes and her feet grew stiff.

The more Jaclyn tried to move from her spot, the stiller her legs were. She tried to kick—tried to *run*—

But any sudden jerk or spasm in her legs did nothing. She felt as if an invisible set of tentacles had been wrapped around her legs, immobilizing them. No matter how hard she tried, Jaclyn couldn't move an inch from the waist down.

"That's right, Miss Ellsworth," the old woman said, smiling with rows of little pointed teeth curling in her mouth. Her grin revealed the blackened gums behind her lips.

Jaclyn's mind was foggy. She was about to faint at the sight of that woman's face, but she was being held upright. Her eyes were kept open. She could feel tiny, invisible wires, thinner than cobwebs, pulling her eyelids wide open.

The old woman's face was a mask of amber scales with tiny flecks of a crusted burgundy scattered between the edges. The flesh around her cheeks and eye sockets had been pulled back.

Her nose had receded back into the skull. The nostrils had changed their shape and started elongating into narrow, vertical ovals.

Thick patches of her curly hair had already fallen out. Most of her scalp was already bare, leaving uneven strands of her scraggly, off-white mane.

Jaclyn couldn't turn away from the pair of oversized, glassy eyes staring back at her. Her head and neck were stuck in place. The enormous pupils and putrid, ripe green corneas burned her retinas.

Another pair of smaller orifices was above her eyes. They were shut tight and reduced to a midnight purple, like they were severely bruised. They were only a millimeter apart, and if one looked close enough—

Jaclyn could tell they were moving.

"He's *here*, Miss Ellsworth," the old woman said. "Your Corey—your so-called 'Corey,' he's *here*."

So-called? Jaclyn repeated it in her mind, unable to grasp what that meant.

Jaclyn wondered if this cult renamed the members. She thought that if it kept such a close eye on people, this was possible too.

"And he's been with *us* for some time. He's *ascended*, Miss Ellsworth! *Much* before the rest of us—"

Jaclyn recoiled at the thought. Not only was Corey among the cult, but *one* of them now? The old woman claimed he ascended like the rest of them. Like her. Like Sabrina. But the tone of her voice was awestruck.

Jaclyn gasped. This old woman was admitting that Corey had already gone down this path of degradation. He was further than most of the cultists here. Whatever her child had become, it was—

BECAUSE OF HER

—something that couldn't be undone.

The building inferno of hate and fear wouldn't pour out of her. She was a volcano that was about to erupt.

She wanted to scream a string of obscenities. She wanted to grab the woman by the back of her scalp and bash her hideous face against the floor until it was a bleeding pulp. She wanted to pull the wrench from her coat and smash the old woman's skull in until she was unrecognizable. Jaclyn knew she'd be ripped to pieces and eaten alive if she did, but in that moment, none of it mattered.

But Jaclyn couldn't do it. The violent rage kept building beyond the point of eruption because of that old woman's gleaming smile. Jaclyn's voice box and her arms refused to move, like the invisible wires kept them immobile.

Her face was directed toward the stage. Jaclyn tried to pivot away, tried to forcefully free herself, but it all still failed. She was just wasting her energy.

The wicks of the candles above the obsidian slab were beginning to smoke. They formed wavering gray tails that rose to the air and dissipated. A collective silence overpowered the room.

After a moment, a faint *click-clack* echoed through the area.

Jaclyn watched as the toes of a pair of all-white Oxfords peeking out of the curtain. Then, a man, six foot eight inches tall, limped onto the stage. It looked like his right foot was permanently injured. His skin was nearly as pale as his suit. It was contrasted only by a scarlet collared shirt with the usual ebony crescent moons on the corners.

His jet-black hair was combed back to perfection. A pair of glasses perched on the long, narrow bridge of his nose. They were thick enough to conceal his eyes entirely. That, and his hollow cheeks made him look like he was in his seventies.

As the man appeared, Jaclyn was astounded to think that he was in his early thirties. Somehow, he looked decades younger in every image she saw before. Even younger than his real age.

His stuck his hands deep in his pockets. Jaclyn thought it was an odd gesture until she looked closer at them. She strained her eyes, realizing he was wearing a pair of white gloves.

Charles raised his left hand out of his pocket and hovered it in the air. He smirked a little, as if to signal the crowd.

The instant he did, they cheered together in a lunatic fury. The atomic bomb of sound paralyzed Jaclyn until it finally died down.

Then, Anthony Charles said in a slow, powerful baritone, "Good evening, my children."

56.

A fanatical, hiss-like cheer exploded from the crowd. Jaclyn shrank away from the overwhelming noise. It wasn't the sight of those surrounding her—but the noise that made her feel the walls of a prison going up around her. The noise down here, and the shrieking she heard just the night before.

As she looked at the towering scarecrow on the obsidian slab, Jaclyn couldn't believe her eyes. This man was supposed to be in his early thirties but looked like a premature relic.

Anthony Charles raised both hands in the air, signaling the crowd to quiet down. They obeyed in an instant. The silence spread across the room like the burst of an invisible grenade.

"My children," he said. "There are new pilgrims with us on this night. And what a night for them to join us. Become *one* with us. *Consume* with us." He lifted his covered hands up, his grin revealed blackened gums and a mouth full of dagger-like teeth protruding from them. "And blessed is the act of consumption."

"Blessed is consumption," the hooded cultists chanted back in a dull unison.

"Consumption is *life*," Charles proclaimed.

"Consumption is life," the crowd chanted back.

"Consumption is *knowledge*," Anthony Charles declared.

"Consumption is knowledge."

Charles balled his fists and shook them in the air as he cried, "Consumption—is—*power*!"

All the scarlet-robed cultists shot their hands into the air at once. When they repeated the final mantra, it was louder than the rest. The echo was potent enough to make Jaclyn tremble. She saw a few of the candles flicker. Charles lifted his face toward the ceiling grinned even wider. He breathed deeply, then exhaled.

Lowering his head, and finally his arms, he smiled at the crowd. The room quieted on his cue again.

After a moment of silence, Charles said, "My children, at last, the moon will be new again. This midnight will be most sacred of all—it marks the beginning of a new Cycle."

Jaclyn furrowed and cocked her brow.

"Where the next sheep to follow us are ready to be chosen," Charles said. "But *first*, there's someone among us who needs to be saved."

A bolt of anxiety struck Jaclyn's heart. Her rage exploded, as she shouted, *"YES!"*

The word escaped her mouth, but she wasn't on her own. Her outburst had been yanked out of her like a stubborn, rotten tooth.

Charles flicked his wrists and the shout was pulled out of Jaclyn's mouth again. She didn't see his gesture but fell dizzy with disbelief. Despite her senses, she couldn't reel around what she'd done—

Or, what had been done *through* her.

Anthony Charles directed his gnarled grin at her and moved his spindly fingers back and forth. "Then come forward, my child, and be *saved*."

Jaclyn felt the invisible threads on her hands and feet now. As the crimson sea parted to make a clear path for her, her right foot was pulled off the ground to take her first step, followed by the left.

Her limbs were being moved in a way that resembled a slow, natural walk. Jaclyn's movements were stilted as she walked down her narrow pathway. She looked more like a poorly crafted wooden doll with every step.

Jaclyn tried her best to scream. It didn't matter that nobody outside the cult would hear her. She needed her voice to act of her own will.

But she couldn't even whisper. It was as if something had sewn her lips shut. Every failed attempt started eating away at any willpower she had left. She was a rat thrashing around in a steel trap.

Each step she took made her shrink as the red sea froze for her, and she approached the black slab. She looked up at Anthony Charles like a frightened mouse—the man who stood at damn near seven feet tall.

It shouldn't have been possible, but his smile twisted and widened even more. His mouth could start unhinging. It hit her as she saw the creases in his teeth.

Jaclyn was finally able to move her eyes.

She searched for anyone who stood out with her limited movement. Anyone who was shorter than the rest. For someone who was about five feet tall. She didn't even need to see a face beneath the hood. It didn't matter—at least not then.

But no such luck. She didn't see anyone below the average adult height. It didn't mean Corey wasn't out there though. Jaclyn didn't even have the chance to examine the rest of the crowd.

When she reached the front of the crowd, Charles stopped moving his fingers back and forth. He straightened and stiffened them, and Jaclyn was stopped at the front row.

"*Rise*, my child," he commanded her. "Stand up *with* me and be saved!" Charles knelt and offered a gloved hand. Charles jerked the fingers of his other hand up.

Jaclyn felt the strings jerk her feet onto the short stage. The pain in her ankle fired off like a shotgun blast. All her thoughts were an explosion of curses, but her physical reflexes had been snuffed.

When she stood before Charles, he still towered over her. Being close to him didn't make a difference. He was a skyscraper that was about to collapse on top of a small bungalow.

"Your name is *Ellsworth*, isn't it?"

Jaclyn nodded, seeing the unusual creases in his face. *And this man's supposed to be thirty-one. He looks like an old man with a full head of black hair.*

Charles announced, "You came to us with a terrible illness, Miss Ellsworth." He peeled off his gloves.

"Illness?" Jaclyn repeated, staring at his left hand and cocking her eyebrow in disbelief.

Though Charles' hands were naturally long, the left showed hints of discoloration and malnourishment. He had small green bruises on his skin. Jaclyn noticed another detail on the surface, more so than the others. It was a mass of bold scar tissue. Along with his eyes and foot, this was the third of his apparent wounds.

Jaclyn couldn't tell if it was a birth mark. It was pink, like an old wound but faded enough to be years—maybe even decades—old. She thought Charles was either born with it and built an obsession around it to turn it into an icon of his own, or it was self-inflicted just after inventing this faith in his head. It was a mark of the solar eclipse, engraved permanently into the back of his hand.

"Yes, my child," he answered, putting his hands firmly on her ribs. "A grave illness, I'm afraid."

57.

"A *grave* illness," Jaclyn repeated, droning to herself. She thought about her coughing fits, wheezing and shortness of breath. "No. That's not true. I have my share of problems, but I don't have anything nearly *that* bad."

As she finished her sentence, Jaclyn uttered a prayer in her head that this man—this *prophet* of the flesh and blood coven was wrong. But the most exhausting thing was acting as if she wanted to be at this ritual at all. It wasn't just knowing she'd be torn to ribbons after making the wrong move—

It was realizing that if Corey *were* out there in the crowd, he'd recognize her. Then, she'd somehow break free of the strings holding her in position and run the Hell out of there. Run the Hell out to start life anew.

Breaking free *was* possible. She needed to believe that. After all, there were stories of adrenaline-stricken mothers finding miraculous strength to lift a car and save their trapped children.

And Corey was either waiting for just the right time to cut through the crowd toward her, or—

Or he'd already begun to resent her and watched her with a cold indifference. At that point, it may have been to late to change anything. For him, at least.

Jaclyn's heart fell to her stomach. If he did feel that way, and saw her with a cold emptiness, she wouldn't blame him.

"It isn't quite the case, unfortunately," Charles corrected her. "You've come here after coughing up blood. I'm wiser than you might think. I *know* you, Miss Ellsworth. Whether you realize it, you've come to us with a cancer."

"A—a *cancer*?"

"Of the lungs, I'm afraid, and the tumors are starting to spread. You've known this already. It's been impossible for you to accept. But that's why you've come here. You're here because you can be saved."

The touch of his hands against her ribs was like dry ice, crawling underneath her skin. She felt her breath stop at the revelation. She managed to look down at Anthony Charles' hands. Jaclyn's eyes widened at his left hand, and the dull ache in her abdomen turned to a beating pulse. The chilling sting spread out and branched like a network of blood vessels. It crawled through her body until it reached her collarbone and pelvis.

Anthony Charles shouted, "*Breathe*, Jaclyn!"

He flexed his fingers. A set of tiny strings that felt like titanium cobwebs jerked her diaphragm and the back of her throat. Jaclyn suddenly gasped for air. A deep, hoarse wheeze followed.

The mark on Charles' hand started changing color. It went from a faded fleshy pink to a deep scarlet. Then, a dark burgundy with flecks of maroon and black.

The air was vacuumed out from Jaclyn's lungs. She could feel them flooding again. It was as if they were being filled with a thick liquid that turned to solid matter.

Jaclyn tried to squirm but was paralyzed from below her neck. She looked at Charles, seeing that his right hand was balled into a twitching fist. Gasping for air, she didn't feel anything moving through her body. She was a fish, stupidly moving its jaw up and down after being plucked from the ocean by a fisherman.

God in Heaven, Jaclyn thought, looking up toward the sky. *Please help me. I think I'm drowning—*

She looked back down at Charles' left hand again. The bruising spread across the entire surface like the bone had shattered from a car accident. The color blossomed into a dark eggplant. Only one thing stood out from it: the mark of the eclipse. It transformed into a full midnight black.

His hand was thinner by the second. The muscle and any traces of fat were wasting away at an unnatural rate. Jaclyn could see the bone and vascular structures protruding from the skin. The knuckles of every digit in his hand would be visible if one looked hard enough.

Circular growths rose through the top layer of his skin. There were a few at first, but they multiplied, covering half the surface of his hand.

It shocked her whole body. She felt as if someone had pushed through the center of her brain.

Jesus, help me. I'm going to die, and I can't even speak—

Charles let go of her, bending down and cringing in pain. Jaclyn felt the solid matter melting and evaporating from her lungs. The small branches of icy pain released their grip on her innards and exited from her throat.

The numerous uneven growths—no, *tumors*—receded. They washed back into Charles' hand and started to vanish. It was like the cancer had eaten itself away.

Despite his own bodily pain, Charles stood back up and lifted his hands in his air. "*Breathe*, Jaclyn!" he exclaimed.

She gasped as if she had been chained to the bottom of a lake and was finally breaking through the surface. Even stranger, she didn't feel the tug of the strings at all. Neither on her throat, nor her diaphragm.

The realization dawned on her. She didn't feel any pain in her abdomen. No wheezing. No shortness of breath either. Not even the slightest grip on her throat to send her into another coughing fit. In fact, she didn't have the urge to cough at all.

When was the last time she felt like *this*?

Jaclyn didn't remember feeling *anything* like this since her teens. She thought that whatever Anthony Charles did to her was a sudden, enormous injection of youth. She thought her lungs didn't match the rest of her body at all. Any minute, her body would reject them altogether.

Jaclyn didn't realize it, but she was breathing deeply for a clear stream deep gasps for air. They transformed into calmer breaths, slowing down with each one.

This had to have been temporary, she reflected. What Charles did couldn't be anything more than a cheap dose of medicine. But she had never breathed this well with any over the counter drug. The evidence of something more was before her eyes and passing through her windpipe—

Yet she still couldn't quite take it in.

Charles hid his left hand behind his body and raised the right. He exclaimed with a grin, "Her cancerous lungs have been purged *clean* by the consuming fire!"

The second he did, the cult slipped into a total uproar. Jaclyn noticed the nearby candles flickering again. As she did, she noticed Charles wasn't moving his hands at all.

That last stunt of his must've been a bit too much, she thought. *But why go through the trouble?*

Jaclyn didn't know if blunt force would break her free of the invisible wires at this point. But at least she could move independently from the neck up.

58.

Jaclyn scanned the frenzied crowd. None of them were shorter than five foot four. But these people were indistinguishable.

Among the cult of flesh and blood, there was *someone* who stood out. She was the only other person not dressed in a full robe. Her body was limp, propped up by the cultists on either side. Her eyes were closed, and her mouth hung open like that of a dead horse.

Was the poor girl—

No, she had just fainted. And no wonder.

The way she described meeting the Anngologists, it sounded like a gathering at a televised church. The moment she fainted was anyone's guess, but it had to have been long before Anthony Charles' stunt.

It could've been the moment she reached the bottom of the ladder and entered the sewer system. Jaclyn was amazed she hadn't fainted herself—especially after seeing the limp-tongued man who followed her down the stairwell. The memory alone still made her shudder. She wouldn't sleep through the night. Not unless she got back to Corey and—

"Trixie!" Jaclyn shot the word like a spastic bullet. *"Trixie!"*

She saw the girl being steadied up again. Trixie's head moved from one side to the other as her body was adjusted. Her eyes opened halfway, looking at the stage.

Thank you, sweet Jesus, Jaclyn thought. *She really is alive.*

She looked closer, and a sudden jolt of fear struck her. Even if she managed to get Trixie back up to the surface and *away* from Dourmsburg—

It would still be too late to save her.

Jaclyn noticed the changes in Trixie when she squinted. Trixie's eyes were beginning to draw back in their sockets. The skin on her face had started to pull back around her eyes and mouth, and already turned a yellowish tint.

And they feed me.

Jaclyn whipped her head around and looked at Charles. His hand in the air was still, and he smiled at his crowd.

"As we get closer to midnight," he said as red sea of followers simmered down, "We must *give back* to our youth, for their dedication and their enthusiasm, as theirs has the most *life* and the most *value*."

A cheer erupted from the hooded audience.

Midnight? Jaclyn thought. *What time is it? How long was I following these people underneath the city? The pain made it feel like it could've been hours, but how was I supposed to know? Is it really close to midnight? Lord, it can't be. There's no way.*

"Just as we give back to the feeble and gray every night *during* each cycle," Charles continued. "We will end it on this night when we anoint our young with blood and save them through consumption."

Jaclyn screamed from the obsidian stage like a lunatic, *"TRIXIE!"*

But that was no use. Even at her loudest, Jaclyn's screams were drowned out by the sea of followers before her. Crowd or no crowd, she was only screaming into oblivion.

Anthony Charles wouldn't look at her. Yet, as if he *heard* her, he rose his arms up and smiled toward the ceiling.

On cue, the front row of cultists went into a statuesque stillness. They converged together in a single horizontal line. Not an inch of space was left between them. As their shadowy faces stared directly at Jaclyn, she gasped.

Jaclyn kicked her right foot back to try and get away. She couldn't move far but heard a *snap* as she did. She didn't sprain her other ankle—

But broke the invisible threads that held it down! Jaclyn *broke* it! She couldn't believe it!

Just as she was thanking her blessings, the combined row of crimson hoods advanced toward her. They walked onto the stage, their arms outstretched. Jaclyn's eyes lingered on their long, undernourished arms. Their hides were completely saffron, covered in scales, with oversized fingers with dark jagged nails.

She caught a glimpse of their faces and let out a deathly shriek. Jaclyn moved her left foot back and felt the strings about to snap. As she stumbled over and her body hit the smooth slab, a wave of pain passed through her back.

The fragments spread throughout her body once both of her feet were free again. Before she could try to stand up again, the legion of gnarled hands grabbed her arms and legs. The invisible strings still gripped her, but she managed to squirm anyway.

A few of the strings on her wrists and legs snapped like thin, weak hair. Most of them held onto her, but they didn't compare to the tightening hold of the cultists. They were squeezing her limbs enough to cut off her circulation. The pain throbbed and sharpened as she kept trying to kick herself free.

But the cultists weren't fazed. All at once, they lifted Jaclyn's body up and carried her to the edge of the stage.

She yelled one more time, *"TRIXIE!"*

The figures carrying her still didn't respond. As they carried her off the slab, she noticed Trixie's face. Tiny scales had already grown on her cheeks, replacing her freckles.

The girl turned to Jaclyn as she was pulled back into the dense crowd. The now-deformed young woman's eyes cracked open again. Just for a second, the two brushed against each other.

Trixie's voice was groggy, but audible enough to hear, "J-Jaclyn?"

Before she could respond, Jaclyn looked to the figures propping her body up, and down at their feet. Between them was a short, lone syringe. Its cap was missing. The metal tip glistened in the candlelight.

A loud *clang* sounded off. It sounded like a combination of an old ruined bell, and an enormous sheet of glass shattering into a million pieces. It was almost enough to make Jaclyn deaf.

Anthony Charles still had his arms in the air with the gnarled, toothy smile across on face. "My children, *midnight* is upon us."

The cultists holding Jaclyn stood still, propping her up, just like Trixie. She imagined a small metal needle pricking the back of her neck, followed by a cold thin stream of liquid.

She wasn't pricked, but the crowd near her shifted. The cultists holding Trixie up as she drifted in and out of consciousness wove through the crowd, past the front row, and toward the corner of the room to the right of the curtain.

One of them let go of her, bent down, grabbed a latch on the floor. The figure pulled it up, as a loud creak echoed through the room. Jaclyn saw a *dark*, narrow passageway beyond the trap door.

59.

He held his right hand in the air to stop the crowd, and followed the cultists who carried Trixie. As he disappeared down the trap door with them, he lowered his hand. He slid them in his pockets, hiding them from the crowd.

Jaclyn saw this and thought, *The bruising on his hand—did any of them even see it? How wouldn't they have noticed it? Or maybe, it didn't matter. Trixie never mentioned it before. Maybe all they cared about was the 'miracle' that happened.*

Most of the crowd followed them, except for the figures holding Jaclyn's arms.

But the mark on his hand, she realized. It changed color. It glowed a strange black, but that's what happened when he cleared my throat and maybe even my lungs. It's not just a symbol these people wear. It must have something to do with how he pulled that off. It was the scar on his left hand. The red sign on it was a catalyst of power—

One of the cult's mantras rang through her head again. Consumption is power.

Just what the Hell did that mean?

The enormous crowd continued to pass by them. They gathered at the trap door like water pooling in a funnel. Jaclyn noticed the red figures at her sides watching them, wondering when their cue to move would come.

When their gnarled fingers loosened around her arms, she jerked to her left. She felt several *snaps* against her right wrist and her arm was free. She pulled the old wrench from her coat pocket and swung it to her left.

It *cracked* one of the cultists' foreheads. She swung to the right and hit against the other cultist's mouth. Jaclyn sprinted and didn't look back. She heard two dull *thuds* behind her.

The other cultists hadn't turned to look. When she moved up closer to them, she heard them mumbling in an indiscernible jargon. Jaclyn thought they must not have heard the sound—or the task was too important to go back.

It must have been the latter. Otherwise, the innumerable members of the legion would've sprung. This realization dawned upon her like a parasite worming its way up her innards and eating away at her heart.

Some of the cultists had already been marked disposable. Her premonitions about Trixie loomed over her head as she moved.

The two she knocked out would get back up any minute. Although Jaclyn had bought herself some time, it was limited. So, looking back to see if they were unconscious was too much of a risk. Either those two were out cold, or they weren't. Going back for *any* reason would take up the precious time she had.

Corey had to be somewhere in the crowd ahead.

She wove her way into the fire red lake. Crouching down, she moved past the outer layer. If Jaclyn kept her body low, she'd be harder to detect. Moving toward the midsection, she tried to formulate a plan.

Even though she hadn't seen him before, *one* of these people had to be shorter than the rest. Anthony Charles said it himself. The Anngologist cult *needed* their young. The fire in their hearts was the very reason for its growth.

Trixie was a fine example of that, Jaclyn thought. *Even if she didn't realize it.*

She'd make her way to Corey and Trixie but find a different route out of this chapel of human decay. Then, through the sewer system and finally, out of Dourmsburg itself.

Going back the way she came wouldn't work. Trying to do that would've made her too obvious. The cultists knew that path by heart. A different way out was little more than guesswork. She realized it was *nothing but* guesswork.

There wasn't anything else to go on. Even then, Jaclyn figured there must've been several other routes away from the chapel. The trap door was enough evidence of that, but if she eventually found her way back up through a different manhole, Jaclyn would still home free.

What did Charles plan for Trixie? God, the thought of it made *her* shudder. They would anoint her with blood, he said.

What they'd do to her at midnight could involve the groaning and muffled cries Trixie heard just last night.

What about getting her away from *Anthony Charles?* He was the man with a cult and other unexplained powers in his spidery fingers. Above all that, the girl was a precious resource to him. A lifeblood of some kind.

Despite the grinding in her ankle and organs, Jaclyn would have to summon the strength to wrestle both her child and the girl away from Charles.

This was a man with the power to move her body around like a fleshy marionette. Lord only knew what else. Charles was weaker for now, but that didn't mean he wasn't capable anymore.

Jaclyn saw his bruises after he pulled her to the stage. It wouldn't take much more to do that again. His left hand was damn near ruined, but that would only last so long.

If Charles managed to make a paralyzed man walk again, it would've done a number on him too. But he recovered from that, and this would've been no exception.

A strange thought occurred to her as she approached the trap door.

Suppose his hand was severed. What then?

Advancing to the front of the crowd, she felt a black apparition overshadowing her—the chances of escaping at all. The odds were bordering on sheer hopelessness.

Taking the two cultists down was a miracle. Even having a weapon like the old wrench was pure luck.

Jaclyn came to the edge of the trap door and peered toward it. She winced but bent further, like she was staring down the eyeless socket of the Leviathan, dwelling at the bottom of the ocean.

She saw the beginning of a rough iron ladder and started climbing down. There was no telling just how deep underground the cult's lair went. There could've been numerous catacombs that went ever deeper than this.

Jaclyn felt the first couple steps wiggle as she got on them. It was even less maintained than the ladder and corridors to the surface.

With each step down, Jaclyn pictured a second labyrinth of pipes, rats and cockroaches. She could see a vague, dim light below. It was more minimal than any other sewer.

As the candlelight grew brighter, so did the markings along the walls. They weren't carvings, but lines made from a reddish maroon substance. It was smeared and dry. The overall painting was erratic and uneven, though it had the same pattern as the chapel.

"Good," she heard Charles say below. "Once the first cut has been drunk, we commence our penultimate feast before the Cycle ends. Then, my children, we choose another pair."

The last words struck Jaclyn. Another *pair*?

Reaching the bottom, she found herself behind a moderate-sized crowd. There were no corridors. She was standing in a single large room, with everyone crowding around the center.

Jaclyn stayed still. Her skin had turned paper white. The blood in her heart was boiling with furious terror. Her stomach was watery. The hairs on the back of her neck prickled and stood upright.

She couldn't breathe. Jaclyn was choking, like the air around her had disappeared.

Near the center of the room, Anthony Charles was drinking from an obsidian goblet. He raised it, drinking with a satisfied greed. His left hand was restoring its natural state. The deep purple bruises were fading to a lighter tint. A drop of glimmering ruby snaked down his chin.

At the center of the room, Trixie lay in the nude on a blocky wooden table. Four cultists stood at its corners, holding her limbs down. Her wrists were spread wide apart, as if she were to embrace someone. Trixie's legs were held together and down to the table by her calves.

Her eyes had rolled up to the back of her head. Jaclyn could only see her yellowing corneas. Trixie's mouth hung open and unhinged, like Donnie Smith's. The gums were faded charcoal, about to become pure ebony. Trixie's teeth had already begun separating and turning uneven.

A stainless-steel dagger lay next to her head. Its edges were soaking wet and gleaming in the candlelight.

Her throat was slashed open like a cow at the butcher's. A pool of fresh blood surrounded it, sliding to the edges of the table and dribbling down to the floor.

Anthony Charles took the empty goblet from his lips. His constant sneer showed that his teeth were stained in deep red. He looked down at Trixie's neck, and then straight into Jaclyn's eyes.

When he directed his left palm at her, she felt something coil around her wrists and *squeeze* like a boa constrictor. He closed his fingers into a fist, and Jaclyn's hands were forced behind her back. As Charles lowered his hand, Jaclyn was pushed down onto her knees with an unbearable force.

Then, she felt a narrow *prick* into the back of her skull. She felt a warm rush of liquid disperse spreading around her scalp.

Jaclyn's vision blurred. She grew dizzy. Her surroundings melted, the colors converging and spinning around her. She lost her balance, turned limp, and felt her body hit the floor.

Charles' voice had a gentle echo around her, though she couldn't see him. "Cute, her thinking she was being sneaky. Luring her down here with the girl only made her do the work *for* us. Await further instructions. I have—*other* plans for her."

60.

When Jaclyn woke up, she saw through a cloudy haze. Everything around her was still a blur of dim colors. A flash of pure white light switched on somewhere around her, burning her eyes.

She squeezed them shut and cursed like that was the medicine for the pain. Even with her eyes closed, the light still burned a bright red.

She lay stretched on her left side. Jaclyn's body wasn't supported by the wall behind her, yet she was almost sitting upright. Once her eyes adjusted, she realized she was slouching over. Her midsection was arched toward the floor. She was too close to it not to fall over. Opening her eyes, Jaclyn knew she was suspended by her arms and sat up straight.

It didn't take long for her to notice that she was bound by the wrists. Whatever was holding her wrists in place had a metal ring tugging against each of her hands. Handcuffs? No, these were too wide to be standard handcuffs. They were wrist shackles.

Jaclyn pulled her hand down, feeling the links of a stern metal chain clicking together. Her heart rose to her throat. She sighed and looked down at the floor. They hadn't taken her out of the room. The real difference was the glare of bright electric lighting from the ceiling. Everything else was the same, as the room where Trixie was—

Oh Jesus—oh sweet Jesus, Trixie—

But her body and the table were both gone. The only remnants of her were the bits of scarlet drying on the floor. Jaclyn hung her head, holding her eyes shut as fresh tears welled up at the thought.

Words were passing through her mind. Her tears wouldn't flow until Jaclyn couldn't hold them back anymore. A pair of hot tears formed, slid down the ends of her eyelashes, and fell, staining the floor.

"Trixie," she said, her voice shaking. After a moment's struggle, Jaclyn said, "I'm sorry. I'm *so sorry.*" Another pair of tears hit the floor. "You just needed someone. And I failed you. I…" Her speech faltered here. "I failed both of you."

Click-clack.

The sound was just loud enough for her to hear.

Click-clack.

The noise was far away from the room—it sounded like it was an unknown distance above and beyond the chapel. But Jaclyn twitched at it anyway. Her eyes squeezed shut even tighter. It was the sound of an approaching storm.

The noise could've been a million other things, she told herself. Anything. Someone who discovered she went down here. *Yes*, another outsider. A person who wasn't another cell of the cult.

The *click-clack* grew louder. Jaclyn's heart jumped. It was getting closer every time.

Corey. That's what the sound was. It was Corey sneaking away from the cultists and coming back for her. Yeah, of course, and he'd find her. Corey was always a smart boy. It had to have been him.

Click-clack. The noise crackled through the floor right above her. Even if it wasn't *him*, it was someone about to take her out of this room. It didn't matter who. Anybody, if it just wasn't—

A deep, smooth baritone murmured right in front of her face. She felt his breath as he said, "Open your eyes, child."

She did and screamed, pressing her back against the cold, rough wall behind her. Anthony Charles was crouching down right in front of her.

His fixed smile was wider than ever. Tiny specs of red stained his abnormally thin lips, black gums, and yellowed teeth that resembled a crocodile's more than a man's.

She stared deep into Charles' glasses. They reflected a blurred, distorted image of her. Jaclyn was gazing into a pair of endless pits where only a stirring emptiness gazed back. She couldn't see his eyes behind them. Only remnants of her own.

The usual attire was gone. Charles had replaced it with a cloak, much like that of his followers. Unlike all the others, his was black as night. The edges were crimson as the blood on his teeth. The hood had the sign from the back of his left hand.

It didn't conceal any part of his face though. The light was far too harsh.

"Wh-Where is she?" Jaclyn asked.

A brief chuckle. Charles replied, "You should already know that. Nothing's changed with you. You've always had a habit of denying the obvious, haven't you?"

Jaclyn struggled to catch her breath. "What do you mean, 'nothing's changed'?

"You've made a lot of talk on the road. A lot of it sounded—*quite ambitious.* I know you've come here, looking for someone. Corey Archer."

A flush of pure rage erupted in her. She pulled against her chains in a furious struggle. Her face was almost close enough to tear into Charles' with her teeth. Thinking about it tickled her.

Charles lowered his hood, giving her a clear chance. He didn't move back an inch. He didn't even flinch.

"You son of a bitch," Jaclyn snarled. *"If you touched him—"*

He broke out into giddy laughter. His mouth stretched down further than a human jaw should. It silenced her. That was the first time she'd ever heard him laugh before. Her blood turned cold like pond water.

"Then you'll do *what*, exactly?" Charles rested his chin on his left hand, reminding her of what he could do.

Jaclyn saw the state of it. Save a few tiny pale green bruises, it had gone back to its natural color. She remembered the small recovery he had after drinking from his goblet.

Observing his face, she had a tougher time believing that a man in his early thirties looked like this. There were several creases in Charles' cheeks, but none in his forehead. There were hints of heavy bags under his bespectacled eyes, as if the man never slept. Most of the little wrinkles were between his eyebrows. They gave the impression of tiny hairs until one looked close enough.

But the folds in his skin weren't anywhere else. If he was lying to seem younger, he would've had creases in the rest of his face. Forehead lines. Crow's feet. Tear troughs. Marionette lines. Creases under the lower lip.

None of those were present. Those parts of his face had a strange youth about them. Then again, Jaclyn considered, his wrinkles weren't caused by aging at all.

She couldn't say why, but Jaclyn felt a strange and deep sense of déjà vu. She hadn't heard the name *Anthony Charles* until his company was already a tech empire. Yet she couldn't help thinking they met before tonight. Something about his face told her it had happened *years* ago.

"You weren't lied to," Charles told her. "The woman you spoke with maybe two nights ago? She was never lying to you."

Scrunching her face, she shut her eyes again, refusing to look at Charles. "She was. She *had* to have been lying."

"And what makes you say that?"

"I didn't see him anywhere. None of these—*people* could've been him."

"You must not have very good eyes," Charles replied, amused. "Then again, who am I to talk?"

He grabbed his thick glasses and pulled them down the bridge of his nose. Jaclyn looked into his eyes, flinching at the sight. His right eye was unnaturally wide, as if it were a glass prosthetic. It bulged out of the hollow socket and quivered on its own.

But Jaclyn knew it wasn't fake. Though the pupil consumed the entire iris, the remnants of the cornea had a pale green tint. Jaclyn peered closer at it anyway, out of a morbid curiosity, a vague outline of tiny purple blood vessels around it. Looking into his right eye was staring into a flickering, black abyss.

His left eyelids were closed all the way. It was surrounded in a wide line of pink scar tissue. Judging from the depth of the socket, he didn't have a left eye anymore. Why he never replaced it with a fake one, she had no idea.

Shuddering at first, Jaclyn asked, "What happened to your eye?"

Charles shivered at the question as if it reminded him of the agony again. He responded with a forced, painful chuckle and replied, "There was an *interesting* run-in with the man I met after I left home." He pushed his glasses back up his nose. "And I didn't want to forget why it all happened."

A moment of silence. "You know that old woman I talked to at the Ace of Clubs?"

"Of course."

"Who is she?"

"One of many," Charles answered. "*Hundreds*, I should say."

"I see. I think I understand. People who were planted. Right?"

Anthony Charles nodded, widening his grimace.

"You said something about Trixie being one of a pair, that she was chosen. I guess that makes me the other person."

A chuckle. "And when did you get so smart?"

Jaclyn paused, then asked, "If that woman was telling the truth, was Corey in Dourmsburg the whole time he's been missing? Obviously, you'd know the answer."

"No. Not for the most part. It was never *nearly* that simple."

"Then, where is he?"

"Still down here, don't worry," Charles answered. "Your kid was one of the first ones to show up tonight."

61.

Hearing that made Jaclyn's stomach turn over. God only knew how far Corey had been sucked into the cult of the red sign. It didn't matter that he was eleven. Fanaticism knew no bounds. There were children his age in the Lyman Family she read about, believing with their hearts and souls that they'd be living on Venus one day.

And God only knew the abuse he could've endured by now. Children in the Lyman Family were punished for things like looking at someone "with that Scorpio soul in your eyes"—pure nonsense.

But how different would it have been? She still had fresh, shameful memories of throwing him out, and for what? Pouring two new bottles of Smirnoff down the kitchen sink moments before she woke up in the middle of the night. Pure nonsense.

Would he be worse now than the morning she found him on the sidewalk in front of the bar just a couple blocks from home? She still remembered the utter dryness in Corey's voice that Monday afternoon. She didn't even ask if he went to school that morning.

Grandpap hung up when I talked about you. He said he'll talk to you when you get rid of the bottle for good. Please let me come back home. I won't let another girl sneak in my room. I'm sorry, I promise. I still don't know what a 'hussy' is. I know she was older, but she's nice.

Anna, that girl's name was. Jaclyn didn't know her last name and she didn't need to. That girl was a brunette, a couple inches too tall for her age and already developing.

But Jaclyn didn't think that was the bad part of her. When Anna came around their house for the first time, Corey mentioned how she was his classmate's older sister. He blushed as he mentioned the worst part: she was thirteen.

The age Jaclyn lost her own virginity. But it wasn't that, Jaclyn had already decided. A strange girl sneaking in to see a younger boy like Corey just conjured up questions. She knew Corey wasn't stupid, but it didn't mean he knew what he was getting into with someone like that.

Someone active at so young an age—maybe someone like Jaclyn.

Yet she never caught the girl in the act. It wasn't something she was prepared to admit, but Jaclyn never heard anything more than the sound of a kiss.

She had no idea if he told her parents about Anna. Doubtful. He never mentioned anything to her about girls. She knew Corey wasn't stupid at all, but how much did he really know? All he seemed to know was what had been relayed back to him.

He said he'll talk to you when you get rid of the bottle for good.

It was too late to make amends with them now. Far too late. She was still amazed the inheritance even went to her. How her mother would've went over her father's head about that would always be a mystery.

So, Jaclyn reflected, maybe it wasn't crazy that a man like Anthony Charles would lure Corey in after all. Trixie had made that much clear. Charles didn't just offer people industry. He also offered something more valuable: acceptance.

62.

"Why won't you tell me where he is?" Jaclyn demanded. "It's not like I'm gonna be going anywhere, so what does it matter to you?"

She didn't *know* that she wouldn't find a way out. Not for certain. Even with her heart pounding in her mouth, she knew the shackles had *some* way out. A key. Every kind of lock had a key, as Jaclyn's father taught her. His words rang in her head:

Once in a while, you might have to make your own key, but no matter what kind of lock you're dealing with, there's a way to open it.

Was there a bobby pin in one of her pockets? She doubted it. Jaclyn didn't have them in her hair often, much less every day. Searching her pockets wasn't necessary to know they were all lighter now.

The wrench was gone without a doubt. She figured it was one of the first things they took. Her phone was gone too, though the battery must have died anyway. Jaclyn didn't feel the corners of her box of cigarettes, neither the smooth metal of her lighter.

They took her cigarettes. She couldn't believe those *fuckers* took her cigarettes too. The lighter was one thing, she supposed, but why the smokes? What in the Hell would she have done with cigarettes?

But if *those* were gone, she wouldn't have a bobby pin left in any of her pockets. She wondered if searching through pockets was a normal practice for them. If it was even routine.

"If you were paying attention where it mattered," Charles answered and stood up, looking down at her, "You would've known already."

"What do you mean? What the Hell are you getting at!?" Jaclyn shot back.

His gleaming smile was replaced by a deep scowl. He said with disgust, "Spare me the emotion. It's a bit too late for anything like that. You won't know anything else unless I *want* you to."

Seeing his face like that put a black pit in her stomach. The grimace on his face was longer than a beaten dog's. His expression was blank, like he didn't have a face at all. Yet every cell in Anthony Charles' body radiated hate. Hate so pure and concentrated to make the devil tremble.

Jaclyn turned away and withdrew to the wall behind her. She shrank away, trying to move further back, but Charles' barrier wouldn't allow it.

His mouth sounded like a legion of little bones snapping as it moved. The grimace disappeared and twisted into an enormous grin again.

Charles reached in his pocket, never taking his eyes away. "I have something you'll find interesting. I think you'll want to see it." He produced a brown wallet made from high-quality leather and dug inside it. "You don't seem to remember coming here before, do you? To Dourmsburg, that is," he said.

"No. It seemed familiar before, like maybe I passed by it at some point. But I don't think I ever actually came into town before," she replied.

"Nothing's really changed with you after all. Is something physically wrong with you, or is it just for the sake of convenience? It's not the first time I've wondered that, you know." He pulled a white plastic card from the wallet.

Charles flicked it out of his hand like a pestering insect, and watched it fall near her feet. The card landed on the floor, face up, and Jaclyn cocked her brow on seeing it. She couldn't read the upside-down text but moved the card around with her foot.

Her breath was still when she read it. It was an ID card. It was worn around the edges and had blurred blue text with a rubbed-out bar code. Just from the look of it, the card was considerably old.

The ID card was from an elementary school—Dourmsburg Elementary. On the left-hand side was a photograph of a boy with dirty blond hair, bangs just reaching his eyebrows and a dusty texture on the left. He had a mouth full of baby teeth, both the front ones missing. He was smiling at the camera, as if trying to hold back the giggles.

Charles sneered and asked, "Look familiar?"

Jaclyn couldn't deny that she'd seen the picture before. Her eyes were drawn to the full name under it. The name stuck out like an open wound: *Corey Archer.*

It was her favorite school picture of him so far. It was from when he started the third grade. She was speechless that Charles would have this, much less in such ragged condition.

Her voice shook as she asked in a harsh whisper, "Where did you get that?"

"I've had it for quite a while. Sometimes you just save things like that. Pure, irrational compulsion, I suppose."

"Before he joined all of you?"

"*Long* before," Charles replied. "Why would I only have it after that point?"

His words felt like a slow, rhythmic drip of venom. Thinking that Charles knew about Corey *years* before he ran away chilled her to the bone.

"Let me ask you," he said. "How old do you believe you are? I've heard you mention it once or twice when you were on the road." He slid the wallet back into his pocket.

The question left Jaclyn dumbfounded. She hesitated before answering, almost as a question, "Forty."

Charles scoffed. "You were when it first happened. You must've ignored yourself quite a bit in the meantime. But that wouldn't be anything new. You know how old habits die hard." He took his phone out. It was the XX—the newest phone to be released on the market, and the best design of the company.

Charles turned it around, showing that the phone was acting as a mirror. There were no filters or any other way to alter the image it presented.

He put it directly in front of Jaclyn's face and asked, "Does that *look* like a forty-year-old to you?"

She gazed into the reflection and watched her face begin to sink. The reflection was filled with wrinkles. The crow's feet and marionette lines were even deeper than her forehead lines and tear troughs. There was a melancholic droopiness to her entire face.

Jaclyn saw a head full of dusty light, pure gray hair that went just past her shoulders. She flinched as if it was a trick in a funhouse mirror. Overall, she felt she'd become something reminiscent of a witch depicted in old cartoons.

Charles said, "Your answer *should* be a firm *no*. That isn't the face of a forty-year-old at all. The face in the mirror is that of a *sixty*-year-old. Everything that happened was *twenty years* ago.

"You've deluded yourself into making the cut a lot less deep than it actually is. The person you started searching for just *now* has been missing for decades. 'Corey Archer' has been off the map for twenty years, and the reason you didn't find him right in front of your eyes is simple. You were searching for a child when it *should* have been a full-grown man."

63.

Jaclyn couldn't take her eyes off him. Her face grew more disbelieving and mortified by the second.

She breathed heavily. "Is—this isn't really me."

"Of course, it is," Charles answered. "No tricks. No magic up my sleeves. It's just a reflection in a mirror. Did you really make yourself see something else in the mirror every day? You must have. You must've frozen the very image of yourself for a *third* of your *life*."

Jaclyn was quiet, but then she replied, "No. Not at all."

"Then you think I'm creating an illusion? Is that what it is? You have to fight about *everything*, don't you? But I suppose it's comfortable being able to predict the next thing to come out of someone's mouth." Before she could interject, Charles continued. "Then I'll *show* you, you miserable hag!"

He turned the phone off and held it up to face her again. Tilting it, Charles let the harsh light reflect off the device. Jaclyn's mirror image was right before her, unchanged.

She wanted to deny the proof staring back at her. She wanted that more than anything. But what was the point? No matter how much she closed her eyes or wished for it to go away, there was no denying her senses. There was no arguing against them. Not anymore.

"And what do you get out of this?" she asked.

"The last thing I need, of course. If you paid attention to the bigger picture for once, you would've already put two and two together by now. Tell me, when *'Corey Archer'* went missing, how old was he?"

"Eleven."

"And that was two decades ago," Charles replied. "So he'd be how old now? I know you like to fudge the truth in your favor, but don't be in denial this time. Just answer me straight—what is eleven plus twenty?"

Jaclyn lowered her head to face the ground and said, "Thirty-one."

"And who do you know that fits the description?" As her eyes widened and her blood froze, Charles snickered. "So, the last runner finally gets to the checkered flag."

"*You—But—*You hardly *look* like him!"

"Surgery. A little cosmetic reinvention, so to speak. That is, after the money really started coming in, and the name change. A few adjustments in the bone structure and hair color. That's all it took, nothing too complicated."

"Why?"

"Simple." Charles bent down and moved his face just millimeters away from hers. When she flinched and tried to move back, he said, "The less I resemble you, the better." He stepped back, limping. "Being off the grid for so long was probably why the Archers and even the Ellsworths stopped bothering with you. The police, *if* you even bothered to call them at all, must have had quite a goose chase."

"Of course I did!" Grief exploded across her face. "I called *every* day until—"

Charles interrupted, "It's always a matter of time until they give up, until they stop giving you any information. Usually, a *short* matter of time. They started hinting that you needed to stop calling even sooner. And then, outright *tell* you."

Jaclyn shuddered at his apparent knowledge. She felt like he had been next to her during every phone call. "You don't know a *damned thing*. And *how dare you* impersonate him!?"

Silence. "'Impersonate'?" He didn't respond, watching as Jaclyn waited for impact, and Charles burst out laughing. He calmed himself down at once. "If you really think I'm faking that…" Charles trailed off at first, but told her, "A really long time ago, Grandma used to have a little garden of sorts in her backyard, where she used to grow tulips and daisies. Even *you* wouldn't forget something like that."

Tulips and daisies, Jaclyn reflected. The memory was true. She remembered more of Dourmsburg too, but it had been so many years ago that it looked like a different town then. The place where she gave birth to Corey and he completed most of elementary school was another time. It was a place with booming businesses with a sunny future. A town brimming with smiling, healthy people.

But then, why did she leave with Corey? She found the answer was the very reason for Dourmsburg's former glory. It was the economy. The economy left Dourmsburg after so many years of living there, but as she started to remember, most people couldn't afford to follow the money.

Becoming unemployed was an inevitability for her. The phone call letting her know that she was laid off made her heart sink. She didn't have a car to drive to the city, or any other township, and every business in town she where inquired said they weren't hiring. Jaclyn knew that sending an application wouldn't help much. But trying in case someone quit didn't hurt.

Thank God for her parents, Jaclyn often contemplated at night. If it hadn't been for them loaning money to her, she wouldn't have been able to leave either. She wouldn't have been able to go with see them with Corey either.

"And it wasn't just the flowers," Charles said. "There were a lot of vegetables, and she taught me how to grow some of them. It's just too bad that the little bit of farming I learned didn't do me any good during my run-in."

In a humiliated, mousy voice, she asked, "What was the run-in, Corey?"

The grin disappeared from his face. That beastly scowl returned, deeper than ever.

Jaclyn cowered against the wall. She clenched her teeth together as her skin grew clammy. She curled into a ball as far as her restraints allowed, and prayed in her head. Her knees were close to her chest. Jaclyn's arms were still locked but trembled like dirt during an earthquake.

A blizzard of disdain spread across Charles' face. He stretched his left hand out and curled his fingers. As the little bruises spread and darkened to a forest green, Jaclyn felt a wide tentacle engulf the outside of her throat.

Charles jerked his fingertips inward, and her air supply was cut off in an instant. When she started choking, his scowl deepened. Her face turned apple red. Tears of struggle welled up in her eyes, and he started blurring in Jaclyn's vision. She squirmed, pulling against her shackles, attempting to pull the strangling force away from her neck.

Even with the rage emanating from him, he spoke in a cool tone, "I can give you the very cancer I took away and double its malice. I can inflict woes beyond your fragile comprehension. You will *not* call me that again."

Jaclyn shut her eyes and nodded. There were no results. She wondered if he even saw her and kept nodding with increasing panic.

God, she thought. *Please make him see me. Please make him let go.*

Charles' grip tightened. She felt it starting to break her skin, like his grip was a set of sharp talons. Jaclyn wasn't sure, but swore she heard a low snicker.

64.

Jaclyn's neck was released. When she tried to speak, her throat was raw. As her eyes cleared, she saw that Charles' hideous grin was wider than ever. This should've been impossible like everything else, yet he made it so.

"And now that you understand your place," he said. "You'll hear only what you *deserve* to know."

He stepped closer to Jaclyn, letting her see some of the folds in his black gums. As Charles met her at eye level, he explained, "The night I left, the first thing I did was sneak to the refrigerator. God knows you hardly kept much in that thing besides the Coors and Smirnoff. There was still bread, a little bit of peanut butter, and a couple of other things.

"I went out through the kitchen window and made sure I was careful not to make any sound. My bedroom window was next to yours, and it would've woken you if I left that way.

"The stupidest thought passed through my mind when I was closing the window. Do you remember Anna, that girl who used to sneak in before? The one you threw me out of the house over because I gave her my first kiss? Did it ever occur to you that it was *me*? That *I* did that, not her? I thought that maybe, by a wild chance, she'd be waiting beyond the dark, and she'd lead me to a better place.

"Of course, that didn't happen. It was just me. Me and the entire, empty world. I never had a phone or money, just the clothes on my back and the little food I could bring. There was never a *plan*. The only goal was to just get away.

"Where was I going to go? I didn't know, but it didn't matter at the time. After wandering down the side of the road for miles and finding just spaced out houses, I would've been fine with settling down anywhere. A school. The police. Just not someone's private property. When morning dawned, the suburbanites told me to go somewhere else.

"After a few nights in oblivion without any food, water, or any idea where I was, someone welcomed me in his own way. I got picked up by someone driving in the middle of the night. It was a charming old man. I guess it was the friendliness in his voice and the warmth in his smile that made me get in the car. He said he'd take me to the police station, and it wasn't much further from where we were.

"I was wrong to believe him. He didn't stop for quite some time, so I fell asleep in the car, and we were deep in the country the next morning.

"He locked me in the basement. It was days before I had another scrap of food. When you're tied up in a stranger's house long enough, a moldy bun becomes a delicacy

"You asked about my eye, and no doubt noticed my foot. Yes, of course you have. These are all thanks that old bastard. It was his handiwork after all.

"I was desperate to escape. I shouldn't have been able to do it, but I managed to undo the knots a little bit at a time. Call it a miracle. Call it survival instinct. But it was a struggle sneaking away with part of my foot gone.

"Just before the bastard woke up, I managed to find a kitchen knife. There was nothing around that house for miles, and nothing but discarded wrappers inside the house.

"After it was done, I cleaned the blade off and hid it, just in case anyone noticed that he was missing. In case anyone snooped around and found the bones.

"I wandered around after escaping. The only thing guiding me in the middle of the night was the moon, but eventually, the police found me. They didn't search for identification, so my name became my choice. From then on, I was somebody else instead. 'Corey Archer' was a ghost at that point. The state slowly became my guardian, but not before I began ascending like the others.

"I managed to hide myself from the public eye until recently. I hired an actor to do most of my interviews. It was incredible how people were willing to accept my money without seeing me at all.

"The key to my ascension though, wasn't just consumption of the body, but the soul." Charles opened his mouth as far as it could go.

Jaclyn could just make out a cacophony of shrill screams before he closed again. She was speechless, unable to wrap her mind around what she was hearing.

Charles said, "It was how the red sign first manifested on my hand. I could never heal what wasn't there anymore. I could at least mend the scars from that bastard's cigarette butts on my hands. It was the first trick I learned."

Jaclyn was paralyzed for what felt like an eternity. It was a feat of strength to imagine a killer child, but she knew that real stories and convictions like these occurred.

She finally spoke. "But if you hate me so much, why would you want to get rid of the cancer?"

Charles' face loosened into something natural. His expression was ordinary but struck her like a torpedo. She'd last seen it twenty years ago. Jaclyn expected to see a solitary roll down his face.

But it never did. His enormous grin returned. "The final person in each Cycle has to be *clean.* When the moon is new again, so shall we begin once more."

He limped to the exit and said, "Twenty years—and your conscious only caught up to you a few months ago. You will not leave this place. I wonder, do you still pray at night? Any prayer you have to offer won't be heard. Your God has already abandoned you, just as He has me."

65.

Jaclyn was alone in that room for nine hours. The garish light overwhelmed her eyes. It could've been hours or even days since Charles left the room—she would've had just as much trouble accepting what he told her. His words danced around her mind like puppets in a stage play. Reality had a way of hissing and sneering at her now.

There was no way out of this place. There wasn't a key. No out of place tiles hinting at an escape tunnel. Just her, the gentle echoes of her whispers, and the engulfing white void.

"I'm in Hell," Jaclyn said. "God, please help me. I'm in Hell."

She repeated this again and again. Her desperate fervor increased with every repetition. It descended downward in a muffled whisper. Little by little, her voice grew quieter. Gradually, she became totally silent.

But her words continued into infinity. The words she mouthed inaudibly continued forever. She closed her eyes as flashes of panic exploded in her chest. They snaked down to the ends of her limbs.

The panic was a shower of rocket bombs in Jaclyn's forehead. It reached the palms of her hands. Then her feet, and she felt her body lift off the cold, hard ground.

"God," she said. "Why have you forsaken me?"

A familiar noise—*click-clack*.

Yet she didn't flinch. She felt a prickly ring of insane terror around her forehead. A strange delirium illuminated her mind.

Click-clack, click-clack.

It sounded like a pair of identical entities was entering the room. The noise descended the stairs toward her, but only one person emerged. Jaclyn assumed it'd be the towering, grinning figure of Anthony Charles.

The man before her was tall, but nothing abnormal like the one wielding the red sign. He stood at five foot eleven with a moderately slim figure. His hair was blonde with flecks of brown, combed and gelled back with unusual attention. His square jaw with a slight underbite was the focal point of his face.

As Jaclyn recognized him, she shuddered, and her mouth dried. She remembered the other striking part of his face being his warm hazel eyes. Now, they were a dull concrete gray.

"I—" Jaclyn stammered. "There's no way."

The man didn't respond in words. He only responded with an inviting smile.

"This is some kind of dream. A hallucination. A big illusion, right?" Jaclyn asked.

"What do you mean?" His tone was comforting, as if the dungeon she'd been in was nothing more than a minor inconvenience—everything was okay with the wave of a magic wand in his jeans' side pocket.

"Because you haven't aged a day," Jaclyn clarified.

The man cocked an eyebrow. "Hm? Since when?"

"Not since—" Jaclyn looked down at her feet, noticing that she wasn't shackled anymore. Somehow, they completely vanished. She was standing upright with no recollection of getting on her feet. "Not since twenty years ago."

"Twenty years ago?" He smirked with an air of reassurance. "I don't understand. What happened then?"

Jaclyn paused, then answered, "The divorce."

"Divorce? You mean us?" He asked.

"Of course. Who else?" Jaclyn replied.

Her husband chuckled. "Divorce? Why would we ever get divorced?"

She looked him in the eyes, smiled, and replied, "We wouldn't. You're right, Tom. That was—really stupid of me."

"No, not at all. People always have those little fears at the backs of their minds. Everyone who gets married has that fleeting concern at some point. You don't need to put yourself down," he said.

"Yeah, I guess so."

Another set of footsteps was approaching her and Tom from the distance. An excited pair of small feet hurrying through the adjacent room and down the ladder.

The final entity was in their presence.

"*Whoa*, settle down there," Tom called out. "If you're not careful, you'll slip and get hurt. This place is pretty old, you know."

"I'll be okay," a child's voice replied. "I never get hurt."

A boy, four foot five inches tall, joined them. He wore a red t-shirt and denim shorts. He had dirty blonde hair with bangs that just touched his eyebrows. He looked up at both of them with his gray, lifeless eyes. Grinning as if he was about to embark on an adventure, he showed off how his two front teeth were missing. It was only a matter of time before the permanent, adult pair took their place.

Tom looked at him and asked, "You ready to get going, Corey? I'm sure your mother is."

He nodded and replied, "Yep, sure am."

"I've been pretty tired lately," Jaclyn said, taking Corey's left hand.

"I'm sure," Tom answered, taking his son's right. "With both of us working, it's not gonna be easy. But we can tough through as long as we stick together."

A large opening with a bright light flowing through it stood before them. It was a new doorway Jaclyn hadn't seen until now. She couldn't believe that she hadn't noticed it, but that didn't matter. She shrugged the thought off.

As they walked toward it, Jaclyn uttered, "I don't know if we'll be able to make rent on time. Maybe if I get a little overtime, I can scrape by."

Tom smiled. "Just cut back on the cigarettes a little. You can do it. You've been doing a lot better with the drinking. It's been a whole two weeks without a drop."

"Are you sure I can do it?"

"I am. I know you can if you really tried," Tom replied as they passed through the doorway. "You just gotta believe in yourself."

"Maybe you're right. I might be overreacting again. I know I do that sometimes," Jaclyn responded.

The red and fuchsia of dawn filled their vision. They were standing on the smooth, mostly even sidewalk. Jaclyn turned her head out of some strange compulsion. There was more sidewalk with a few manageable cracks behind her. A manhole was across the street, its cover fit snugly over its top.

Somewhere in the distance, she could hear a faint sound. She cupped her left hand around one ear, listening closer. It was music.

After a couple seconds, Jaclyn recognized it. Sybil Thomas was singing a tune from Jaclyn's youth. She smiled at the vocals carried through the wind. She looked over and saw it was coming from a stereo on a resident's green lawn. A middle-aged woman lay asleep on a lawn chair in front of the house.

"Free me from these chains, save me from this misery—"

Jaclyn fixated on the manhole but had no idea why. She looked away from it again, shaking her head. It had been a long week at the hotel where she worked. Housekeeping the ideal job, but it was the only available work for now. Just moving around was a chore, but today had been her day off. After running around nonstop for the past five days, it was always a well-deserved break.

"Maybe I need to start looking for a different job," she said.

"I don't know," Tom replied, the confidence from his face disappearing. "It doesn't seem like places are hiring, and I hear businesses are leaving Dourmsburg. But it wouldn't hurt to try anyway."

They approached a small sandwich shop called Cooper's. It had just opened this year, and Jaclyn always made a note to stop by at some point. It was one of those places that made her curious, but she always fluttered away from it like a butterfly.

The music continued, and for some reason, it was slower by a beat per minute. The difference was far too minute for Jaclyn to notice. All she heard were the vocals.

"Save me, baby. Rescue me—"

There were spaced out, single-storied houses before them. They looked like they didn't cost much. But they managed to look new and had a unique charm about them. Jaclyn thought it could've been their pastel exteriors and glistening windows that gave a vibe of happy, young families expecting a first child.

The fleeting thought of owning one some day made her grin. It'd be a Hell of a time even saving enough for a down payment, but it was always possible.

A sky-blue Ford Focus stood further down the sidewalk. It was Tom's so-called *new* car. It was old, but she had to admit it was a steal. Tom had bought it after seeing an online ad for a grand. Not a penny more.

The Ford didn't have any problems. The man selling it just wanted to get rid of it because he started a loan on a new Honda.

Selling it for actual market value wasn't a concern. Evidently, the seller was thinking of getting it off his hands *fast*.

Jaclyn asked, "What if we end up short though? I guess we could ask my parents."

"No," Tom answered. "I don't want to just take their money. They're wonderful people, but I don't want to burden them. Your parents are already paying for Corey's school lunch. We'll find a way to get by. We're probably getting worked up over nothing anyway. That's what it usually is."

She paused and replied, "Alright. I'll just look at applications to be safe."

A passing thought occurred to her. She had to go get something. The memory was right outside her grasp. The penny was about to drop—

But it dissolved and escaped her.

There was the sound of a thousand tiny bones snapping to her left. Corey's face was twisting into an enormous sneer, too wide for the human jaw to achieve. The absence of front teeth was being filled by a pair of little daggers. His other teeth were contorting to match them. An array of deep, unnatural wrinkles appeared on Corey's cheeks and under his eyes. There was a pair of thick glasses on the bridge of his nose.

Trixie, Jaclyn thought. *It was somebody named Trixie! That was it! But why does that name sound familiar? Someone at work? No, that's not it.*

She pondered for a moment but couldn't place the name. It wasn't one of her coworkers, much less a manager. Coworkers asked for a ride every now and then, but it wasn't often. There wasn't anyone in the Ellsworth *or* the Archer family with that name.

None of her friends were named Trixie, so why did it come to her with such familiarity? She thought about it but couldn't answer. It was a silly thought. Nothing more. Another fleeting butterfly.

As they stopped in front of the car, Tom produced his keys. He unlocked it by pressing the button on his key and slipped the set back into his pocket.

"Ready to go home?" he asked, smiling.

"Yeah," Jaclyn answered. "I'll look around and see who I can go to." She turned to Corey with a smile of hope and apprehension. "What do you think?" She put her arms out, about to embrace him, but felt her feet bind together.

As sharp pains wracked her flesh and she writhed in agony, Corey said in a smooth baritone, "You poor, deluded hag. We already have someone new headed into our embrace, very young but *so* enthusiastic about us. A young girl and her friends. She told them—*all about us.*"